W9-BUQ-295

DATE DUE

NO
SAINTS
IN
KANSAS

NO
SAINTS
IN
KANSAS

AMY BRASHEAR

SOHO
TEEN

Published in the United States by Soho Teen,
an imprint of Soho Press, Inc.
853 Broadway
New York, NY 10003

Library of Congress Cataloging-in-Publication Data

Brashear, Amy, author.
No saints in Kansas / Amy Brashear.

ISBN 978-1-61695-683-7
eISBN 978-1-61695-684-4

1. Murder—Fiction. 2. Criminal investigation—Fiction. 3. High schools—Fiction. 4. Schools—Fiction. 5. Family life—Kansas—Fiction. 6. Capote, Truman, 1924–1984—Fiction. 7. Lee, Harper—Fiction. 8. Kansas—History—20th century—Fiction. I. Title.
PZ7.1.B75154 DDC [Fic]—dc23 2017021387

Interior design by Janine Agro, Soho Press, Inc.

Printed in the United States of America

10 9 8 7 6 5 4 3 2 1

For my mom, my dad, and my brother, Alex

AUTHOR'S NOTE

Dear Reader,

On November 15, 1959, a family of four was brutally murdered in the quiet town of Holcomb, Kansas. The Clutters—Herbert, Bonnie, Kenyon, and Nancy—were shot execution-style in their own home. The senseless crime made national news. It quickly attracted the attention of a writer from New York City, Truman Capote, who traveled to Holcomb to investigate. The book he wrote about that experience, *In Cold Blood*, has since become a classic.

In 1991, at the age of nine, I moved to Garden City. It's only six minutes from Holcomb, but a metropolis by comparison. Everyone was eager to talk about the Clutters, pillars of the Holcomb community. The first person we met at church mentioned that her husband was a relative of Bobby Rupp, one of the original suspects. It was a strange introduction to a place I'd call home. I began to wonder how Holcomb might feel to a newcomer, like me, at the time of the murders. When I finally read *In Cold Blood*, that wonder turned into a consuming interest—and ultimately inspiration.

The result is teenager Carly Fleming. She's one of the few fictional characters in a novel otherwise populated by the real people who are forever seared in the nation's memory—the victims, their friends, the police, the investigators, Truman Capote and his friend Harper Lee . . . even Arthur Fleming, one of the real-life court appointed attorneys for the culprits. In my novel he is Carly's father.

I remain grateful to the woman we met at church that day because she also made me fall in love with a phrase that stuck with me when I read *In Cold Blood* for the first time: "Out there." It showed me the truth about how lonely home can feel—anyplace where the fence posts are all the same height, where the wind always blows the same way—in the wake of tragedy.

With thanks,
Amy Brashear

NO
SAINTS
IN
KANSAS

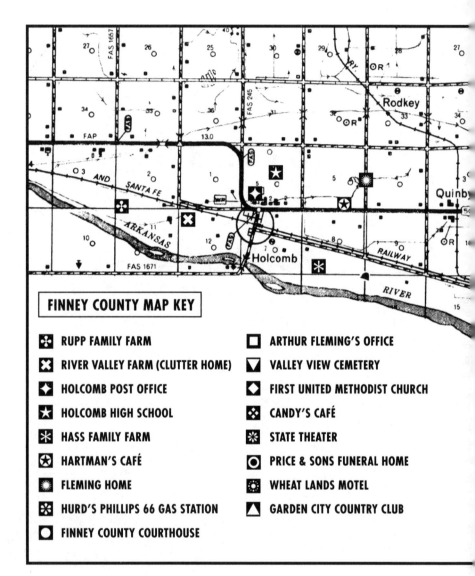

FINNEY COUNTY MAP KEY

- ✵ RUPP FAMILY FARM
- ✖ RIVER VALLEY FARM (CLUTTER HOME)
- ✦ HOLCOMB POST OFFICE
- ★ HOLCOMB HIGH SCHOOL
- ✳ HASS FAMILY FARM
- ✪ HARTMAN'S CAFÉ
- ☀ FLEMING HOME
- � HURD'S PHILLIPS 66 GAS STATION
- ◘ FINNEY COUNTY COURTHOUSE
- ☐ ARTHUR FLEMING'S OFFICE
- ▼ VALLEY VIEW CEMETERY
- ◆ FIRST UNITED METHODIST CHURCH
- ✤ CANDY'S CAFÉ
- ✳ STATE THEATER
- ◉ PRICE & SONS FUNERAL HOME
- ✸ WHEAT LANDS MOTEL
- ▲ GARDEN CITY COUNTRY CLUB

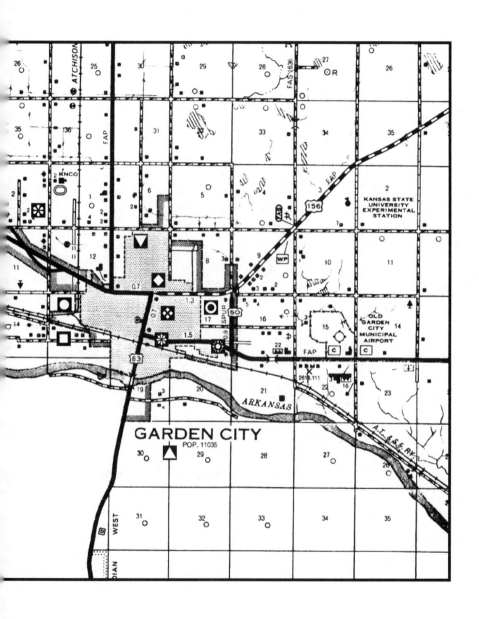

GARDEN CITY

POP. 11035

CHAPTER ONE

I CAN SMELL THE KEROSENE. The police tape is the only thing that separates me from the men loading a pickup truck with blood-stained blankets, sheets, pillows—even a couch. I grip the bicycle handlebars so tight my knuckles turn white.

There are a lot of volunteer men here. And there are a lot of people like me, standing behind this barricade, crying. I use the sleeve of my coat to wipe my eyes and my runny nose. All around I hear sniffling and whimpering. Two blood-soaked mattresses are chucked onto the pile. Foreman Taylor puts a teddy bear in the back and digs for his keys in his pocket.

He starts slowly down the lane. I push my bike across the grass and lean it up against a fence post. He drives right through the police tape, straight across the road, into the wheat field. We lookie-loos turn and watch him unload it all. After everything is stacked into a pyramid, the teddy bear's placed on top, like a star on a Christmas tree. He lights a match and tosses it. Smoke fills the air as everything that once belonged to my friend and her family burns.

"You shouldn't be here," Mr. Stoecklein says, walking up behind me.

"Then where should I be?"

"Well, not here," he says, crossing his arms.

"But Nancy—"

"Is dead."

CHAPTER TWO

Mrs. Walker's history class doesn't seem to matter now. I walk in late while she's lecturing about President Lincoln's assassination.

"'On April 14, 1865, John Wilkes Booth, an actor and a Confederate sympathizer, fatally shot President Abraham Lincoln at Ford's Theatre in Washington, DC.'" Mrs. Walker is reading from a book.

Nancy was shot, too. Nancy's dead. I care about that. Lincoln? Not so much. Not even a little bit. I don't know him. I know, I mean, I knew Nancy.

Sue Kidwell and Nan Ewalt found them—the entire Clutter family—Sunday morning, on their way to church. Sue was Nancy's best friend. She's not even in school today.

Nancy promised I could borrow her red velvet dress for the Sadie Hawkins dance; she was bringing it to Sunday school. Reverend Cowan told the congregation the god-awful news. *"This morning, I was called out to Holcomb to the River Valley Farm. There has been an incident,"* he'd said, pausing to rub his eyes. *"I'm saddened to report that the Clutter family—Herb, Bonnie, Nancy, and Kenyon—are deceased."*

I cried when I first heard. I cried again at the crime scene. It feels like some part of me hasn't stopped crying since. Especially at the headlines.

CLUTTER FAMILY SLAYINGS SHOCK, MYSTIFY AREA

Everyone likes—I mean, everyone *liked*—the Clutter family. Well, I guess not everyone.

People in town think that Bobby did it. You know, killed the Clutters. But I know that Bobby didn't do it. Bobby is, *was*, Nancy's boyfriend.

Mrs. Walker taps me on the shoulder. "Hon, the bell's rung."

"Yes, ma'am." I grab my bag, leaving a tissue behind.

Mary Claire stands in the hallway with her books to her chest, staring at a photo of Nancy on a wall next to a row of lockers.

"Carly, can you believe it?" she says. "Things like this don't happen here."

CHAPTER THREE

My boyfriend, Seth, has to go to Garden to run an errand for his mom, so he puts my bike in the back of his truck. It's a ten-minute drive, and once we get there, he parks on the square and goes inside a store while I stay fiddling with the chipped knob on the radio, moving it back and forth, trying to find something to listen to on the AM stations. Anything but farm reports and market reports. I don't care what the going price of cattle and wheat are at the moment. I hear a no-nonsense voice, stern and to the point, and stop moving the knob. The reception is low, static mostly, but a news bulletin breaks through.

"*A local family was found murdered Sunday in their home—*"

Click. That goes off.

I look out the window and see Bobby's truck, and he's sitting inside with the engine turned off. Mrs. Parker, or as everyone in town calls her, Mrs. *Nosy* Parker, walks by and glares at him before rushing down the sidewalk and into a nearby store. People in town have been giving him that look. A knowing look. A look of *I know what you did*. Before I know it, I'm walking over there. He's alone, staring out the windshield. I knock on the window but he doesn't move; he stays facing forward. I climb inside and slam the door shut.

Bobby and Seth are considerably different in appearance. Where Bobby is tall and muscular, with dark curly hair and light green eyes, Seth is short, pudgy, with blond hair and dark brown eyes. Bobby's cuter than Seth. Yes, I said it. Everyone knows it. Bobby's out of my league. But it doesn't matter anyway. He belongs to Nancy—belonged to Nancy. Besides, I'm still the new girl in town. Seth was the first boy to ask me out to go cruising around on this square on a Sunday afternoon. Seth's popular, and being the new girl, I wanted to be popular. Really, I wanted Holcomb to be like Manhattan, even if everyone around me agreed that my Manhattan is the wrong Manhattan. This, they tell me all the time.

"You probably don't want to be seen with me," he says.

"Why?"

He looks over at me. "You know why."

"I don't believe what I hear."

"Yesterday, we were supposed to go cruising around town."

"Bobby—" I touch his hand, the one that rests on the steering wheel.

"I was at home when I heard. My pop told me." He sniffs and rubs his forehead. "My brother and I drove out to the farm. There were emergency vehicles everywhere. They surrounded the house and blocked the entrance. I went home and called Sue." He squeezes the steering wheel so hard that his knuckles turn white. "That night we went to the funeral home in Garden—"

"Bobby, you don't have to talk about it."

"Do you think if I don't talk about it, it'll just go away, that I'll forget?"

"No."

The clouds part, sending rays of late-fall sunshine directly into my eyes. I pull down the visor to shield my face.

"Nancy was lying there in that casket. Not moving. She was wearing the red dress, the one that she made for 4-H—"

"I was supposed to borrow that dress. She was bringing it to Sunday school."

"Carly—"

"Now she's going to be buried in it for all eternity."

"It's just a dress," he says.

"It's not. It's Nancy's dress."

"We wanted to go see the spook show on Saturday night. But her dad said no. What if . . . ? Nancy wouldn't have been home." He turns to me.

I look out the passenger-side window. Seth's walking out of the store and down the sidewalk toward his truck. Seth nods at Bobby and then nods at me to get out.

"We'll talk later," I say, glancing over my shoulder as I open the door.

He shakes his head. In the sunlight I notice the dark circles under his eyes. "You say that now."

"I say that always."

Seth's waiting with the engine running and the volume to the radio turned up high. "Come on, Carly, you know better than that," he says, eyeing Bobby's truck.

"What?"

He puts the truck in reverse and takes me home.

CHAPTER FOUR

THE FIRST THING I DO is throw my book bag on the kitchen table and grab an oatmeal raisin cookie from the cookie jar. I pour myself a glass of milk and then lean against the counter, right next to the phone on the kitchen wall, waiting for Mary Claire to call. She always calls once she's done with her chores out on her family farm. I stare at the rotary dial; the ring of white circles is like a clock that's stopped ticking. When the phone bursts out with a shrill ring, I jump.

"Hello, Fleming residence."

"Darling!"

It's not Mary Claire. It's my mother's younger sister, Trudy. Unlike Mom, she decided to stay close to her East Coast society roots—wisely, as far as I can tell.

"Aunt Trudy, we're fine."

"Oh, thank God," she says. "I read about the murders and just hoped that it wasn't a spree."

I sit my empty glass on the countertop. "How do you know about the murders? Did Mom call? Did Dad?"

"Oh, no, *The New York Times* had a clipping. When I read it this morning over coffee, I just knew that I had to call."

I almost smile. The real clock, the one on the wall next to the refrigerator, just hit four o'clock.

"I know. I know," she adds. "I should have called sooner, but I had a date for tea at the Plaza Hotel with a certain someone special. Time just got away from me, darling."

Aunt Trudy calls everyone darling. I think it's because she can't remember anyone's name. She's always calling me Carol, Cory—or my favorite, Charley—but never Carly. It's better than what my brother gets: "the boy," "that boy," or just "boy."

For someone who always gets our names wrong, she makes sure everyone knows hers. She's also a mirror image of my mom. Thin, blonde, pretty. Always has her makeup on, red lips that match her nails. Her hair is curled and always in place. She carries around a pair of dark sunglasses to hide her late nights that turn into early mornings. She wears too much mascara, which runs when she cries. She always cries. Cries because she is sad or cries because she is happy. My mother says I take after her in that regard. Emotional. Too emotional for our own good. We, as in Aunt Trudy and I, always get worked up over things that are out of our control.

"I was shocked—I tell you, *shocked*—to see something about Kansas in *The New York Times* that didn't have anything to do with the farming that you people care so much about out there."

"Out there" is what she calls anything past the Mississippi.

She came out here once, a few months after we moved. Mom begged and begged for her to come. Aunt Trudy took the train from New York City to Kansas. She got off in Dodge City, mainly by mistake. Dad drove the fifty miles to pick her up. She couldn't believe the smell. How the air smelled like cow shit, even if you didn't see any cows. It's an acquired smell. I still haven't gotten used to it. Most people say it's the smell of money. And the nastier the smell, the more money's being made.

She spent a good portion of her time in Holcomb stuck inside our house, venturing out only for food, which she quickly dismissed. She announced, like she was delivering the Gettysburg Address, "I am a vegetarian!" The smell does mess with your sense of taste. At dinner one night, she squeezed her nose shut with her fingers while attempting to eat a salad. She glared at my mother. "Smells like cow poop. The whole town. How is that even possible? How do you live like this?"

Aunt Trudy stayed exactly three days before she came up with some excuse to get back to New York. Now she calls, writes letters, and sends presents, mainly books. All kinds. She thinks being "out there," or "hours from civilization," as she puts it, I don't get to read anything besides the Bible. I told her we have a library but she doesn't listen. So she sends me books and leaves notes inside.

"I'm so glad that you're safe," she says. "The article says that they had a girl who was sixteen. She was your age, Coley; did you know her? Was she a friend?"

I sigh at the name Coley. "Yes. She was."

Aunt Trudy draws a sharp breath. "Not a *best* friend?"

"Not really, but she could have been."

"Well, if there's anything that I can do for you all, don't hesitate to ask. I'm just a phone call away."

"Wait!"

"What's that?" she asks.

"Aunt Trudy, can you send me that *New York Times* piece?"

"Sure thing, darling. It'll go in the first-class mail tomorrow, along with a book. But hide the book from your mother," she says.

"It's kind of risqué. It's about this man named Norman Bates—you're going to love it."

Great. Another thing to hide. Under my bed I've got the Ouija board Aunt Trudy sent me last year—she swears that it really works because she "went to a séance, Carrie, and saw a spirit!" (her words)—a camera that miraculously produces instant photographs, and a pair of blue jeans.

I know the Ouija board will scare the Methodists, but Aunt Trudy specifically instructed me to hide the camera because "it will threaten Arthur Fleming, Esquire." Her words again, although I'm not sure how instant photos would threaten Dad. He's a defense attorney. As I see it, Dad's job is to prove that people accused of a crime are really innocent—so if anything, instant photos might help. But Aunt Trudy's logic plays by its own rules.

The most scandalous Aunt Trudy gift of all, of course, is the jeans. My mom thinks a lady should never wear pants.

"Thanks, Aunt Trudy."

"Stay strong, Carlotta."

"Carly," I say.

"No, darling, it's Trudy, Aunt Trudy," she says. "Well, look at the time."

I look at the clock. It has barely moved at all. "Do you have to go?"

"Sadly, I do. Don't worry, child. Things will be back to normal, just you wait and see."

CHAPTER FIVE

ASHER COMES THROUGH THE BACK door and tosses his gym bag on the floor.

He's fourteen, a sophomore, but since Sunday he's seemed so much older. He walks around with his head low, his lanky frame stooped. He doesn't make eye contact with anyone. When he does talk, he speaks in short phrases. His eyes are red; he claims it's because he's not feeling well. His oxford shirt, which is usually tucked in, is sticking halfway out. Asher doesn't want to show his emotions to anyone. Kenyon was his best friend. Kenyon was the first one to introduce himself to my brother when we moved here. He got Asher to join the 4-H. They had secrets and inside jokes.

Kenyon was nice to me. When he came over to our house, he always made conversation, asked me how I was. Maybe he was just being polite.

What I know for certain is that Asher considered Kenyon to be his best friend, and from what I could tell, the feeling was mutual.

"Basketball tryouts were canceled," Asher says, opening the refrigerator and taking out a pitcher of cucumber water. He pours himself a glass and gulps it down. "I wasn't ready anyway." He pours himself another.

Kenyon was on the Longhorn basketball team. This season Asher was supposed to finally make tryouts, to be his best friend's teammate. Sunday afternoon, Kenyon was supposed to give Asher some pointers on what the coaches are looking for this year.

"I don't think I'll make the team now," Asher says.

I nod.

"Thanks for the vote of confidence," he says, placing his empty glass in the sink and leaving the kitchen.

"Asher—"

"Forget I mentioned it," he yells, slamming his bedroom door shut.

I pound my head gently on the counter.

CHAPTER SIX

MATH EQUATIONS LOOK EVEN LESS appealing now. Who really cares what x plus y equals? My mind's not in it at all.

Dad walks into the house from the garage. He tries to hide it but I can tell he's upset.

"You okay?" I ask.

"Of course."

I know he's lying. His voice is hoarse and his eyes are red like mine.

"Dad, do they have a suspect yet?"

His lips form a b sound and I stop him.

"Bobby didn't do it."

He gives me that look. He tilts his head and lifts an eyebrow while twisting his bottom lip with his front teeth, as if he's biting away the words to tell me that I'm wrong.

"It's pure laziness to think that the Garden City Police Department would go after him like this," I add.

Dad sighs. "Carly, he was taken into custody this afternoon."

"What?" I pound my fist on the kitchen table. "But I just saw him—"

"Carly, don't do this."

I'm breathing hard. Dad's face softens. He stands behind me, leaning over, trying to give me a hug.

"Dad, do you think he did it?" I ask.

He kisses me on the top of my head and leaves the kitchen without answering my question.

Yesterday, after church, Dad went with a few of the men who knew the Clutter family over to the farmhouse. When he came home, he sat in the rose-colored wingback chair in the living room and didn't say a word for the rest of the night. Mom asked. Asher asked. And I asked, too. But Dad wouldn't tell us what it was like, what he saw. We had to read it in the newspaper the next morning.

CLUTTER FAMILY SLAYINGS SHOCK, MYSTIFY AREA

After dinner, I sit on the sofa reading *Breakfast at Tiffany's*, the last book that Aunt Trudy sent me. Her call reminded me that I'd started it and forgotten about it. I also forgot I'd used her note as a bookmark, on page 55.

Dearest Darling—I was the inspiration for Holly, or at least people tell me. The author is an eccentric man but I do call him an "acquaintance." Be well.

Love, Trudy

Instead of reading, I'm really trying to eavesdrop on my parents in the kitchen. Dad is adamant that whoever murdered the Clutters had to know them.

"It was personal. Herb's throat was cut. That's personal," he whispers.

Mom pokes her head into the living room, probably to make sure I'm not listening. She's on her third martini of the night. My eyes dart away from her and back to the page.

Most people in town have already convicted Bobby for the murders, all because he was the last person to see them alive. It says so in every news article out there: *He had been visiting the home, and left around 10:30 P.M.* To me, that just means that he was there and then he left. He didn't kill them.

He couldn't have.

"Those poor children," Mother says. "Thank goodness Eveanna and Beverly don't live at home anymore."

Eveanna lives with her husband and child in Illinois and Beverly attends college in Kansas City. She wants to be a nurse. She's engaged to be married the week of Christmas.

"I cannot imagine," Mom adds.

I'm not looking at her, but I know she is clutching her pearls. I hold the book so tight that the pages start to crumple. There's a shadow behind me. I can feel Dad staring at me from the kitchen, too. But I'm not going to look at him or my mom. I'm just going to keep on staring at this passage on page 55.

I have a memory of spending many hither and yonning days with Holly; and it's true, we did at odd moments see a great deal of each other; but on the whole, the memory is false.

Then, at the appropriate time, I'm going to turn the page.

CHAPTER SEVEN

THE NEXT MORNING AT SCHOOL, I hear a commotion as soon as I walk in the door. A Garden City police officer is causing a scene in the hall, taking all of Bobby's things out of his locker, shoving everything in evidence bags. Including his tennis shoes.

I spot Paul, a son of one of the Clutters' handymen at the River Valley Farm. He's lived in Holcomb his entire life. His face is blank and ashen, like everyone else's. He's in overalls, chewing something, shaking his head. Of course, while it's true that his father worked for the Clutters, it wasn't as if Paul knew Nancy or Kenyon—not socially, anyway.

"Why are they doing this?" I ask Paul.

"I have no idea," he says, not making eye contact.

"What do they think he did? Write his plot to kill the Clutters in between math and science?"

"So you think he did it, too?" he asks, his gaze still fixed on the police officer and the locker inspection.

I feel the same surge of anger I felt last night. "He loves Nancy; he wouldn't kill them," I hiss. "Let alone her—"

"Why not?" Paul interrupts in a lazy drawl. "He was the last one to see them alive."

"You're wrong."

"Am I? You know I was in that house."

I step back, clutching my books against me. "The Clutter home? When?"

"Sunday morning, before Nan and Sue found them," he says so matter-of-factly, it's like I should know this already. He turns to me. "Our dad sent me and my brother to the farm to milk the cows. We put the milk in the creamer in the utility room and the rest in Mr. Clutter's icebox. I walked right by the basement door. Who would have thought that Kenyon and Mr. Clutter were dead down there?"

"Paul—"

"We were in a hurry. We were going pheasant hunting. We were doing our job, that's all," he says, looking me right in the eye. "I guess that makes me a suspect, too."

"Paul—"

But he's already making his way down the hall.

"Carly," Mary Claire says, running up to me with today's newspaper in hand.

"I want to see it."

POLICE ASK CITIZENS FOR HELP IN SOLVING THE MURDERS
HOLCOMB—What was termed "the goriest murder in Kansas" appeared no closer to a solution Monday night.

Finney County Attorney Duane West said he had no further announcement concerning the members of the Herb Clutter family Saturday night.

"Can I have this?" I ask.

She shrugs. "If you want it."

Careful as I can, I rip the article out, fold it, and stuff it between the pages of my English composition notebook.

Seth approaches as the police officer passes him in the opposite direction. "I heard the police drove up to the Rupp farm and put Bobby in the backseat of a patrol car," Seth whispers, glancing over his shoulder. "Bobby even took a lie-detector test."

"He's your friend."

He turns back to me with a scowl. "Yeah, I know he's my friend."

"Well, you aren't acting like it," I say under my breath.

"They say they're going to drag the river to find the murder weapon."

"That's stupid," Mary Claire says, shaking her head.

"Why?" Seth asks.

"The killer didn't throw the murder weapon in the Arkansas River."

"And how do you know that?" he presses. I want to slap that leering excitement off his face.

Mary Claire frowns at him. "It's common sense. A true marksman would never throw their gun away in a body of water, especially a dirty river."

I almost smile. I'm no marksman—I've never even held a rifle for longer than a minute—but I can tell Seth believes her, too. He chooses to ignore Mary Claire. "Carly, do you want to come watch the police drag the river?" he asks.

I shake my head no.

"Well, if you change your mind, we'll be out by the truck after school." He takes his books out of his locker, kisses me on the cheek, and heads down the hall.

CHAPTER EIGHT

I'M SLUMPED OVER IN MR. Hendricks's English class when there's a knock at the door. He doesn't even get a chance to answer it because a man wearing a dark blue suit and striped tie takes it upon himself to come on in. He holds a folder in his right hand. I can make out a *C* and most definitely an *F*.

"May I speak with Carly Fleming?" he asks.

"Aw, Carly, what did you do now?" Alex Baker asks in a stage whisper.

A few kids giggle. I shoot Alex a glare, resisting the temptation to ask him if he ever changes his clothes or bathes. He's worn the same plaid button-down shirt, sleeves rolled to his elbow, since the school year started. His hair is smashed thanks to his cowboy hat, which he keeps in his locker. He's worn the same condescending smirk, too. And the same sweaty odor.

"Carly, this man would like to speak to you," Mr. Hendricks says, as if I didn't hear the man at the door say my name.

I stand, grab my bag, and walk up the aisle slowly, slapping Alex on the back of the head as I go by. His black-rimmed glasses fall to his desktop. The same kids who giggled now giggle again but fall silent when Alex shoots them a menacing glare.

"Carly's in trouble now," Karen Westwood says out loud. She trips me a little as I pass, crossing her legs, playing with the end of her long brown braid.

"No, I'm not," I snap at her, knowing full well that I might be. I hurry into the hall.

"Sir, this won't take long," the man says to Mr. Hendricks. He shuts the door.

I stare at the folder. It has my name on it. What did I do to constitute a folder? "Who are you?" I ask him.

"Agent Church with the KBI," he says. "Nothing to worry about. This is just routine."

The Kansas Bureau of Investigation—the state version of the Federal Bureau of Investigation, the FBI—showed up yesterday to lend the local law enforcement a hand. I guess today, the KBI is using the principal's office to conduct their "routine" interviews. Routine? As if any of this is routine.

"What do you want with me?"

"Agent Dewey would like to have a word with you," he says, ushering me down the hall toward the principal's office.

"What does Agent Dewey want with me?"

He doesn't answer. The secretary sits at one of those waiting-room chairs and Principal Williams sits at the secretary's desk. He looks at me, smiles, and nods as I walk past him and into what used to be his office.

Agent Church stands outside the door, like a guard dog, his hands in his pockets. I can feel his eyes on me. I'm about to jump to my feet and confess for the fear of it all. Behind me a man coughs and places a hand on my shoulder, startling me. Sitting up straight, I cross my legs at the heel, like a lady would do, and get ready to say yes sir or no sir, at rapid speed, even if the question doesn't really need an answer.

Agent Dewey straightens his black tie and lays it flat on his crisp white shirt. He pulls his coat sleeves down, looks at me, and nods. "Carly, I'm not here to interrogate you," he says, placing a file in front of him and sitting in Principal Williams's chair.

"Then why am I here and why do you have that with my name on it?" I ask, pointing to the folder in front of him.

He doesn't answer my question; instead he asks one of his own. "You were friends with Nancy, weren't you?"

"I thought you said this wasn't an interrogation."

He smiles. "Not an interrogation. I just want to understand your relationship with Nancy Clutter."

I cross my arms. "We were friendly," I tell him. "Very friendly." But even as the words come out of my mouth, I think of the passage from the book Aunt Trudy sent me.

It's true, we did at odd moments see a great deal of each other; but on the whole, the memory is false.

CHAPTER NINE

IT HAD BEEN TWO WEEKS since I'd moved here, and we'd just got back our geometry tests. Mr. Bailey said I could take the test and see where we were at with my knowledge of geometry. When I got it back with $A+$ and a smiley face written at the top, along with *See me after class*, I was kind of surprised and also kind of frightened. Did students who got $A+$ grades have to see the teachers after class a lot?

So I waited until all the students left—well, not all. Nancy was waiting at the front of the room. She looked sick. Her test was balled up, and it looked like she had been crying.

"Nancy Clutter, do you know our new student?" Mr. Bailey asked her gently.

"No," she said, shaking her head.

"Well, I was thinking you two might want to get better acquainted." He smiled at me. "I have an idea."

Nancy sniffled. "This is unlike me, Mr. Bailey. I'm a good student."

"I'm sure it is for your other classes. But Nancy . . . this is becoming a problem. This is your fourth D in a row. I think you need a tutor."

Her eyes shot up. "A tutor?"

Mr. Bailey nodded.

"I don't need a tutor," she said. She wasn't crying anymore.

"Yes, I think it would help."

"I think Carly—Carly, right?"

"Yes, it's Carly," I said.

"Well, I think Carly would be an excellent tutor for you."

Nancy stood there, frozen. Then she started crying again. Her face was wet. Tears were streaming from her eyes. But it was like watching June Allyson act. The waterworks were on full blast. Like they were on cue. The tears were real, but she was most definitely acting. And while Mr. Bailey comforted her, I stood off to the side, awkwardly holding my A+ test.

I coughed as if to say, *I'm still here.* They looked at me. Nancy shrugged, took a deep breath, and sighed.

"What do you think about helping me out with geometry?" she asked, even though it wasn't her idea. "But it'll be our little secret."

"Okay," I said, probably a little too eager for the new girl.

And that's how we became best friends. From that moment on, we were inseparable. We were attached at the hip. At lunch, at 4-H club, every school event, double dates, sleepovers, I was popular by association.

I wish.

I started tutoring her the next day. I'd go over to her house once a week and then twice a week when there was a scheduled quiz or test.

Finals were rough. I was over at her house until really late one night, when she asked, "Why don't you sleep over so we can do more studying in the morning?"

I said yes, too quickly as always, even before we got permission from our parents. I knew her parents were nice. Sure, kind of strict, but whose parents weren't?

My parents were thrilled when I called to ask them. This was the first time I slept over at a friend's house, at least here in Holcomb. I didn't have many friends here. Mary Claire was the only one who initiated any sort of friend relationship. My family was "city folk" and Nancy's family was "country folk"; at least that's how she described it. She didn't exactly know how to act at my house, and I didn't know how to act at hers. Eventually it got easier, but at the beginning—whew.

That night, I hoped things might change. Once I got my parents' permission, I tried to keep my excitement in check.

"We don't need to tell anyone that you stayed over, though," Nancy said the moment I hung up.

"Oh, okay," I said, trying not to rock the boat.

"Good." She nodded. She went to her sister's room and found an old pair of pajamas. "My sister doesn't wear these anymore. They might be a little small."

"Thanks," I said.

"Bathroom's down the hall."

I changed quickly and we were back to studying. No gossiping. Or making cookies. Or anything you normally do at a sleepover. But that was okay. Even if she was adamant about keeping our friendship a secret, she was talking to me. Even if no one else knew. I was her tutor, not her friend. She was afraid of not being seen as the perfect girl, and me having to tutor her in math certainly did not make her perfect. But maybe this was the first step to becoming her friend and not just her tutor.

We stayed up past midnight. Mr. Clutter woke us up with the smell of pancakes.

"So, New York City," he said at breakfast, pouring a cup of coffee for his wife. He didn't drink the stuff.

"Yes, sir," I said. I tried to keep smiling as I cut a piece of butter.

"What brought your family out here? Does your family farm?" Mrs. Clutter asked.

I shook my head as Nancy passed me the syrup. "My dad's a lawyer."

"A good one?" Mr. Clutter said with a smile.

"He's a defense attorney, so . . . it can go either way."

He laughed.

"Why did you choose Kansas?" Nancy asked.

"What's wrong with Kansas, dear?" her father asked, arching an eyebrow.

"Nothing." She sounded bored, or maybe just tired. "It's far away from where she came from, that's all."

"My dad spent a lot of summers visiting his great-aunt Lucille and uncle Olin out here. They lived near the Colorado border," I said.

"Well, that's nice," Mrs. Clutter said.

"When a case went bad, he decided he didn't want to deal with capital murder cases anymore," I said, pouring syrup all over my pancakes.

"Oh. Do you mind if I ask which one?" Mr. Clutter asked.

"He has a morbid curiosity," Nancy said with a smile.

I shook my head. "Frank Beggett."

"Yes. So, your father defended him? I remember reading about that case in the newspaper." The "defended him" implied judgment.

I slowly nodded. I was trying to stay cheery.

"We all need good defense attorneys, even when we get to heaven. Do you go to church?" he asked, probably thinking that this New York City lawyer and child were heathens.

"Yes, the First Methodist Church in Garden City."

That seemed to shake Nancy out of her doldrums. "You do?" she asked. "I don't think I've ever seen you."

"We usually sit in the back," I said, cutting my pancakes.

"This Sunday, sit up close, so the good Lord and all of us can see you," Mr. Clutter said, handing each of us a napkin.

Kenyon came down a little later. When he saw me, he said hello right away. He knew me, of course. He'd been over at our house a lot. Apparently, Asher can make friends real fast. Me? Not so much.

When we'd finished, Nancy took our plates to the sink. Her father nodded approvingly. "I'm proud of you, Nancy, for befriending a new student. Doesn't Nancy make the best tutor?"

"Tutor?" I echoed slowly.

"She's a good student," Nancy piped up. She grabbed my hand, ushering me out of the kitchen and up the stairs. "I'll do the dishes later, Dad," she yelled from the landing.

"But I'm tutoring you," I said as she closed the bedroom door.

"I know, but I can't let my dad know that. It'll ruin my reputation."

I stared at her, baffled, as she flopped down on her bed. "So you'll let him believe a lie?"

"It's not a lie. I can tutor you in something, too," she said.

"What subject are you struggling in? How about Kansas history? You know nothing about Kansas history, since you're an outsider."

"Kansas history?" I repeated. I almost started laughing.

"Yes! I taught everything Sue needed to know."

I took a moment to consider what Nancy had just let slip out. Sue Kidwell was practically joined at the hip with Nancy when they were out socializing, at the 4-H or at school. But thinking about them now, I realized Sue always seemed to follow Nancy's lead. It was always Nancy asking Sue, "Doesn't this sweater look pretty?" or "What do you think of Bobby's truck?" And Sue would nod or shrug or laugh or shake her head. She'd give whatever response Nancy was looking for.

"Sue's not from here, either?" I asked.

Nancy shook her head. "She's from California."

"Righto."

"California. Doesn't it sound exotic?"

Then I did laugh.

"New York sounds exotic, too," she said, smiling back at me.

"It can be."

"But not like here. We have blizzards," she said.

"So do we. I mean, when I lived there, we did."

"Yeah? But not like here."

Now Nancy had a cover. We didn't even have a class on Kansas history. It was just a ploy for her parents—really, her dad—so he wouldn't find out that she was failing geometry. But it worked. Her grades went up. And what do you know: I learned some interesting facts about Kansas. Like, Dodge City was dubbed the "Wickedest Little City in America," so that's why Dodge City High School's mascot is a Red Demon. The Arkansas River is pronounced "R-Kansas," not like the state of Arkansas at all. And cow patties aren't some pie or cookie, and a cow-chip toss isn't some game where you eat with your hands afterward.

She *did* tutor me in her own way, I suppose.

Beyond the fake class, I learned a lot of hands-on Kansas stuff by joining 4-H, which I wouldn't have known about if it weren't for Nancy. My dad thought it was a good way to make friends and Mom thought it was a good way to get involved in the community. She's a big fan of community involvement. She was right, too, because that's where I got to know Mary Claire.

I KNEW WHO SHE was before I started going to 4-H, so that helped. The first time I officially met Mary Claire, though, was when her dad hired my dad for some legal matter. Some land dispute that he had with a neighboring farm. Mr. Haas came by our house to sign some papers and brought along his daughter.

Mary Claire's family owns Haas Feed Yard. With over forty-five thousand head of cattle, it's one of the biggest in the state. The first time I ever saw a cow slaughtered was at her house. It was a year ago, October. Mary Claire had just showed her Texas Longhorn at the Kansas State Fair in Hutchinson. She got a ribbon, but if I remember correctly, she wasn't too happy with the judge's decision with the color she got. Most people were showing their Herefords and Holsteins. Mary Claire assumed hers was unique, but the winner ended up being Brandon Dalton, a boy who lives in Cimarron. He had the newest breed, a Charolais—a French cow. Mary Claire had never liked Brandon; this pushed her over the edge.

Once we got back to Holcomb, she declared her losing Texas

Longhorn, appropriately renamed B.D. (after Brandon Dalton), would be slaughtered. Mary Claire's got a dark side.

That morning, I stood off to the side with Nancy. She made her famous award-winning cherry pie for dessert. B.D. would be the main course. We watched as Mr. Haas loaded his .22 rifle and aimed for the kill shot, an invisible X above the eyes. He squeezed the trigger. I couldn't look. I grabbed Nancy's hand and, like Mr. Haas, squeezed hard.

"You don't want to watch?" Nancy asked.

My entire body shook. "No," I squeaked out.

Nancy laughed. "City girl."

Then there was screaming. At first I didn't realize that it was me.

Mr. Haas looked at me and shook his head. "City kid," he said.

B.D. fell to the ground with a loud thud. Nancy grabbed me by the arm and pulled me closer to the fallen Texas Longhorn. I didn't want to, but I didn't want to just be this "city kid." I watched as Mr. Haas handed Mary Claire a hunting knife and let her cut B.D.'s throat. The blood drained out onto the ground. I thought I was going to throw up.

"Come here, girls," Mr. Haas said to Nancy and me.

Nancy and I moved toward dead B.D.

"I need the both of you to pump the leg up and down a few times to help get the blood out," he said, showing us what to do.

Nancy got down on the ground and I did the same. I wanted to ask for gloves but thought that would be a "city kid" thing to do. I grabbed the front leg and started jerking it up and down, watching as the blood poured out of B.D.'s neck.

"See, you can do this," Mary Claire said, wiping the bloody knife on her apron.

The rest of the girls were inside with Mrs. Haas, cutting

potatoes and carrots for the sides. I wished that I had stayed inside to help with that chore.

"Did that move? Did his back leg just move? Oh dear lord, he's still alive . . ."

Mary Claire laughed at my jabbering. So did Nancy. Thank goodness Mr. Haas had walked away and wasn't in earshot any longer, or he would've, too, and then called me "city kid" for good measure.

"It's just his unconscious reflexes," Mary Claire finally said.

"His what?"

"Even decapitated animals will kick."

"I don't think I want to see a decapitated animal." I blew my hair out of my face.

Mary Claire and Nancy looked at each other and snickered. Mr. Haas walked out of the barn, carrying a large saw.

"Ready?" he asked.

"Let me! Let me!" Mary Claire squealed.

Mr. Haas shook his head. We three moved out of the way and watched as Mr. Haas cut off B.D.'s head with sharp, straight motions.

"Oh my God, what in the world just happened here?" I said, covering my mouth.

Those were my last words before I passed out.

When I woke up, Mr. Haas was removing B.D.'s testicles, while Mary Claire and Nancy were removing the front feet and lower legs.

"Welcome back, city slicker," Foreman Taylor said, lending me a hand.

Foreman Taylor is tall and always wears overalls. The cowboy hat he wears all the time kind of smells like pee. He supervises everything on the Haas family farm.

I stood and wiped the dirt off my pants.

"Don't worry," Mr. Haas said. "I've got the most important job for you yet."

I tried to smile.

Foreman Taylor and Mr. Haas loaded up B.D. on the tractor and took him to where they could finish butchering him. Mary Claire, Nancy, and I followed slowly behind.

"You still look white as a ghost," Nancy said.

"Yeah, you do," Mary Claire agreed.

I was real quiet. I didn't know what Mr. Haas had in store for me. We entered the slaughterhouse; B.D. was hanging by a shackle. Foreman Taylor had already started to skin him.

"Let Carly," Mr. Haas said.

"Dad, I don't think that's such a good idea," Mary Claire interjected, trying to save me from this torture.

"Nonsense. She's got to learn how to live off a farm."

"But her dad's a lawyer," Nancy said. "If we're doing stuff our parents do, she's just got to learn how to defend people."

"Yeah, I need to learn how to do lunch and get a person off," I said, shaking.

"Still, everyone should know how to slaughter an animal," Mr. Haas affirmed.

I didn't even want to know the reasoning behind that.

"Come on, Carly, I'll show you how it's done," Foreman Taylor said.

I took a deep breath and climbed a small ladder to stand beside Foreman Taylor. He grabbed my waist so that I wouldn't fall into B.D. Nancy and Mary Claire cheered me on from down below.

"Quiet, girls. Carly needs to concentrate so she doesn't cut herself," Mr. Haas said.

I didn't even think about that. Foreman Taylor handed me the sharp knife and showed me where to cut into the cowhide. I took another deep breath and laid the knife onto the hair.

"I'm so sorry, Brandon Dalton," I said, making my first cut.

"Don't talk to it," Mr. Haas said.

Mary Claire and Nancy laughed. A long piece of skin fell to the ground.

"Good job," Foreman Taylor said.

I handed the knife to him and made my way back down the ladder. Foreman Taylor and Mr. Haas finished up B.D. while Mary Claire, Nancy, and I made our way to the main house. Once outside, I threw up.

"Are you all right?" Nancy asked as I wiped my mouth on my apron.

"Uh-huh," I answered.

"I can't believe you apologized to B.D. before you skinned it," Mary Claire said.

"How polite of you," Nancy said with a laugh.

"Next weekend, I'll have you milk a cow," Mary Claire chimed in.

"Milk a cow?" I asked.

"Yes, milk a cow," she said, showing me how with her hands. "You know some weird guy was doing some dirty stuff when he discovered milk came out of udders."

She and I laughed, but Nancy just rolled her eyes.

CHAPTER TEN

HERE AND NOW—A LIFETIME (FOUR lifetimes) away from that day on the Haas farm—Agent Dewey pulls out a little black notebook from inside his black jacket and flips it open. "When was the last time you talked to Nancy?" he asks.

"Saturday night. I called the house to remind her about bringing the dress to Sunday school."

"Dress?"

"For the Sadie Hawkins dance on Friday. She made this red velvet dress for 4-H and promised me that I could borrow it for the dance. I'm going with Seth Patterson."

Her math grade went up a whole letter grade, I add silently. I know she was trying to say thank you in her own way. Lending me the dress wasn't a public acknowledgment that we were friends, but it was a step in that direction.

"And what time did you call her?" he asks, ready with a pen.

"I don't know, maybe around eight o'clock. She said that Bobby was over at the house. We didn't talk long."

"So that was the last time you talked to her?"

I stare at him for a long while. I guess I never thought about it like that. Agent Dewey waits for me to answer his question.

"Yes, sir. She said that she would write herself a note so she wouldn't forget," I tell him.

Agent Dewey opens the folder and pulls out a clear plastic bag marked *EVIDENCE* in scary black capital letters. Inside is a note written in Nancy's handwriting.

Remember dress for Carly

"I had to know what this meant," he says. He sticks it back in the folder and closes it before I can take a closer look.

"Can you think of anyone who would want to harm the Clutters?" he asks.

"So does this mean that Bobby isn't a suspect anymore?"

He narrows his eyes. "Excuse me?"

"Bobby. He was her boyfriend—"

"Carly, I'm sorry," Agent Dewey interrupts me, "but I can't discuss an ongoing investigation with you."

"But you want to know my opinion about who did it?"

His face softens. "I do."

"Honestly, I can't think of a single soul who would want to harm the Clutters. Can you?"

CHAPTER ELEVEN

AFTER SCHOOL, MARY CLAIRE CONVINCES me to meet Seth and
Alex. She's curious to see where the police are dragging the
Arkansas River. I admit I'm a little curious, too. It's blocked off,
though, and you can barely see the boat out on the water.

Mary Claire explains the situation to the boys, who clearly
have no clue what's going on. A net latched to a hook is pulled
through the water and dragged along the riverbed. The police
hope a gun will get caught in the net. But Mary Claire bets they're
just pulling up vegetation and rocks.

"I bet they find it," Alex says.

"I bet they don't," Seth says.

This goes on for a good five minutes before Mary Claire gets
annoyed and practically gets on her hands and knees, begging me
to go with her to get a pop at Hartman's Café.

"I'll see you at the funeral tomorrow, right, Seth?" I ask.

He turns to Alex and mumbles something under his breath.

"Seth, you're going, right?" I ask, with my hands on my hips.

He doesn't answer at first, but I finally wear him down enough to
confess that he and Alex are going fishing tomorrow. I stand there,
my shoes covered in mud, my mouth wide open, unable to say a word.

SITTING IN A BOOTH at Hartman's Café,
I lay it all out there while slurping down a chocolate milk shake.

"My boyfriend has to be the biggest jerk ever in the history
of jerks. His friend is dead and all he can think about is going
fishing," I say, loudly enough that people in the café turn and
stare.

"You know that's Seth," Mary Claire says, dismissing everything I just said with a shake of her head. She leans close, her eyes
sparkling mischievously. "I talked to Sue last night."

"Is she all right?" I gasp.

She shrugs. "How could she be? She saw her best friend's brains
outside of her best friend's head."

"Mary Claire Haas!"

"What?"

"Who do you think did this?" I whisper.

"I think they have a suspect."

"But he didn't do it."

"Why do you care? Nancy told me that you two aren't
friends—"

"I know that we aren't friends," I say shortly, cutting her off.
"*Weren't* friends."

For a long time, there's silence between us until I break the
tension by tossing twenty-five cents on the table and scooting out
of the booth. "I'll prove to everyone in town that he didn't do it,"
I say, throwing my scarf around my neck.

"How are you going to do that?"

"I don't know. But I will."

Turning, I walk right into Landry Davis.

CHAPTER TWELVE

I'VE KNOWN LANDRY EVER SINCE his family moved here from Olathe, right after his uncle Thomas died. It was a runaway tractor accident last spring. They found him "a little bit to the south, a little bit to the north, and a little bit to the west" on the Davis farm. Those were Mary Claire's words. She thought they were funny. They were a little, I guess.

His funeral was the first I'd ever been to. We went because my dad was his lawyer. He handled his estate. Mary Claire and I sat a few rows back from Landry. I remember stealing glances at the back of his head, wondering who he was. It was a strange service. You were sad that the man was dead but also wondered what was in the casket. Since they didn't exactly find a whole body. What were they burying?

This man I didn't know, Thomas Davis, was dead. I don't think I really understood what was happening. Death was a stranger to me. My parents tried to explain it. Heaven. Hell. But it didn't make sense. I just remember thinking that I hoped I didn't become acquainted with it for a very long time. Besides, it was a freak farm accident. Nothing malicious about it. The police didn't suspect foul play. But no one knows exactly what happened that day in

April. Lots of theories, but no one was there to prove if any of them were true.

Foreman Taylor found him—well, pieces of him. It ended up being quite a jigsaw puzzle. The coroner arrived, laid out a white sheet on the ground, and started to put him together again—just like Humpty Dumpty. Or so says Mary Claire. Thinking about it makes me sick, but she loved to needle me with details. It was hard. The pieces were tiny, bloody, and crushed. It was impossible. *All the king's horses and all the king's men couldn't put Humpty together again.*

Teddy, the Clutters' dog, ventured over to the property. He was more of a hindrance than a help. He found Landry's uncle's right foot and he buried it. So who knows what other body parts Teddy found. He's no Lassie. He didn't quite save the day. I called Aunt Trudy and told her what happened. She didn't believe me at first. She thought I was telling a story that I made up. But it wasn't fiction. When I mentioned how they'd found the head on an anthill, she finally did believe, and she excused herself from the phone for a while. I swear I heard gagging in the background. When she returned she said something so profound it has stayed with me ever since. *"Death is a test everyone passes. But sometimes you get extra points for creativity."*

Sometimes—not very often—Aunt Trudy can come up with words of wisdom at the right time when nothing else makes sense.

I thought of her words at Uncle Thomas's funeral. Mary Claire wondered why they didn't just cremate the body, or at least the parts they could find. And since I had never been to a funeral before and didn't quite grasp the concept, I had to ask what "cremate" meant.

"Reduce to ashes. Burn. Set fire to. Incinerate," she whispered, like a thesaurus.

I was sorry I asked.

A few people wondered if he was *truly* dead. I mean—it *was* him. The head proved it. But a few hoped he faked his death. Maybe they were wishing he'd walk in through the back doors of the sanctuary and say hi. We'd get a nasty shock when he showed up, but we'd get over it. He'd be alive.

But he didn't.

"We are gathered here to mourn the death of Thomas Davis; farmer, a man of his word, friend," the minister said.

I burst into tears, and I wasn't even sure why. Mary Claire sat on the other side of me, staring at the casket, which was draped in flowers. "How many body parts did they actually find?" she asked in a whisper.

"*Shhhh!*" Mrs. Parker sounded without turning around in her seat.

Uncle Thomas never went to church, but he had a will and it said that he wanted a funeral to make things right with the man upstairs, so just in case there was a God, Thomas'd have his bases covered.

I leaned over to Mary Claire and whispered, "When I die I want one of those New Orleans types of funerals, the kind in the movies, where there's singing and dancing."

She shook her head and said with a laugh, "Carly, you're not going to die. I'm not going to die. We're young; we've got too much to do for that to happen anytime soon."

Now I think about death every day.

I first met Landry—for real, I mean, as in I spoke to him—when Nancy and I went to pay our condolences to the family. Nancy had just gotten her driver's license and was looking for an excuse to skip our tutoring session. So she drove us out to the Davis farm.

She took one look at Landry sitting on the front porch, elbowed me in the side, smiled, and said, "He's a stud, all right."

"He's cute, but I don't think a stud."

"Seth's no stud," she said, shaking her head.

"Bobby is," I said, staring through the windshield at Landry.

"Do you have a crush on my boyfriend?" she asked.

I turned to her. "No."

"Good. He's off limits."

Before we got out of the car, she grabbed my arm and said, "You know you can do better than Seth. He's a dipstick."

Landry sat on his front porch, shucking corn. His shoulders were sunburned. They were big and muscly, bulging out from underneath his overall straps. The first words out of my mouth were, "Sorry your uncle got ran over by his tractor."

"Me too," he said. He looked at me, maybe smiling, maybe not.

"She's Carly," Nancy said, walking up the stairs. She didn't bother to say hello, much less offer any sympathies.

I followed her, wondering why she was acting so rude and haughty. It was embarrassing. Maybe *she* was embarrassed. After all, her dog had found some of Uncle Thomas. Maybe this was her way of avoiding that unpleasant fact. "I'm Landry," he said to me.

"Usually, I would bring my best friend, Sue, but I think it would be nice for you to meet another outsider," Nancy announced.

I frowned. Landry caught my sour expression and I quickly turned away. My face felt hot. But I'd caught another glimpse of a sort-of smile playing on his lips.

Nancy and I sat on the porch swing. Landry kept on shucking. None of us said a word. I tried not to stare at him. A little while later, Mrs. Davis came out with three mugs of hot chocolate and a couple of blankets to cover us. It was starting to get cold. Spring came late in Kansas.

"Carly's from New York City," Nancy said once Mrs. Davis was back inside. "Her dad executed some spies back in '53."

"My dad didn't *do* the executing," I protested.

"He helped get them there, didn't he?"

I wasn't sure what to say to that. "Anyway, she's been here since the ninth grade, so she knows what it's like to be new," Nancy added.

Landry chuckled. "City kid, huh? Sounds like I might have to pick your brain . . . Carly, is it?" I nodded. With both hands I lifted the mug to my mouth and took a big swig. Bits of marshmallow stayed on my top lip.

"Carly, you've got some right there," Nancy whispered, pointing it out with her index finger.

"Oh my God," I said, wiping it with my coat sleeve.

Landry dropped the corn and hopped to his feet. "I can get you a rag," he said, going inside the house.

"What are you doing? Are you trying to embarrass me?" I hissed, scowling at her.

She shook her head. "Don't have a cow."

"Cool it," I said.

He came back with a dishrag. I took it, trying not to hold on to his hand.

"So are you two paper shakers?" he asked.

Nancy flashed a big smile. "No, we're not cheerleaders," she said. She sounded as if she were suddenly in front of an audience. "I'm the sophomore class president and Carly's on the yearbook staff. She wants to be the editor next year. She usually talks more than this."

I smiled, but I really wanted to run *her* over with a tractor.

He went back to shucking. "Well. I guess that doesn't give either of you a whole lot of time to go on dates, then, does it?"

My face felt hot again. "I'm dating Seth Patterson," I blurted out. I was furious with myself. Why did I just say that?

"Oh," he murmured, not lifting his eyes from the corn.

"Do you need some help?" I asked, desperate to change the subject. "Honestly, I'm an excellent shucker."

Before he could answer, I jumped off the porch swing and crouched beside the crate. I grabbed a piece of corn from it and started pulling the husks from the cob, stripping it clean in a matter of seconds. I tossed it into Landry's finished pile and moved on to the next one.

"Hey, look at you," he said gently. "Not bad for a—"

"City kid," we finished at exactly the same time.

I turned to him. "Jinx, you owe me a Coke," I said.

We were close, huddled together over the mess on the porch. I could see his eyes were more hazel than brown. I knew I had a big goofy smile on my face. But I didn't care. He did, too.

CHAPTER THIRTEEN

"Where are you going in such a hurry?" Landry asks me now.

"That traitor . . ." I begin. I point at Mary Claire, who's putting on her coat and standing up from the table. My shoulders sag. "You don't think Bobby did it, do you, Landry?"

"It's not like I *want* to believe he did it," Mary Claire says, placing her arm on my shoulder. "If you want, I'll help you prove that he didn't."

"I'll help, too," Landry offers.

We stand in the middle of Hartman's Café, the two of them staring at me, as if I have any clue what we should do. I try to think of what my dad would do in a situation like this. Actually, I have no idea what he'd do, other than grumble, "Real life isn't like *Perry Mason.*"

"We need to find some evidence to prove that someone else did it," I tell them. I walk out of Hartman's Café and they follow me. We stand at the curb on Main Street. "Like on *Perry Mason,* we need to go to the scene of the crime."

"But it's blocked off," Landry says.

Mary Claire turns to him. "How do you know?"

He stuffs his hands in his pockets, looking down. "My dad

and I went snooping last night. They have the road to the house blocked off."

"Did you see anything? Anything at all?" I ask him.

He shakes his head, sheepish. "It was dark."

I wonder if he regrets opening his mouth. If he's ashamed, he shouldn't be. Everyone in Holcomb is curious about that house.

"Any detail at all would help. If the person were a local, they would know the land. If the person were an outsider, then they wouldn't." I start to pace. "It's daytime. We'll be able see anything out of the ordinary with the sun still out."

"But Landry just said it's blocked off," Mary Claire says.

I pause. "That's not going to stop us, is it?"

Landry looks up at me. We both look at Mary Claire.

"Fine, I'll drive," she groans, pulling her keys from her coat pocket.

THE RIVER VALLEY FARM is a few miles from town, so it takes a while to get there. We drive in silence. I think of Nancy as the car bounces along. The trees lining the two-lane highway are mostly barren now, branches naked except for the last few dead leaves. The sky is gray. It suits my mood. Maybe theirs, too. I think it's just too much for any of us to carry on a conversation.

When we arrive, I see that Landry was right. Police have roped off the entire drive with yellow tape. It's impossible to get close, like I did that first night. I don't know what I was expecting.

"Now what do we do?" Mary Claire asks, peering over the steering wheel.

"Who put me in charge?"

"You did," Landry says from the backseat. "I've never even watched *Perry Mason*."

Mary Claire keeps going and eventually pulls over on the side of the Arkansas River Bridge. She puts the car into park and turns to me.

I shrug. "I don't know what to do," I say.

She sighs. We sit for quite a while. I can hear the faint rumble of the river behind the closed car windows.

"Do you think the person dropped their shotgun here?" I ask in the silence. "You know, threw it in the water? Because that's what the police think."

"What are you getting at?" Landry asks.

I get out of the car and run over to the bridge. It feels colder now; the wind has picked up. I wrap my arms around myself, squinting down at the black current.

"Carly, what are you doing?" Mary Claire calls. She steps outside the car, watching me lean over the guardrail.

"Give me a second."

I gaze back across the bridge and toward the farm. I try to imagine that night. The person came across this bridge to get to the Clutter farmhouse. Four shotgun blasts—then out of the house and back down this road. One way in; one way out. If the killer had gone toward town, he would have been caught. If only one of the Clutters had escaped and chased after him . . .

"Four gunshots," I say out loud.

"Yes," Landry says. I hadn't even noticed he was standing right next to me. "Carly, what are you getting at?" he repeats.

"What did it say in the papers?"

He shakes his head, confused. "What part?"

Mary Claire runs up to join us.

"Four gunshots, four dead bodies. But they were all tied up, and Mr. Clutter's throat was cut, right?"

They both nod.

"How could one person tie them up and then make Mr. Clutter and Kenyon go to the basement?"

Mary Claire's eyes grow wide, and I know what she's thinking.

I can usually read her from the way she looks at me. Narrow eyes mean she's untrusting. Rolling of the eyes means she's disgusted. Moving her eyes from side to side means she's questioning my motives. Closing one eye and looking at me with the other means she's plotting. She's an open book when it comes to her eyes. That's why I know what she's thinking, and that's why I have to say again, "It wasn't Bobby. And there was more than one."

The blank stare that she's giving me, the kind where no blinking occurs, the kind that means *I can't believe you're actually right*; well, she's giving me that one right now.

I turn to look again at the rushing water. "I have a theory."

"A theory," Mary Claire repeats. But she's nodding. She's having an epiphany moment.

"Wait," Landry suddenly cries. "If it was just one man, Mr. Clutter could have met him at the top of the stairs with his twelve-gauge shotgun and some buckshot. Nancy and Kenyon would be alive, telling us how their dad killed an intruder . . ."

I stop listening. Something under the leaves at my feet has caught my eye: a dark splotch on the pavement. I stoop down and sweep the leaves out of the way with my gloves. There's a gooey substance on the ground . . . It kind of looks like dried ketchup. No. Something else. Thicker. My heart starts thumping. I think I know what it is. It's too much of a coincidence for something like that to be here. Way too much.

"Carly, what is it?"

They peer over my shoulder to take a look at the dark reddish-brown substance. I get on my knees and lean over and take a big whiff.

"Carly, that's disgusting," Mary Claire says.

My heart is beating so fast I can hardly breathe. "It smells rancid," I manage. "Coppery, too, like a roll of pennies."

"Carly?" Landry whispers. "Is that . . . ?"

"I think I found blood."

MARY CLAIRE DRIVES TO Garden to get the sheriff while Landry and I stay put to make sure no one comes along and disturbs the evidence. We sit together on the other side of the bridge. We can't stop staring at the ugly spot beside the opposite guardrail.

"When did you hear about Nancy?" he asks me.

"At church," I say. Landry isn't Methodist like Nancy and me. He's Catholic like Bobby. Before Bobby and Landry, I'd never met a Catholic before. Or if I had, I didn't know it. Before moving to Holcomb, I never went to church. I don't see the big deal about the different types of religion, but apparently other people do. Nancy told me she would never be able to marry Bobby because he's Catholic. According to Mr. Clutter, faiths couldn't mix. I may be naive but I don't get it. My family's going to the Methodist church only because a client of Dad's recommended it. We were new to town and we were trying to fit in.

"What about you? When did you hear?" I ask.

"From Mrs. Parker, she was making the rounds."

"Do you think the blood belongs to them—the murderers?"
I ask.

"Maybe," he says.

I shiver, wrapping my arms around myself. "Or it could be
from . . . you know, one of them."

"Could be. Or it could be from an animal," he says.

I blink and turn to him. That hadn't occurred to me. He shrugs.
"Maybe an animal was hit by a car."

"Like a deer?"

Before he can answer, sirens fill the air. A police car turns onto the
bridge; Mary Claire's car is following closely behind. Sheriff Robertson turns off the sirens and lights. He gets out of the patrol car
and walks toward us. He's an older man with bushy black eyebrows
that stick out over his wire-rimmed glasses. He pulls up his black
pants, lays his dark tie on his belly, and straightens his tan cowboy
hat. An officer with him opens the trunk and pulls out a briefcase.

"Carly, Carly, Carly," Sheriff Robertson says. "Carly, you
shouldn't be out here."

"But, Sheriff . . ." I start.

He stands before me, his hands on his hips and gun, his expression stern and unflappable. He's never been a fan of the Fleming
family.

Living in the city meant that every time you heard the sound
of a gunshot, you did the most logical thing: call the police. They
would do the most logical thing: come to investigate. But in
Kansas, the first time we heard the sound of a gunshot, we called
the police and they did come, but all they did was mock us. Two
officers stood on the front porch, shook their heads, and laughed.
Sheriff Robertson taught us a valuable lesson that night. In the
city, when you hear a gunshot, you call the cops; in the country,

you better have your own. Dad went out and bought one the next day. To my knowledge, he's never fired it.

"Sheriff Robertson, I found blood," I say, pointing near the bridge.

The officer stands in front of the sheriff and waits for his instructions. I can tell that Sheriff Robertson doesn't exactly want to indulge me, a fifteen-year-old girl.

He sighs. "Take a sample."

I feel somewhat vindicated even with his disapproving stare.

"Again, Carly, you shouldn't be out here," he says.

"I just had to—"

"Carly, leave it alone."

"We're trying to clear Bobby's name."

The officer bends over and opens his briefcase. "That boy's not a suspect."

"Deputy," Sheriff Robertson scolds him.

"Sir?" he asks.

"But, Sheriff, you brought him in as one," I say.

"Carly," he says with a sigh. "I shouldn't be telling you this, but he passed his polygraph test."

"Passed is a good thing, right?"

He nods. I breathe a sigh of relief.

"Now, Carly: promise me you won't go looking where you don't belong. You understand me, girl?"

"I promise."

He nods, satisfied. Of course, he can't see my gloved fingers, snugly crossed behind my back.

CHAPTER FOURTEEN

I SIT ON A WOODEN pew next to my parents on the left side of the church, staring at the four cold gray steel caskets in a row in front of the pulpit. People I don't even know are sitting near me, whispering, spreading rumors about how they died. Two hundred seventy people live in Holcomb; lots of them could have done this.

"Did you know the deceased?" a man dressed in black sitting directly behind me asks a grief-stricken woman to his right.

"No," she whispers. "Did you?"

"No, ma'am," he says in a soft voice. "I'm from out of town, just wanted to pay my respects."

I want to stand and scream at these funeral crashers, *YOU DIDN'T KNOW THEM! GET THE HELL OUT OF THIS CHURCH.* But I don't.

I think Nancy would have hated this.

My aunt Trudy once said, "People always think highly of the dead when they're dead. It's definitely not how they thought of them when they were alive."

They canceled school today so anyone who wanted to come to the funeral could. Mary Claire's here, along with Karen. So is Audrey Phillips. She doesn't go to HHS. She attends church here.

That's how Audrey knew Nancy. Audrey's with her parents. Her dad's a deputy with the GCPD. He was one of the first on the scene.

Seth's not here. He chose fishing with Alex instead of being here, with me.

"God bless you," Mrs. Parker sobs to Beverly Clutter, one of the two surviving daughters as Beverly walks by on her way to the front pew. Rumor has it Beverly and her fiancé are thinking about moving up the date of their wedding to this weekend. Everyone's already in town and the family needs a shred of happiness during this horrible time.

Mrs. Parker sits beside me without asking if the seat is taken. She goes to all the funerals, whether she knows the deceased or not. She always makes an appearance, carrying that oversized purse of hers. She reaches over and touches my knee with her thick hand. "Everything's going to be all right. She's in a much better place."

I laugh.

"Carly Fleming, this isn't the time for jokes," she says, and my mother pinches my right thigh.

I don't know why people say they're in a "better place" or any other phrase of comfort, encouragement, or just plain Kansas niceness. It doesn't make sense. "You know, they look at peace," some people say. You just want to reply, "Why, yes, they do, because they're dead." No comforting phrase can make up for the fact that we shouldn't be here today.

DESPITE THE FACT THAT there isn't an empty seat in the sanctuary, people keep coming into the church.

They stand in the aisles and up against the walls, anywhere there isn't a seat. I see Sue sitting across the way. She sees me. We smile and shake our heads. This shouldn't be happening.

Reverend Cowan stands at the pulpit and talks about the Clutter family. Everything he says we already know. Everyone has a Clutter family story, especially if you live in Holcomb. The Clutter family was a whole. Together they worked hard, supported each other, supported their neighbors.

Then he talks about each family member, starting with Kenyon. He starts to speak in short dramatic bursts. About the boy's love of basketball. About the boy's devotion to his friends. Asher starts to bawl beside me. I find that I am crying, too.

Mom and Dad are stoic.

Next comes Nancy, "the town darling," as the reverend calls her. By now he's almost crying himself. I don't blame him. Funerals are rare around here.

Reverend Cowan draws a deep breath and intones Nancy's virtues in a shaky voice. How she respected her parents. How she was a beacon, the embodiment of "what we in Holcomb call the Christian thing to do." How she took it upon herself to befriend everyone in the community. On and on he goes about what a nice, sweet, good girl she was.

Suddenly I'm not crying anymore. I'm almost laughing. My mom pinches me as I fidget. True, Nancy was the "town darling." She knew it. But she was also a liar, and she knew that, too. Does anyone here know that she smoked cigarettes? Sometimes when I tutored her, she would sneak a smoke. If her parents smelled it, she would blame it on Kenyon. And I think of the way she acted at Landry's house that day I first met him, the way she laughed at me when I couldn't handle Mary Claire's slaughtered cow. But no one knows any of these things. *I* probably shouldn't know these things. These things are meant for a friend to keep secret. They're not meant for someone who would betray you after you were murdered.

And she would have been my friend, if we'd just had a little more time. I've had this thought more than I'd care to admit.

The service is coming to an end. Reverend Cowan prays for peace at this time and hour; he petitions the Lord to give us power to understand the sins of a mind that has confusion. My dry eyes dart around the sanctuary. I spot two men I've never seen before, in front. They're hunched over; hair greasy and unkempt. I wonder who they are and why they're here. I don't know them from Adam. Maybe they're just strangers to Holcomb, like I was. Are the murderers here? Did they come to gloat? A camera clicks as the choir sings. A hymnal drops to the floor with a thud. A noisy diesel truck drives past the church. A few people whisper to their neighbors, *"How dare they drive down the street on this day, don't they understand we're trying to mourn here?"*

We say a final prayer and leave. Asher stays behind; he's a pallbearer for Kenyon. He's dressed in a black suit he's never worn before—one of Dad's. It's a little big. Asher's grown a lot. Mom didn't think he would need a new suit anytime soon, living in Kansas. A friend's funeral isn't an occasion you plan for. His eyes are puffy like he's been crying, but he isn't crying now. Probably all cried out. Unlike me, Asher actually *is* crying over a friend.

Four black Cadillac hearses are parked in a row, waiting for the caskets. The bodies come out of the church in a line. Nancy's is brought out first, followed by Mrs. Clutter, Mr. Clutter, and then Kenyon. Mom grabs my hand and holds it tight.

THE EVENING PAPER IS on our door-
step when we get home. $1,000 REWARD FOR INFORMATION ON
CLUTTER KILLERS is on the front page of the *Gazette*. *The Hutchinson
News* is offering a reward for any piece of relevant evidence to the
case.

"I bet everyone, whether they know something or not, calls
them," Asher grumbles. "No matter how stupid or useless. Or
untrue."

He's so bitter now.

I want to comfort him. I want to tell him that there might be
real leads, that there are plenty of Good Samaritans in Holcomb.
But what do I know?

"Mail," Dad says, handing Mom the letters and keeping the
bills for himself.

"Carly, you have something from Aunt Trudy," Mom says,
handing me a package.

I run upstairs as I tear it open. Inside is a half-written note on
beautiful personalized stationery. I slam the door behind me.

Darling,
Here's the piece from the Times, and Psycho, the novel. Be well.

Love,
Aunt Trudy

P.S. Don't tell your mother.

I toss the book on my bed and pull out the clipping from
The New York Times. Mr. Clutter's photograph is displayed with the
headline, WEALTHY FARMER, 3 OF FAMILY SLAIN.

H. W. CLUTTER, WIFE AND 2 CHILDREN ARE FOUND SHOT IN
KANSAS HOME

I hear heavy footsteps. "What do you have there?" Mom asks from behind the closed door.

I know I can't lie. "It's about the murders."

"Now, Carly."

"I asked her to. I wanted it."

"Carly, I don't want you to become obsessed with all of this."

I whirl and scowl at the door. "All of this? Really?"

Mom sighs, and I hear her plodding back downstairs. I wonder how she'd feel if she'd been Mrs. Clutter's tutor? Obsessed? And what about Asher? Is he obsessed with Kenyon's death? I try to return to the article. I hadn't even realized I've crumpled the newspaper clipping into a ball with my right hand.

CHAPTER FIFTEEN

"They found blood out on the Arkansas River Bridge," Seth tells me, as if he's letting me in on a secret.

We're sitting side by side at the counter at Hartman's Café. He knocks my arm with his elbow, almost spilling my cherry limeade.

"Careful," I say. I try to edge away from him but can't. The stools are built into the floor, close together.

"Did you hear what I just said?" he asks.

I take a sip of my drink, my eyes roving over his pudgy face, his beady eyes. There's something mean in his smile. I can't put my finger on it. Dirty satisfaction. Or maybe I'm just thinking those words because his flannel shirt is so grimy. When was the last time he washed it? It occurs to me, sitting there: I find him repulsive. I take a last slurp of the sweet, slushy liquid and place my glass on the counter.

"I know they found blood on the bridge, because I was the one who found it."

He rears back and frowns. "What?"

"You heard me. Mary Claire, Landry, and I went searching for clues."

"Landry," he says with a laugh. "Why are you hanging out with that rectangle?"

"He's not a rectangle."

Seth's lips turn down. "You're right. He's worse."

I roll my eyes. "Why weren't you at the funeral?" I ask, changing the subject. "Was fishing more important?"

"Listen—" he says, grabbing a menu from the stack next to the napkin dispenser. "I want to remember them alive, not like that, not forever lying in those death boxes. Plus, seeing dead bodies." He shivers, waving the waitress over.

I WAS FOOLISH EVER to have gotten involved with this boy. It was Mary Claire's idea. The only reason I began dating Seth Patterson was because he was best friends with Bobby, and Bobby was dating Nancy. I was the new girl, the outsider in this small town. I needed all the help I could get when it came to making friends.

"It's easy . . . Date Seth," Mary Claire said as she sat on my front porch flipping through back issues of *Teen* magazine. She smirked at a cover headline from July:

DOES FATHER REALLY KNOW BEST?

"I don't even know Seth," I said.

"Yes, but he knows you." She kept her eyes on the magazine.

"How does he know me?"

"You're exotic."

"Exotic? I'm from Manhattan—"

"Yes—and not the good one."

The whole good-versus-bad Manhattan was made abundantly clear each time someone brought up that I wasn't from Kansas.

You know how, in *The Wizard of Oz*, Dorothy talks about Kansas and how great it is, and you can tell that the Tin Man, the Cowardly Lion, and the Scarecrow don't exactly care? That's me. But in reverse. New York City is my Kansas; Holcomb is my Oz. The whole talking-about-my-home thing became a drag. Mary Claire made it pretty clear that New York City was as boring to her as a wide-open prairie was to me.

"He likes you," she said, grinning but still not looking at me.

"Seth likes me?"

"Yes."

"But he doesn't even know me."

"He'll get to know you."

"Is that how 'like' works out here?"

That made her lift her head. "Out here?" she asked.

"Past the Mississippi."

Mary Claire rolled her eyes. "If you don't want to be forever known as the outsider, then yes, it's how we do it out here."

The problem was that dating Seth didn't make me an insider. Bobby may have liked him, once, for reasons I'll never know. But Nancy could not stand him. She once told me that the thing that annoyed her most about Bobby was his loyalty. He refused to cut anyone loose, to grow apart. Bobby's friends were friends for life. "Like the chicken pox," she said. "Once you catch it, you'll always have it. Bobby gets infected with people that way."

I didn't think loyalty was like a disease then, and I don't now, either.

Seth's problem with loyalty is that he has none. He didn't even go to her funeral.

⌒

"WHAT WOULD YOU LIKE?" the waitress asks him.

"Cheeseburger and a Coke, and she'll have—"

"Don't bother," I interrupt. "I can't believe you can be this heartless." I grab my bag, take a dollar out of my wallet, and throw it on the counter.

"What?" he asks, staring at me as if *I'm* the one who lost my mind.

"Don't act so surprised," I say, putting my purse strap around my shoulder. "And by the way, the caskets weren't open."

He starts to laugh. "Why do you even care? It's not like she was your best friend."

"Jerk," I say under my breath.

Walking to the exit, I look in the mirror next to the door. I see Seth pocket my dollar bill, like I left it for him.

CHAPTER SIXTEEN

POLICE, CONTINUING THEIR INVESTIGATION of the tragic Clutter family slaying, have requested that anyone with pertinent information please contact the sheriff's office.

Seth is right, as much as it burns me. But just because Nancy and I weren't exactly best friends, it didn't make me care any less that she's dead. We never got the chance. I was never going to tell anyone that she needed tutoring. I would have kept that secret. I've kept Mary Claire's secrets. I would have done the same for Nancy. I *did* keep her secrets, the ones she let me in on without even knowing.

Night has fallen and it's cold out, but inside my car it's warm and quiet. I cross the Arkansas River Bridge and roll to a stop once I hit the dirt road. The police barricade has been torn down. Slowly, I make my way down the Chinese elm–lined drive.

The Stoeckleins' porch light's still on. I bet he sees my car, but I don't even care. He could be calling the cops for all I know. But he didn't call them that night. Why didn't he hear anything? Why didn't he do anything to stop it? He lives right here; so close. He must have heard the gunshots. He must have heard them scream. I don't understand. I don't understand at all.

There's this eerie feeling, like someone's watching. It's dark, though, so anyone could be nearby. In the glove compartment there's a flashlight. I step out of the car with a shiver. The flashlight's beam is weak; it doesn't give much light as I walk up to the porch. The door's unlocked. There's a single light left on in Mr. Clutter's office.

"Anyone here?" I whisper. Thankfully, no one answers.

I close the door behind me, as silently as I can, and tiptoe toward the light. Inside, boxes are stacked on each other. Some are filled with trinkets, and picture frames are stacked ever so neatly on the floor. The Venetian blinds still cover the windows; papers are spread on the desk. Mr. Clutter's sweat-stained gray Stetson hangs on a hat peg on the wall. Even his coats are tucked on posts on the coatrack. It's just the same, as if they still lived here. Grabbing his Stetson off the peg, I put it on my head. The brim falls just below my eyes. Pushing the cowboy hat back, I sit in his oversized chair, which is against the wall. I try to determine if anything is missing. The desk looks exactly as I remembered it, everything in its place, except for his binoculars. They're gone. Maybe they've already been packed away. I hang the hat back on the peg.

In an empty house all you can hear are the creaks and moans. Holding on to the railing with each step, I climb the stairs.

There are four bedrooms on this floor. One is Eveanna's room, and one is Beverly's. Kenyon's room is just as I remembered it. Pale gray and green walls; his Hardy Boys books still on the bookshelf, along with his plastic cars from model kits. Pictures of his prizewinning sheep hang on the wall. But his radio's gone. It could have been packed up, but nothing else looks out of place.

Nancy's small bedroom is across the hall. Like her father's

study, there are brown boxes stacked on top of one another. But photos of her friends and clippings from the school newspaper are still pinned to the cork bulletin board. A nightstand, a wooden chair, and a bed frame are what remain. The paint's faded where someone took soap and water to it, but no amount of scrubbing could get everything clean.

I drag the wooden chair across the hardwood floor and sit next to the nightstand.

Nancy kept her diary in the top drawer. I won't read it. Just holding it in my hands will be enough. But reading something that she wrote will make her alive again. Authors always say that when they die, they'll live through their words. Can that be said for one's diary?

It doesn't matter; it's not there. Nancy's sisters must have taken it.

My hair falls in front of my eyes. Hoping to find a bobby pin, I dig through the drawer. Tucked at the back is a hairclip. It's probably been there for years. It's one that we made in the ninth grade during Home Ec. The paint's faded but it's still in one piece. A clip with an old button painted green, yellow, and brown to resemble the state flower. I twist my bangs and pin them to the side.

In the middle of the room I sit in complete darkness.

There's a crash downstairs. It makes me jump. The chair shifts and slides against the hardwood floor. Mr. Stoecklein doesn't need to come in and find me here. Shaking, I hold the flashlight in both hands like a weapon. Slowly, I tiptoe across the creaky hardwood floor, out of the room and down the stairs to the front door. The sound of the back door snapping shut stops me.

I spin around, swinging the flashlight like a club. The sound of objects crashing to the floor makes me regret that.

Bending over, I pick up Mr. Clutter's Stetson and place it back on its peg.

There's another noise. It sounds like it's coming from the kitchen. Holding the flashlight out in front of me, I feel my way to the back of the house. The moon shines through the curtains. Outside I hear an engine starting. Peering out the glass panels on the door, I don't see a truck. There's a red substance smeared along the brass knob. I bend over to take a closer look. It smells metallic. My stomach clenches. I know that smell.

Shining the light at the floor, I see blood droplets leading to the basement door.

Using the railing and the flashlight as my guide, I make my way down into the basement. The light catches a faded bloody print on one of the wooden stairs. Bending, I run my index finger over it. It's dry.

I shouldn't be doing this. My palms are clammy and I'm shaking. But I don't stop.

I keep walking.

There's an imprint on the floor where the couch sat, the same couch where I sat on Friday night during the *Tom Sawyer* cast party.

WE WERE ALL LAUGHING and sipping punch and eating sugar cookies in the shape of Santa Claus. Nancy pretended she'd chosen Santa Claus on purpose as a gag, that she thought it was hilarious. Everyone believed her. I was the only one who knew the truth. This was the only cookie cutter the Clutters owned; I'd seen the insides of their kitchen cabinets and drawers and pantry. Funny how she'd rather make up a lie about all the many cookie cutters her family had at their fingertips than admit the truth. But by then I knew that it was much easier for her to lie in certain situations.

"Everyone wants Christmas early, right?" she said.

I sat on the couch talking to Landry, who'd built the sets. Seth was in the corner with Bobby, watching me. I caught him a few times rolling his eyes. I made the mistake of mentioning to Landry that I'd been here a couple of days ago.

He asked why, naturally surprised, since no one knew that I was Nancy's tutor.

I covered it up quite well. "Dropping off something for her dad from my dad," I told him without missing a beat.

Besides, it *could* have happened. My father was always advertising his services some way or another, through letters or leaflets or pamphlets. If anyone in this town ever got on the wrong side of the law, they'd think of only one lawyer to call.

It was fun lying like that, I have to admit. I'm just as good at it as Nancy was. At that moment I felt like I was in a play with her. We were both acting, inhabiting our parts. I think I'd be good at *that*, too—acting, I mean. I'm the only one around here who has seen a Broadway show. I could see myself at home on a stage.

After the party, a group of us went to a midnight spook show at the State Theater in Garden. I went because Seth wanted to go. We had to get permission from our parents. We were supposed to go on Saturday night, but Mr. Clutter didn't want Nancy to be out too late and fall asleep in church the next day, so we went on Friday instead.

Since it was a group thing, he allowed it. Nothing scandalous could happen in a group. We stayed out past three. I didn't wake up until close to noon the next day. I had no idea I'd never see

Nancy alive again. That Saturday would be Nancy's last full day on earth.

THE LIGHT FROM THE flashlight moves across the room and falls on a faint red stain on the wall. Touching the rough concrete, I close my eyes, my mind playing like a movie reel of what might have happened to Mr. Clutter and Kenyon. All at once I feel like throwing up. I turn to run up the stairs but bang my knee on a dresser. Bending over in pain, I see little droplets of something on the floor. When I touch them with my index finger, they're wet.

Someone's in the house.

Rushing up the stairs, I face-plant. My eyes smart. I rub my palm against my nose. That metallic smell and a rush of pain hit me.

I sniff to stop the blood from dripping out.

Mr. Stoecklein's porch light comes on when I reach the landing. Standing in the middle of the kitchen, staring out the window, I turn off the flashlight and wait for a flashlight to be shone on me. The porch light goes out.

A hand covers my mouth; an arm grabs my waist, pulling me away from the window.

"Be quiet," the voice whispers.

It's a boy's voice. Trying to wiggle free, I bend my leg back and kick my captor in the crotch. He falls to his knees. Quickly I flip on the flashlight and shine it in his eyes.

"Landry, what the heck?"

He has tears in his eyes. "Carly—"

"What are you doing here?"

"Can you shut that light off?" He reaches for my hand. He's grimacing, squinting up at me.

I drop my arm. "Landry—"

"I'm okay."

"No, you're not," I say, looking at the gash on his arm. I lead him to the bathroom. I turn on the light once I close the door, and examine his now bloody arm. "What did you do?"

"It's nothing."

"It's not nothing."

I rummage through a cabinet and find a couple of washcloths, one for him and one for me. I turn on the faucet and soak a washcloth with cold water, then wring it out.

"It doesn't hurt," he says. But he winces when I lay the wet washcloth on his arm.

"Sure."

"I tripped. I must have caught my arm on a rusty screw in the—"

"You should get this looked at."

"We've got more important things to worry about," he says.

I start to dig through drawers, trying to find a bandage. "What do you mean? Mr. Stoecklein?"

"I found shells . . . empty shells." Landry's voice is hoarse.

"Where?"

"Outside."

"Show me."

"Carly," he says, grabbing my arm. "Your nose . . ." He takes the washcloth that I have in my hand and runs it under the water. "What happened to you?"

"I fell up the stairs."

"That's a new one," he says, trying to stifle a laugh.

"I'll live."

I try to take the washcloth from him, but he shakes my hand off his and does it himself. I open my mouth to breathe while he presses on my nose. A sharp pain rushes through my body. I want to cry out, but I don't. His other hand brushes my hair out of my face. His skin is rough against my cheek. He's a farmer, and farmers' hands are not known for their softness. He looks in my eyes and smiles.

"Your nose is going to make it," he says, balling up my bloody washcloth and stuffing it in his jeans pocket.

I sniff and rub my hand against my nose. It's a little sore.

"Ready?" he asks.

I nod.

I follow him to the back of the house. As he grabs the door-knob, I notice the telephone sitting on the edge of the counter. The wires look frayed.

"Hold on," I say, picking up the receiver.

"Who are you going to call?"

"No one. It's dead."

"Maybe they canceled the service."

"Maybe, but I don't think so." Gently placing the receiver on the hook, I take the wires in my right hand and feel them with my left. "They've been cut."

"What?" Landry asks, moving to see for himself.

"Look. Someone cut the phone line. Which means the murders were premeditated. We have to tell the sheriff."

"He probably already knows."

"Probably, but maybe not."

"Let me show you the shells."

I swallow. I'm not sure why this sends a chill down my spine. The shells have long been emptied. "Right. The shells."

We crouch near where the tall grass stands at the side of the barn, shining the light on the ground. A couple of shells lie hidden in the scraggly grass. I see them only when the beam from the flashlight catches the shiny gold metal.

"They're empty," he says, poking them with a stick that he found next to the fence post.

"Maybe they dropped them when they left."

"Maybe—"

"I've called the sheriff," a man hollers, cocking his shotgun.

Landry and I don't move. We're frozen, hunched over the shotgun shells.

"Turn around, let me get a good look at the two of you."

We turn slowly. I shine the flashlight in Mr. Stoecklein's face as he aims the shotgun first at Landry and then at me.

"What the hell are you two doing?" he screams, his finger on the trigger. "Y'all are trespassing on private property. I can shoot you. I have that right."

I hear a police siren in the distance. It's approaching fast.

Mr. Stoecklein walks toward us, his eyes slits. "Carly Fleming, is that you?"

"Let us go, we won't come back, I promise," Landry begs.

"Landry Davis." He snorts. "I thought I heard your busted old Ford." He's pointing the gun at Landry now.

"Please—Mr. Stoecklein—don't kill us," I plead frantically.

The siren is deafening now, bright headlights bearing down on us from the drive. A police car skids to a halt, spraying gravel. The driver's door flies open, and a shadow emerges, hidden in the glare. Mr. Stoecklein laughs, aiming the shotgun in the air and firing off two shots. I flinch at both. "Next time, it'll be you," he says.

But his smile vanishes when Sheriff Robertson runs up beside him and wrestles the shotgun out of his hands.

"What are you doing?" Mr. Stoecklein yells. "They're on my land."

Throwing the flashlight on the ground, I shout, "It's not *your* land!"

Mr. Stoecklein steps toward me. I take a step back. He looks at me and then at the sheriff. "Give me back my gun," he says. But the sheriff stands his ground. Mr. Stoecklein tries to pry it loose from the sheriff's grip. "Let me have my gun," Mr. Stoecklein says again.

"Sir, you need to calm down," the sheriff says.

"Me? They're on my land."

"It's not your land!" I say again.

Mr. Stoecklein backs off. He stands off to the side with his arms crossed over his chest.

"Carly, why on earth are you out here on the Clutter land?" He looks over at Mr. Stoecklein, who's muttering something unintelligible. "And at this time of night?"

"I . . . we found something," I say, bending over.

He grabs his flashlight off his belt and shines it on the ground right where I'm pointing.

Taking the stick from Landry, I pick up one of the shells. "See, Sheriff Robertson? Clues."

"Carly—"

"The telephone wires were cut, too."

"Drop it," the sheriff barks at me.

I open my mouth and he shakes his head, waving Landry and me out of the way.

The sheriff goes to his patrol car and returns with a couple of small plastic bags. Then he takes his flashlight and hands it to Mr. Stoecklein.

I'm desperate to be heard. "The blood on the bridge," I begin. "It was . . ."

"It was animal, not human," the sheriff finishes.

"What?"

"A farmer said that he butchered a hog on his place last week and dumped the entrails in the river." He sounds tired and fed up as he tells me this. Then he turns back to Mr. Stoecklein and asks him to focus the light on the empty shotgun shells.

I don't understand. It made sense. I thought we could help. The blood on the bridge was a good lead, evidence that would clear Bobby. My father always manages to get his defendants off on seemingly random discoveries like that. But then I'm reminded of what Dad always says about *Perry Mason.* I look at Landry. He's standing off to the side, next to the patrol car, with his hands in his pockets. I got us in trouble . . . for what? I wipe my nose. I'm bleeding again.

"Here," the sheriff says, handing me a handkerchief from his pocket. "Now, you two get home," he orders. "*Straight* home."

Landry walks me to my car.

"Do you think it's weird that Mr. Stoecklein could hear us but not the killers?" I whisper.

"I don't know," he grumbles miserably. "I just wish I hadn't come here."

I open the door and start to get in. "You do?"

He holds the door open before I can shut it. "Carly, don't go and get yourself—"

"Arrested?"

"Yeah. But I was going to say killed." He closes the door for me.

I get in the car, start the engine, and drive slowly back down the Chinese elm–lined lane. When I turn right on the Arkansas River Bridge, I see headlights in my rearview mirror. My hands strangle the steering wheel. It's Sheriff Robertson; it has to be. I see lights on top of the car. I travel down the road slowly, stopping at the stop signs rather than pausing like I usually do. Every turn I make, the car behind me follows. I turn onto my street. A streetlamp catches the roof of the car, and I want to be anywhere but here. I pull into the driveway and shut off the engine.

The sheriff's waiting at the curb. I give him a questionable look and make my way up to the house. He follows right behind me.

"I thought we had an understanding," I say without turning.

"So did I, young lady," he replies.

"I left, didn't I? I don't need an escort. Please just go."

"Can't do that, Carly." He's side by side with me now.

I start to grab the doorknob but the sheriff jumps forward and knocks loudly, three times. My shoulders slump; I close my eyes and shake my head.

After a minute, Dad answers the door.

His reading glasses are perched on the bridge of his nose. He was in the middle of something. He looks at me, then at the sheriff, and then back at me again. With a heavy sigh, he invites Sheriff Robertson inside.

CHAPTER SEVENTEEN

IT'S PHEASANT SEASON. HUNTING STARTS before dawn. Not that I slept very much last night, anyway, with the world of trouble I am in, but every time I hear a shotgun blast, I jump and my blood pressure rises.

"Don't these hunters have any manners?" I say, grabbing my coat from the closet. I hate this coat. Back in New York I had an overcoat. This is one of those big fluffy coats that makes me look like the Michelin Man. I have to get out of this house. I'll go to school early. I don't want to be late for school, either. "I wish they would just go home."

"I know you do," Dad says from the couch in the living room. "But remember, Carly, this *is* their home."

Always with a lesson, I think. I roll my eyes, turning to the door so he can't see. "Can't they hunt somewhere else? It gives me the willies," I say.

"Now, you know the rules, right, Carly?" Dad asks, his voice louder.

I nod. Of course I do. After the sheriff left, Dad lectured me while Mom sat on that same couch, dabbing her eyes.

"I'll repeat them to make sure," Dad says. "Do not go back to the Clutter farm. Stay out of the police business. They don't need your help. And after school, come straight home."

"Yes, sir," I say.

Asher bounds down the stairs. "I'll be home late," he announces. "I've got tryouts,"

He grabs his own fluffy coat. Another shotgun blast resonates through the house. He doesn't even blink. He zips up, his jaw tight. I stare as he fumbles with his bag. I want to leave, but he's dug out a notebook. It's full of little handwritten diagrams, Xs and Os on a basketball court.

"Are you okay?" I ask.

"I'm fine," he snaps. "Just worried about tryouts, that's all."

"You don't have to try out."

He glares up at me. "Of course I do. For Kenyon."

Dad gets up and joins us in the hall. Then Mom appears from the kitchen. Both have their eyes on Asher. He shoves the notebook back in his bag and turns to the door.

"Carly, someone from the Lock Shop is coming out around four o'clock to install new locks," Dad says. "Since you'll be home, you can let him in."

"I'll be running errands," Mom chimes in, hands at her aproned hips. "Unless I need to postpone them," she adds pointedly.

"So we're those people now," I say. "People who lock up." Dad's jaw drops. He turns to my mother, whose face is a mask of disgust. She whirls and stomps back into the kitchen. Dad's eyes blaze as he turns back to me and throws open the door.

"You're this close, young lady," he whispers. "Don't get into any more trouble." He musters a thin smile for Asher. "Good luck at tryouts today, son. I'm proud of you."

But Asher is already at the sidewalk.

Dad slams the door behind me. I run to catch up with my brother.

When people found out about the murders Sunday afternoon, they started locking their doors. This was a new thing; no one ever locked their doors around here. People trusted each other, I guess. When we moved here in the ninth grade, we were one of the very few families that would lock up even if we were home. Eventually, we stopped. It felt safe. Not anymore.

The hunters are farther away now, but the *pop, pop, pop* echoes more clearly outside the house. Asher and I make our way to the bus stop. Silence falls except for our footsteps. It's cold and nearly wintertime; it's especially quiet. There are hardly any birds, even. There's another distant shotgun blast, and I wince.

"Get a hold of yourself," Asher snaps. "It's only a shotgun."

It's only now I see Asher isn't an outsider anymore. Asher was Kenyon Clutter's best friend. Asher is an up-and-coming basketball star. He's comfortable with the sound of pheasant hunting. He doesn't confuse or conflate.

"So you say," I mutter.

His face twists in anger. "Maybe you shouldn't put your nose where it doesn't belong."

When the bus comes, Asher takes his seat near the front, next to his friend Grant, another basketball player. I walk to the back and find my usual empty spot—a whole seat to myself with no companion. I'm the only one who sits alone. We ride in silence, all twenty-one of us, to school. The whole time, I think of Mary Claire, who lives close enough to walk.

CHAPTER EIGHTEEN

Mary Claire stands at her locker, talking to Landry. They're hunched over a newspaper. "They probably just belong to some hunter," she's saying.

I approach, but slowly.

"But they're from a twelve-gauge shotgun," Landry argues, stabbing his index finger at the print. He reads aloud, "'According to West, another gun theft in the area is being checked for possible connections with the Holcomb shootings. A twelve-gauge shotgun was reported stolen last week in Dodge City.'"

She shakes her head. "But—here; look what it says." She reads, "'Police caution against rushing to judgment. Shotgun pellet casings are more difficult to match to a specific weapon than bullet casings, and require more time from ballistics experts.'"

"So?" Landry asks. "They always say that. They can identify a shotgun casing from other things, like the firing pin."

Mary Claire sniffs. "How do *you* know? Are you a ballistics expert?"

Landry shrugs. "I saw it on *Perry Mason*, okay? But I bet it's true."

On any other morning, I might have laughed. Now I just feel

sick. I listen to their conversation, but I don't dare interject. Mary Claire and Landry look like they could come to blows over an article in the *Garden City Telegram*. I don't want to get caught in the crossfire.

Too late. Mary Claire turns and sees me there.

"Hey, Carly, what's wrong?" she asks.

"I was the one who found the shells last night," I hear myself answer.

Landry folds the paper and cocks his head at me with a frown.

"Sorry, *we* found the shells," I correct.

"Excuse me?" she says.

"We found the empty shotgun shells," Landry clarifies.

She smirks. "I'm not dumb, I understood."

I lean in close and whisper, "Last night, we went to the farm—"

"You did what now?"

"Went to the farm and—"

"You didn't do that. Tell me you really didn't do that."

I straighten and look her in the eye. "I had to see it for myself."

"You could have gotten caught."

I grin miserably in spite of myself. "We did, by Mr. Stoecklein and the sheriff."

"Mr. Stoecklein almost shot us," Landry adds.

"You guys," she says, pausing as Mrs. Walker passes. She lowers her voice. "I've been to enough funerals for my lifetime."

"But we finally have a lead," I whisper back. "Even though I'm on the sheriff's radar now, and have been warned and threatened by my parents to stop, to stay out of the police's business—"

"And the KBI's investigation," she interrupts.

"Yeah, them too . . . but as I said, we finally have a lead."

She shrugs.

"What's *that* supposed to mean?" I ask, mimicking her shrug.

Mary Claire doesn't answer. Instead she takes the newspaper from Landry and reads, "'Boris E. Bailey, forty-eight years old, Hodgeman County rancher, died Wednesday of injuries received when the car in which he was riding veered out of control Tuesday night, throwing him into a barbed wire fence.'"

"That doesn't have anything to do with the case."

"True, but what a horrible way to die," she says, looking first at me and then at Landry.

"Mary Claire Haas!" I gasp.

Landry slams his locker shut and marches off to class.

She watches him go. Then she gives me a sly smile and shoves the newspaper into my chest. "That'll teach him to put himself in danger. Carly, tell me you didn't go inside the house?"

"Well—"

"I told you not to tell me."

CHAPTER NINETEEN

AFTER SCHOOL, I STOP AT my locker to get my homework, though I have no interest in doing any of it. I see Asher going into the gym for basketball tryouts. "Good luck!" I yell. He does one of those half shrugs and half smiles.

Mary Claire is sitting on a bench outside, next to where the buses line up. "Hey, Carly," she calls, waving me over. "I've been waiting for you."

Pushing the strap of my bag over my shoulder I walk toward her.

"Are you going to apologize?" I ask.

"For what?" she asks.

"For being so mean to Landry."

"I'm not going to apologize," she says.

"Then why did you call me over?"

"To warn you."

"Warn me?" I ask.

Mary Claire leans toward me. Her eyes are big and bright. "Doesn't it make you nervous that maybe—just maybe you find out whoever did this and it changes everything forever?"

Her tone makes me nervous. "How so?"

"It might be one of us; did you ever think about that?"

"Bobby? Because——"

"Stop. I'm not saying him. I'm saying it could be any one of us. I know how to use a shotgun, and so do you."

"Any one of us?" I repeat.

"Yes," she says.

I open my mouth, but I can't think of an argument. Mary Claire is right. Most people in Holcomb own a shotgun. Including us. And I know from my dad that even the ones who don't own shotguns have been borrowing spares from their neighbors who do.

Funny: Seth was the one who taught me how to shoot. Or tried, anyway. Dad never touched our shotgun after he bought it. At first, I couldn't get the hang of it. The shotgun flew out of my hands, I landed on my butt, and Seth laughed real hard. He said it took him a while to get used to the pull, too. He had to have his shoulder popped back in after a couple of false starts. Maybe I'd dislocate *my* shoulder, he said, but it was worth it to bag a pheasant. I still hear the ringing in my ears.

"What I'm saying is . . . just be careful," Mary Claire is telling me.

I nod.

She sticks her hands in her pockets and watches the stream of kids piling onto the buses. "I need to go to Garden to the Vogue Shop to get some new nylon stockings for the Sadie Hawkins dance Friday night. I tore a hole in the only nice pair I have yesterday at the funeral."

"I don't think I'm going to the dance," I say.

"Why not?"

"I'm grounded and anyway Seth and I had a fight."

At first she's quiet. "Did you guys break up?" she asks. Her voice is gentle. I wonder if she's remembering the reason she got me to date him in the first place—to get in good with Nancy.

"I don't know. Maybe. I . . . don't know."

"Well, no matter, you're still going with me to Garden."

"I don't think I should. My parents were really mad when the sheriff talked to them," I say. "I'm grounded. I have to let the lock-smith in at four."

"It's just to Garden."

"Um—"

"I'll buy you a cherry limeade at Candy's."

I turn to Mary Claire—to get a look at her face and those eyes that always tell me what she's thinking. Her eyes never lie, even when her mouth does. She smiles, and I smile back. And I know she's thinking the same thing I am. Those cherry limeades at Candy's are pure heaven in a glass.

ON THE DRIVE OVER, my happiness melts away. I'm afraid I'm going to get caught. Like my dad is going to come out of his law office and see me, or my mom will be shopping at the Vogue Shop at the same time Mary Claire's purchasing her nylons. I keep a panicked eye on my surroundings. As we pass the Finney County Courthouse, I spot a crowd of men in overcoats and fedoras.

"Mary Claire, stop!" I yell.

She slams on the brakes and I go sliding straight into the dashboard. "What is it?"

"Can we make a pit stop? It won't take long."

She sighs. "Where?"

I stretch my arm behind me and point to the courthouse, where the men are clamoring up the steps and disappearing through the building's big double doors.

"Car-ly," she says, dragging out my name like my mom does when she's upset.

"Please."

She throws the truck in reverse, nearly running over a straggler as he crosses the street. I recognize him; it's Mr. Brown, the editor of the *Garden City Telegram*.

"Sorry," she yells, waving as she pulls into an empty spot close to the square.

I'm desperate to find out whatever scoop he's chasing. Mary Claire's never panicked or paranoid. She'd be the first one into a burning building. I'm usually the cautious one. The one who is always afraid of getting caught or into trouble. But since last Sunday, I've grown a spine—or as Mr. Haas would say, "a pair." I've had a gun pointed at my face and had the sheriff escort me home. But Mary Claire doesn't want to be here. She lingers in the truck. I have to walk over to her side and practically pull her out.

We race up the steps, pushing our way inside the two heavy doors, and head down the long hallway. There's a marble staircase at the end. The men all gather at the bottom of it, waiting for someone to descend and make an announcement. I know they're doing this because I've seen my father do the same thing. But he's not here, thank goodness. At least not that I can see.

"Since when have you been afraid of us getting into trouble?" I whisper.

"Since when have you not?" she asks.

But I brush her off and try to find a spot off to the side, where we can be relatively invisible. I hold my breath, listening to scraps of conversation.

"*The Kansas City Star*," one man says to another.

The man nods. "*The Denver Post.*"

I turn to Mary Claire. "What paper should we say we're from?"

"Carly, be serious," she groans.

I hug the wall and slide farther into the mob. I've never seen the courthouse so crowded.

Agent Dewey appears at the top of the staircase. Everyone surges forward and suddenly I'm swept up in the current from behind, separated from Mary Claire, who had the good sense to stay back and not get caught up in the stampede. Oh well. I'll slip out once I hear what I need to hear.

"Agent Dewey, over here, question, over here," one man yells, raising his arm.

Just like that, everyone's yelling over each other. I catch the names of dozens of newspapers: *Dodge City Daily Globe, The Hutchinson News, The Wichita Eagle, The Hays Daily News, El Dorado News-Times, Great Bend Tribune, Garden City Telegram* . . . another KBI agent joins Agent Dewey at the top of the stairs. Both men stand with their hands in their pockets. They look unnerved. Finally, Agent Dewey pulls his hands free and gestures for the crowd to quiet.

"Please, please," he calls. His voice is scratchy. "Agent Nye and I will take questions after I make my statement." The place turns quiet. All eyes are on him as he pulls a scrap of paper from inside his jacket and starts to give an update on the case. His hands tremble slightly. I listen, but there's not a single piece of new news. He finishes with, "Shotgun shells were found in the vicinity of the Clutter farm."

I glance over my shoulder and shoot Mary Claire a slight smile; she's shaking her head.

"What about the blood?" someone yells.

"The blood found on the Arkansas River Bridge was in fact hog blood, not human . . ."

As I turn back around, a man pushes me forward and I hit another man, who pushes into another man, then another, and another—until I hear a high-pitched yelp. Everyone laughs. For a second I wonder if some other girl from school had the same idea I did. Then I hear a woman's voice, low and deep, with a strong Southern accent.

"Truman," she scolds.

Once the crowd splits in two, I catch a glimpse of the yelper. My jaw drops. It's not a schoolmate; it's a *man*. He's shorter than I am, with a big head and glasses. His outfit is ridiculous. He's wearing a pristine white suit in the middle of winter and a long coat. It touches the ground even as he straightens himself, his tiny mouth twisted in a scowl. The ensemble is topped off by a colorful scarf, wrapped around his neck at least three times. A woman with a fancy bonnet towers over him, shaking her head, as if he were her child—though she looks younger than he is. Agent Dewey's not deterred. He pointedly ignores the strange little man, turning instead to Mr. Brown.

"Your readers at the *Garden City Telegram* will probably like to know that Mrs. Bentley took Teddy, the Clutters' dog," he says. "Now if there's nothing else, we have to get back to our investigation . . ."

There's a nudge from behind. I turn and see Mary Claire, who's squirmed her way through the crowd. She looks miserable. "If only that dog could talk," I say to her.

"What's that, little girl?" the tiny man calls to me, peering over his thick eyeglass frames. His voice is so squeaky and nasal, it's hard not to stare.

"Who you calling little?" I retort.

More laughter. Even Mary Claire chuckles.

Agent Dewey and Agent Nye glance at each other. Someone shouts about the thousand-dollar reward that *The Hutchinson News* is offering. The rest of the journalists start to chat among themselves, shoving their notebooks back into their pockets. It's clear that this press conference is over. No new leads, no new clues. At least none that the authorities are sharing.

I elbow Mary Claire in the side. "I'm going to ask a question," I whisper.

"No, don't," she hisses.

I raise my arm.

She turns to me. "What are you doing?" she mouths, pulling at my arm.

"Agent Dewey, Agent Dewey!" I call over the din. A hush falls over the crowd. Heads turn in my direction. "And what paper is *she* with?" the tiny man squeaks.

"Holcomb High School," I say, lowering my arm. "The Longhorn yearbook staff."

Agent Dewey sags a little. I can sense Mary Claire doing the same beside me, probably wishing she could melt right into the floor.

"Carly, what are you doing here?" Agent Dewey asks tiredly.

"On a first-name basis . . . impressive," the tiny man says.

There's some laughter, but Agent Dewey just glares at him, annoyed.

"Carly, you shouldn't be here," he says, turning to me and crossing his arms over his chest.

"Why did the police clear out Bobby's locker at school if he's not a suspect? Why do you need his tennis shoes? Does it have something to do with that bloody footprint in the basement?"

Agent Dewey is glaring at *me* now. He no longer looks annoyed. He looks angry.

"Bloody footprint?" the tiny man cries. "What bloody footprint?"

Agent Dewey places his hands on his hips. He chooses to ignore me. The room is dead silent now.

"Now, what paper are *you* with?" he asks the tiny man.

"I'm not with a paper," the man says.

Agent Dewey squints, looking him up and down, lingering on the outrageous scarf. "Then what are you doing in Finney County? I reckon you're not from around here."

The man shakes his head. "I'm from civilization. I write for *The New Yorker.*" He looks around the hallway, taking in a sea of blank expressions. "It's a *magazine?* My name is Truman Capote. I'm a *writer?*"

His tall companion sighs loudly. She glances toward the exit.

Truman. That name! The name she called him! It hits me all of a sudden. Grabbing hold of Mary Claire's coat, I start shaking her. "He's the author of my book!"

"I'm glad you're reading; now let me go," she says, squirming. She couldn't care less. Like Mr. Capote's tall friend, Mary Claire clearly wants to get out of here, too. No one else is impressed by the fact that a real-live famous author is in our midst, either. And the real-live famous author looks like he's personally offended by this fact.

"Well, I'm here to tell *your* story," Mr. Capote harrumphs.

"And how do you suppose you're going to do that?" Agent Dewey asks.

"Don't be silly. I'm here to help." He coughs. "I'll do as you do—investigate. Did Herb have any enemies?"

"Not that we know of at this time," Agent Nye chimes in. "Now, if there's nothing more, we have to get back to work—"

"One more thing," Mr. Capote interrupts. "When will we be permitted to enter the house for a look-see?"

"You will do no such thing," Agent Nye replies, his voice harsh. "This is an ongoing investigation. The Clutter home is still a crime scene, and we intend to handle it as such."

Mr. Capote's companion nudges him, but he shakes her off. "I'm not going to get in the way," he whines.

"Someone's got their panties in a wad," one of the reporters says. The hall erupts in laughter once again.

"You want to see?" Mr. Capote says without missing a beat, unbuttoning his suit coat.

"Come on, now, there are children present," another reporter snaps.

Mr. Capote shoots me a smirk before turning back to the stairwell. "My apologies to the children."

"There is one statement I'd like to make," Agent Nye calls loudly, silencing everyone. All the reporters turn to face him, ready in a flash once more with their pens and paper—well, except for Mr. Capote, who just listens, still grinning. "There have been several false claims and exaggerated stories circulated. The Clutter slaying victims were not tortured or mutilated. Each was shot in the head, and the throat of the father was cut. The women were not molested. That is all. And I would appreciate if you would print every word that I just said for your readers. Thank you." He turns and disappears up the stairs to the second floor. Agent Dewey turns and follows. I try to catch his eye but fail.

Mary Claire tugs at my sleeve again. "I guess we better leave, too," she says.

"In a minute."

"Carly—"

"I have to tell Agent Dewey what I know."

"What do you know that he doesn't?"

"Wait here. I'll be right back."

"Carly!" she cries.

But I'm already shoving my way toward the stairwell.

UPSTAIRS, THE HALL IS completely deserted. The doors are closed, except for one. It's the office of Duane West, the Finney County prosecutor. I swallow as I tiptoe toward it. Mr. West is a little scary—even my dad admits it. He's six foot four, with perfectly combed dark hair and thin lips that never smile. My dad says he takes every crime as a personal insult.

When I reach the door and poke my head inside, I nearly slam right into Agent Dewey.

"Carly, you know you shouldn't be here," he says.

"Agent Dewey, I have to tell you something," I whisper back, trying to poke my head around him to catch a glimpse of Mr. West, who's deep in conversation with Agent Nye.

"Carly, not right now," Agent Dewey says with a sigh, as if he's tired of me. He moves to close the door on me, but all of a sudden the office falls silent.

"Miss Fleming, what are you doing here?" Mr. West asks, standing up. He has a pile of folders in his arms.

I seize the opportunity, jumping past Agent Dewey. "Mr. West, I just need to tell someone what I know, please." I nearly trip over a box. I see now that the whole floor is littered with photographs and boxes full of papers stacked to the rim.

"What's all this?" I ask.

"Leads," he says sharply. "Now, what do you want me to know?"

I stand straight, and, taking a deep breath, I admit that I trespassed onto the farm and in the Clutter house.

Now it's Mr. West's turn to sigh. He glances at Agent Dewey, who bows his head and shakes it. Agent Nye just sneers and looks at his watch, as if I'm wasting their time.

"Carly, Carly, Carly," Mr. West scolds. "Does your father know?"

"Yes, sir—and so does the sheriff."

Mr. West's eyes widen over the rims of his glasses. "My goodness, young lady. Do you know how much danger you put yourself in—"

I interrupt him before he can reprimand me any further, spilling everything I saw: how the telephone wires were cut, how the binoculars that belonged to Mr. Clutter weren't in his office, how Kenyon's radio wasn't in his room, where it always is. Lastly, I tell him about Nancy's diary not being in her nightstand drawer.

"Who would want to steal her diary?" I ask.

He sits back down. "I'll look into it," he says.

"You believe me, don't you, Mr. West?"

He begins to organize the papers on his desk. "We have it."

"You have what?" I ask.

"The diary," he says.

"Are you going to read it? Because it's private. You shouldn't be reading Nancy's diary."

The room falls silent again. Agent Nye glances at Agent Dewey, cracking a slight smile.

"Carly, I'm busy," Mr. West snaps, peering at me over his glasses. "Stay away from that house."

I clench my fists at my sides. "Well. Thank you for your time," I say, holding myself back from running over and pushing everything off his desk. I whirl past Agent Dewey and slam the door shut. I feel the glass shake with the impact. Walking back down the hall toward the staircase, I notice that another door is cracked open, but only slightly. Inside I see a table covered with plastic bags.

"Carly, wait!"

I'm surprised when I turn around. It's Agent Nye. I stop dead in my tracks.

"Don't mind us; we're all just frustrated with the case. I promise I'll look into it."

"What's in there?" I ask, pointing to the room.

"Evidence," he says, reaching past me and pulling the door closed. "You know what, Nancy Drew?" he says with a laugh, locking up. He digs into his back pocket and takes out a steno notebook, then tears out the first page—scrawled over with sloppy handwriting—and hands the rest of the blank notebook to me. "If you want to help, take notes. Write them down. Anything can be a clue."

He's mocking me, but I still take the notebook and shove it into my coat pocket.

"Thank you, sir."

Mary Claire appears at the top of the stairs just as Agent Nye vanishes back into Mr. West's office. "You finished?" she whispers. "I've got to get me some nylons." She grabs me by the arm and pulls me down the stairs before I can get into any more trouble.

CHAPTER TWENTY

AFTER GOING TO THE VOGUE Shop and waiting and waiting for Mary Claire to pick out some nude nylons, we sit in a booth at Candy's Café, drinking cherry limeade. Flipping open the steno notebook, I pluck out the tiny pieces of paper stuck in the spiral binding.

"Where'd you get that?" she asks.

"Agent Nye."

"That was nice of him," she says, biting the cherry garnish off its stem. "I was sure he was going to arrest you."

"But he ripped off the front page," I mutter, flipping it closed.

"I guess it was important, huh?" she says.

Her words get my wheels turning. Of course it was important. Then I remember something Perry Mason did with a piece of paper and a pencil when he was deprived of important information, too. Maybe it will work in real life, despite what my dad says. "Ma'am?" I call to the waitress. "Can I borrow that pencil?"

She picks it out of her hair and holds it out for me to take. Scooting out of the booth I practically run over to her.

"Bring it back, 'kay, hon?"

Leaning over the steno notebook I open to the first page, where

Agent Nye's notes have made a barely noticeable imprint. As lightly as I can, I make tiny brushstrokes over the lines of invisible text. My heart starts to pound as words appear. "I've got it, Mary Claire, I've got it!"

People stare. My face gets hot and I lower my voice to a whisper. "Look."

She leans over and tries to read upside down. "What does it say?"

I squint at the paper. "'Great Bend—hunting knife. An abandoned car. Two Negroes were seen driving, '53 or '54 Mercury, Colorado license plates. Bloody western-style shirt with the sleeves cut off found in ditch north of Hugoton.' That's all."

"What does it mean?"

I look up and smile. "Clues. Anything can be one, you know."

WHEN MARY CLAIRE PULLS up in front of my house, a man in work boots is sitting on the front porch reading the paper, a tool kit at his side. My elation over the notebook vanishes. I forgot all about the locksmith. My parents are going to kill me.

"Shoot! I'm late," I whisper, sick to my stomach. I can't bring myself to open the passenger door. "I was supposed to be home at four."

"Just tell your dad that you had to run an errand with me," Mary Claire says calmly.

"Yeah, I don't think so. I'm grounded. I'm supposed to be at home—thinking about what I've done."

"Tell him it's all my fault. I forced you to come with me to the Vogue Shop. He won't be too mad." She laughs. "Your dad likes me."

It's true. Dad has always liked Mary Claire. I can tell that he likes her better than he likes—than he *liked*—Nancy. He's talked about how he gets a kick out of her, of how she loves to have fun and how she wears her heart on her sleeve. Mom, too.

"Yeah, I'll just conveniently leave out the part about running into the courthouse," I joke grimly, half to myself.

"Sounds like a plan," she says with a smile and a wink.

"I was being sarcastic," I grumble.

"See you later, Carly. Hopefully."

She drives off, leaving me alone with the man on my front steps.

"I'm sorry I'm late," I offer.

He lowers the newspaper so at first I can only see his eyes. They're dark brown and they don't look friendly. He folds the paper in half and stands up. "You Mr. Fleming's daughter?" he grunts.

"Yes, sir," I say.

"Your dad said four, right?" he asks, looking at his pocket watch. Then he grabs his tool kit. "I've got places to be."

"I know. I know. I'm so sorry." Grabbing the key from my bag, I unlock the door so he can get started. He tosses the paper on the chair after I've let him in, then eyes the lock. He crouches down.

"Everyone's doing this, aren't they?" I ask, watching him unlock his tool kit.

"Ever since Sunday morning. Did you know them—them being the Clutters?"

"Yeah, I knew them, did you?"

He shakes his head. "But that doesn't mean I don't care." He takes out a screwdriver and starts loosening the screws. "Righty tighty, lefty loosy," he says under his breath.

Picking up the newspaper, I sit with my feet under my butt. I flip through until one word catches my eye: *deaths*.

"'Mr. and Mrs. H.W. Clutter, Nancy, Kenyon Clutter,'" I read out loud.

"The obituary," he says.

"Did you read it?"

He nods. "It's sad, isn't it?" He pulls the new knob out of a brown paper bag.

"They don't say how they died . . ."

"In obituaries they usually don't," he says.

"But that's not right. It's important to know how they died."

He stops working on the door lock and looks up at me. "But is it more important to know that they lived?"

CHAPTER TWENTY-ONE

APPARENTLY BEING GROUNDED ONLY MEANS being shackled to my family. I, Carly Fleming, am free to hit the open road, as long as my parents and brother supervise.

Asher and I are in the backseat of the Desoto. We travel the 146 miles to Hays in silence, though once we're close, Mom starts to talk and fidget. One of her old prep-school friends is speaking at Jefferson West High School, and then I remember what we're doing here. Mom convinced Dad to drive all this way because she wants to see a friendly face from the past. I don't blame her. It's been way too long since we've seen anybody from back east. We all could use a break from Holcomb.

"I can't believe he came all the way to Kansas," Mom says, applying more lipstick to her already-stained lips.

She's transformed all of a sudden. In fact, the way she's acting now reminds me a lot of the way Nancy used to act when she was looking forward to seeing Bobby—oblivious, lost in a mirror with herself. I don't share these thoughts. I'm not even sure what they mean.

Asher's asleep. Mom and Dad assume it's because he's tired from the grueling basketball tryouts. He'll find out if he made the team this weekend. But I know he's tired because he can't fall asleep at night. I can hear him pacing in his room. He won't talk to me about the reasons why. Anyway, he's sleeping now. That's what matters. Best to let Mom and Dad run this little sideshow. It was their idea.

Mom looks at her watch.

"We'll make it, don't you worry," Dad says, making a right turn off the highway.

"I know, I know. It's just, I haven't seen Jack in forever."

"Him and your mom were *friends*," Dad says to me in the rear-view. He emphasizes the word *friends* in a dry voice.

He hasn't looked so content or relaxed in a long time, either. I try to be content for him. But mostly I'm annoyed and restless and bored.

"Friends, just friends, that's all," Mom says, shaking her head.

"Right," Dad says.

Mom slaps Dad on the arm. They laugh. "Who's this Jack fellow, anyhow?" I ask loudly.

"An old friend of your mom's," Dad begins. "He—"

"Jack and my brother used to get into trouble at Choate," Mom interrupts. "Your uncle Carlson was a part of the Muckers Club."

"A group of boys that got into loads of trouble," Dad clarifies with another smile.

"He brought Jack home one weekend while I was at home from Rosemary Hall," Mom adds.

"Your uncle was one of the orchestrators of a notorious stunt at Choate," Dad says, focusing on the road. Now that we're off the highway, we're passing farmhouses and roadside shacks, the telltale outskirts of a small Kansas town. We're close to the end of this endless journey. Which is good, because Dad can't hold in his laughter. "He took a firecracker and exploded the toilet seat—"

"Oh, please," Mom interrupts. She shifts in her seat and turns to me. "Jack's speaking to a sold-out crowd," she says, getting back on topic. She waves her left hand over her head, fingers crossed. "He could well be the next president of the United States."

MOM AND I FIX our dresses and Dad and Asher straighten their ties. Both Mom and Dad, Mom mostly, are more insistent than usual that we look presentable to her old friend from back east: Jack, the presidential hopeful. She doesn't want us to embarrass ourselves or, more importantly, embarrass her. As Dad hands the man at the door our tickets, Mom scoots past us and jets to the back of the stage. We find our table and sit. I take a sip of the warm water and a bite of the crunchy burned garlic bread.

Asher still seems half asleep, or at least dazed. Dad is in a daze, too, until he spots Mom hurrying back to find us, teetering on her heels.

"He's still so handsome," she says, her face flushed. She sits and places a napkin in her lap.

"I'll pretend like I didn't hear that, dear," Dad murmurs.

Asher is awake now, all of a sudden. He taps his fingers on the table. He sits up, his lips twisted in a scowl.

"What's wrong?" I ask.

"I should be at home practicing. I need more time," he says. "Why am I here?"

I have no idea what to say. I glance at Dad, but he's focused on the stage.

Glasses clink. Everyone else's attention is focused on the stage now, too.

"Governor Docking," Mom whispers excitedly, half standing, holding her martini in her left hand.

The spotlight falls on a pleasant-looking man with thick curly hair at the podium. A hush falls over the crowd as he introduces the night's keynote speaker: "John Fitzgerald Kennedy." Jack, as he is known to my mom. I crane my neck and squint toward the stage. Even from this distance I can tell that Mom is right. Jack *is* handsome. Even more handsome than Governor Docking.

For the next half hour, the "esteemed senator from Massachusetts" (the governor's words) stands at the podium and speaks in his funny New England accent about the farm way of life and the threat of the Soviet Union.

Asher's stabbing his cheesecake. I'm picking at the tablecloth. Like my brother, my mind is somewhere else. I didn't tell Dad that I was late to meet the locksmith. Dad didn't ask, so I didn't tell. I don't want to get into any more trouble than I already am. Besides, Asher is right: he and I weren't supposed to come to Hays. But no one wants to be home alone with a murderer on the loose. If it happened once, it could surely happen again.

Just when I'm about to burst, the room explodes with applause. Mom and Dad leap to their feet. So do I. Asher stands as well, the last one up. Onstage, Governor Docking beams beside Senator Kennedy and shakes his hand.

"A good team, a mighty good team," a man yells from the back of the room.

The room clears. Dirty dishes are left on tabletops; cloth

napkins dot the floor. Before I know it, Mom's engrossed in conversation with a man she calls Liam. He's wearing shiny black shoes. His suit reminds me of New York. But what strikes me most about him is how he ran up to Mom after the speech and kissed her flat on the lips. Dad didn't seem too upset, but I was stunned. Asher didn't even notice, of course.

Now he's looking at me. Mom blinks several times, collecting herself.

"Liam, these are my children. Carly, she's fifteen," Mom says.

I shake the man's hand.

"I can't believe you have a fifteen-year-old," he says with a laugh. "It's seems like yesterday that your brother . . . you know what I mean." He shakes his head and waves for her to come on. "He'll want to see you. I just know it."

We follow them to the back of the stage, where people are crowded around the governor and the senator. But once Jack catches a glimpse of my mom, he disengages and runs over to her.

"Becca," he calls with a toothy smile. "I'm glad you're here." He kisses her on both cheeks. "You traveled all the way from . . . where are you living now?"

"Holcomb," she says, sighing. "A very, *very* small town."

Standing off to the side, I spot *The Hays Daily News* stuck between a cheese platter and a pitcher of iced tea. OFFICERS CHECK SHOTGUN SHELLS IN CLUTTER CASE. It's interesting to read what other newspapers have to say about what you've been living with for the past week.

Liam walks over, stands beside me, crosses his arms, and looks down at the newspaper. "Is that not the worst thing that you ever did read?" He shakes his head. "I read about it in *The New York Times*. It's a shame."

"How do you know my mom?" I ask him.

"I went to school with your uncle Carlson," he says.

"I never met my uncle."

He puts his arm around my shoulder and pulls me into him. "Your uncle was one of the greatest men I ever knew."

Uncle Carlson was killed over in the USSR during the Battle of Stalingrad. He was a part of the lend-lease program with the US Air Force. German forces shot him down as he was delivering American-made boots requested by Stalin. He was killed on impact. They say that he didn't feel a thing. He's buried at Arlington.

"You're named after him; don't you know?" Liam asks me.

I nod. I almost laugh. All that, and still my aunt Trudy can't remember that I'm Carly. But maybe that's why. She doesn't want to be reminded of her dead brother.

"Carlson was my friend." Liam looks at me with sad eyes. "It's hard to lose a friend."

"Did my mom tell you what happened in Holcomb?" I ask.

He nods.

"It's hard to lose a friend," I echo.

Then all of a sudden, Mom is introducing me to Senator Kennedy, and I shake his hand. I can't bring myself to look him in the eye for more than a second. His grip is firm and hearty, and I'm surprised by how dry his skin is. It feels like warm sandpaper. Maybe that's what happens after you shake a hundred thousand hands.

"I can't believe how big your children are," he says to Mom.

I muster the courage to meet his gaze. "Is it true that you, Liam, and my uncle blew up a toilet with a firecracker?" I ask him.

He glances sheepishly at Governor Docking and whispers, "Yes."

Everyone bursts out laughing. My mom's face is flushed. She once said that I'm a lot like my uncle Carlson. Since I've never met him, I couldn't tell if she meant it as a compliment or not. But judging from the way the senator and Liam are acting, I think I know now.

"Give my best to Jackie," Mom says, hugging the senator one last time.

"I will," Jack says.

"Promise me you'll make your way to Manhattan soon," Liam says, hugging Mom.

"Sooner if this one runs for president," Mom replies.

Jack flashes a bright smile. "I haven't made any decisions."

"Oh, you know you're going to run—"

"Becca," the senator interrupts. He punctuates her name with a glance born of old times I can only imagine. But then he shrugs, the intimate warmth fading. "Besides, there wouldn't be any point if half the country thinks I take orders from the pope."

"Or that you'll build a tunnel to the Vatican," Liam adds.

Jack nods. "Exactly, and that is the problem," he says stiffly. "I have to convince people what you already know. I serve my country. Not as a Catholic. I serve as a Democrat who happens to *be* Catholic."

Mom's adoring eyes are fixed on her old friend. "You have to run," she whispers. "You do have a lot of support out here. Look at that crowd tonight . . . They want you to run."

Jack relaxes for a moment. "To be honest, I'm shocked by that. I can't imagine being a Catholic out here. You'd almost be an outsider. People eye you differently and they suspect you do horrible things."

"Pig-headed people," Liam points out.

I want someone to agree with him. But the grown-ups have moved on with their hugs and good-byes, bantering away. Anyway, I've stopped listening. At the word *suspect*, a terrible thought occurs to me, one that hadn't even entered my mind until this very moment. But now I wonder, do people think Bobby's a suspect in the Clutter murder only because he is Catholic?

CHAPTER TWENTY-TWO

Tonight's the Sadie Hawkins dance. Skinning an entire cow by myself sounds like more fun than going, but my mom thinks that if I don't go, I'll end up regretting it. It's actually been a big fight between my parents. My dad doesn't want me to go since I'm grounded, but Mom thinks it'll be good for me to be around people who knew Nancy, too. I overheard my parents discuss me in a tone I really didn't care to hear again, one that made me sound like a criminal.

"She could have been in more trouble if the sheriff wasn't so understanding. She could have gotten herself killed," Dad said.

"Yes, I know, dear, but it's just a dance. She won't get into any trouble at a dance. She'll still be grounded after it," Mom said. "Who knows how she'll suffer here alone?"

After some tense negotiation, they emerged with smiles, not knowing I'd eavesdropped.

So I'm allowed to go. Funny that I don't really want to go. And I tried telling my parents that. Even using the "I don't have a thing to wear" excuse. But that's a lie. Aunt Trudy sent me one dress. A designer label—a Chanel—a thing that you can't get at Penney's. It's a black silk lace chemise dress, sleeveless. It has a swoop neckline and goes just down to my knee. The dress that

Nancy was going to let me borrow, the one that was found draped over a chair next to her bed, is now buried six feet under.

Mom lets me pick one of her handbags, while Dad prepares to take my picture with his new camera. It's a Kodak something-or-other. He's very proud of it. He mounts it on a tripod and fiddles with it, trying to look like he knows what he's doing.

"You do look fantastic," he says reluctantly. Before he can start snapping way, Asher bursts through the front door. It's cold outside, nearly winter, but he's wearing gym shorts and a basketball jersey under his coat. He's drenched in sweat.

"I made the team," he announces, collapsing on the couch beside me.

I grimace. He stinks. As in: literally. He *reeks*.

Mom pinches her nose. "You smell like a boys' locker room," she says in a nasal voice.

"Now, how do you know what a boys' locker room smells like, dear? Do tell," Dad says with a smile, looking up from his camera adjustments. At least my father's mood has improved.

"Don't ask questions you don't want to know the answer to," Mom says, laughing.

I turn to Asher, careful not to wrinkle my dress. "Good job," I tell him.

"Thanks," he says. He stares at the camera and scratches his sweaty scalp. He doesn't look excited about being on the Longhorn basketball team, not like he should be. Not that I can blame him. But something else is clearly bothering him, something beyond missing his friend.

"What's wrong?" I ask.

Asher grabs the basketball beside him and brings it to his chest and sits his chin on the logo. "Nothing's wrong," he says.

"Something is. Tell me."

"It's nothing," he says.

I wait for him to continue. Dad sees that he forgot to load film, so he and Mom scurry upstairs to fetch it.

"Kenyon . . . he should have been there with me," Asher says.

"He was."

"Not really."

"*Really.*"

Asher sniffs. "You know what I mean."

"I do. So tell me what's really bothering you."

Only then does he shift on the couch to look at me. "Some of my new teammates are going over to the captain's house," he murmurs under his breath so that Mom and Dad can't hear as they bound back downstairs. "Should I go?"

"Kenyon would want you to be happy you made the team. You two worked hard."

"Exactly. *We* worked hard. Celebrating feels wrong—"

"Carly, your dress," Mom yells, shattering the moment. She throws her hands every which way, motioning for me to get up. Dad is back at the tripod, trying to shove a roll of film into the camera. I exchange a glance with Asher, who shrugs.

I smile. I hope the smile says what I'm thinking: *Kenyon wouldn't want you to feel like this.*

Asher smiles back for the briefest instant, but that might only be because our parents are making complete jackasses of themselves.

AFTER SNAPPING WHAT SEEMS like a zillion photographs, Dad gives me a ride to school. Before I get out of the car, I'm reminded of the rules:

Rule number one: come home right after the dance because you're grounded.

Rule number two: no going out cruising on the Garden City square because you're grounded.

Rule number three: do not do anything that results in having the sheriff come to the house.

"Do I make myself clear?" Dad asks as I open the front passenger door. A blast of frigid air greets me. Shivering, I place a heel on the pavement, eager to escape. Has it gotten colder?

"Yes, sir," I say.

Funny that my dad is starting to sound like Nancy's dad when it comes to rules. Or maybe not so funny.

"And Mary Claire will drive you home—"

"I know, I know," I interrupt. "Mom already talked to her parents. I'm allowed to have fun until eight-thirty, and then I'm grounded again. Like Cinderella."

THERE ARE APPARENTLY ONLY two boys left in the school without dance partners at the Sadie Hawkins dance. Ronald and Patrick. They have chosen to lurk nearby. Then they close in. Now they stand on either side of me—Ronald on my right; Patrick on my left—next to the refreshment table, each slurping his punch. I hope and pray that neither of them asks me to dance. They do give hints, lots of hints. "Carly, you look pretty" and "Carly, that's such a nice dress," but neither of them comes right out and says *Carly, please ask me to dance.* Thankfully it's traditionally up to the girls to ask the boys, and I won't dare ask.

Seth is on the other side of the gym. I watch him. Maybe he

sees me, but he doesn't look at me once; he's standing with Audrey Phillips. I can't help but feel annoyed. She doesn't even go to our school! But she jumped at the chance to take Seth to the dance when she found out we had a fight. I guess that means we really have broken up.

My angry eyes scour the brightly lit gym floor, then the shadowy places at the top of and alongside the bleachers. I spot Karen Westwood dancing unenthusiastically with some tall boy I've seen at the 4-H. I spot Mary Claire trying to hide—probably from Alex Baker, whom she'd invited only because I'd originally invited Seth. There's no sign of Bobby, though.

Should I have asked Bobby to the dance?

I shudder at the thought. Of course not. That's sick. He's in mourning. He lost his girl.

"Hey, Carly?"

Alex Baker is suddenly standing right beside me.

"I know the girls are supposed to do the asking, but I thought I'd ask anyway," he begins.

His acne stands out in stark relief under the harsh overhead lighting. I can see a smudge on the black plastic frame of his glasses. He pulls his red suspenders out with his thumbs for no reason I can possibly see . . . If he wants to appear relaxed, he appears more like a grandpa.

"Do you want to dance?" Alex finishes.

I'm not sure how to answer that question. Marie Claire asked *him*, and he's Seth's friend, so why is he asking *me*? What's his endgame?

I shake my head.

"Oh, okay," he says awkwardly. His hands fall to his sides.

I whirl toward Mary Claire. Thank God she spots us. She

motions me over with her punch glass. I nod. Luckily the song is coming to an end, and Seth breaks free of Audrey at the same moment. He waves at Alex to go outside for a smoke. This is my chance. I'll beg Mary Claire to drive me home immediately; I'll tell her I don't feel well. I race across the gym floor so fast I nearly trip, and when Mary Claire hands me some punch, I spill it all over my new black silk lace dress.

IN THE GIRL'S LAVATORY, standing in front of the basin, I stare in the mirror at the big wet stain splattered across the dark fabric. I grab a paper towel and run it underneath the water, adding a small drop of soap. But when I try scrubbing the stain until it's soapy, I'm left with a huge wet discoloration. It feels cold against my skin.

"It's not going to come out."

Mary Claire is standing right behind me. Did she follow me in? I didn't even notice. I have to laugh: people seem to be materializing tonight at all the worst times.

"I know," I groan.

"It's a pretty dress. Is it from Aunt Trudy?"

I nod.

Mary Claire's eyes brighten. "I knew it! She has the finest taste. But black? Come on, Carly, you don't have to be in mourning."

"I don't?"

She lowers her gaze.

I turn to face her. Neither of us says a word.

"They should have canceled the dance," I remark in the silence, mostly to fill it.

"Honestly, Carly," she murmurs, looking sideways at me.

"Think about who's here and who isn't. You could have stayed home if you were upset."

I open my mouth, then close it. She's talking about Bobby, of course.

"Nancy wasn't a good friend, really," Mary Claire continues. Her throat catches. The words are a shaky whisper, but her stare is unflinching. "You tutored her. She pretended to be your friend for the good grades that you got her."

My jaw drops. "How do you know I tutored her?"

"I may look oblivious, but I'm not stupid," she says, blinking.

"No one was supposed to know."

"Carly," she says hoarsely. "You and Nancy had nothing in common. You're taking her death way . . . you're taking it way too hard for someone who barely knew her."

I swallow. My eyes start to sting. "That's mean."

"The truth hurts sometimes."

"Don't you care that she's dead?" I turn back toward the sink and dab my eyelids with a tissue.

Mary Claire's face goes pale in the mirror. "How dare you ask me that?"

I spin to face her, but she's already halfway out of the lavatory.

The door swings shut behind her. My shoulders slump. *What am I doing?* I ask myself. *Why am I hurting my friend?* My teary eyes wander back to the mirror.

Leaning forward over the basin, I stare at the pimple that's popping out on my chin. Standing up straight, I smooth the wrinkles out of my dress. The stain mocks me. I try to smile, but all I can do is sneer. It isn't going to get any better than this.

I need to apologize to Mary Claire, though. That will help. I collect myself and stride to the door.

When I swing it open, I find Karen Westwood standing right there, as if she were waiting for me.

AGAINST MY BETTER JUDGMENT, I let Karen drive me home. Mary Claire must have left the dance, because I couldn't find her anywhere. Serves me right.

Karen's driving is a cross between Aunt Trudy's and Lee Petty's, the 1959 Daytona 500 winner.

"I heard about your sneaking into Nancy's house," she says, slamming on the brakes at a stop sign. "I bet that was really spooky."

"Spooky?" I repeat.

"You know . . . because they died . . ."

"Yeah, I get it."

Karen Westwood and I aren't exactly friends. Nancy Clutter and I *knew* each other at least, even if we were only friendly in secret. But the only thing Karen and I have in common at all is 4-H.

On the other hand, I feel like I know Karen as well as anybody else in Holcomb.

She's of a type. She likes to stir up trouble, to spread gossip and rumors, especially if they're not true. When my family first moved here, I was the hot commodity. Everyone wanted to know the new girl from New York City—the girl who didn't have a drawl, who overdressed, who didn't like the smell of cow manure. But that air of glamorous mystery, that potential, quickly dissipated. I was the *weird* new girl who didn't have a drawl, who overdressed, and who didn't like the smell of cow manure. I was the outsider.

"You know people think that you had a part in it," Karen announces.

I shake my head, too tired to put up a fight. "No, they don't."

She steps on the gas with a screech. "Yes, they do. Why would I lie about that?"

"Just try not to kill *us*," I croak. "Okay?"

"Don't be so melodramatic."

I make sure my seat belt is fastened. She's not wearing hers.

"Why do people think I had a part in it?" I ask.

"Because you're an outsider."

"I've lived here for three years," I counter, even though she's just confirmed every thought I've ever had about my status.

"That's really not a lot of time to get to know someone," she says. She turns to wink at me. Her smile is bright in the darkness of the car.

"Come on, Karen. Keep your eyes on the road—"

"Come on, Carly . . . if that's your real name."

I clutch the door in panic, but I still manage to laugh. "Not everyone believes that he's innocent," Karen adds.

"Who's *he*?" I ask.

"You know."

"Well, if we're talking about the same person, he is. Innocent, I mean."

Karen chuckles as she picks up speed again. "So *you* say."

"So the evidence says."

"Evidence? What evidence?" She glances at me, taking a curve with the gas pedal on the floor.

"Nothing. Just please look where you're going."

"People don't die for no reason."

It takes me a petrified moment to realize that she's turned onto my street. I'm home. I made it. Alive. I let out a gasp of relief. "You're right," I say as the car lurches to a halt. With trembling hands, I unbuckle my seat belt and glare at her. "Some people only die if someone kills them." Karen just smiles at me wickedly, clearly not getting the subtext.

"Get out of my car," she says.

My eyes narrow. I can't believe the gall of this girl. Grabbing the door handle, I shake my head. "Can I ask you a question?"

"I guess."

"Do *you* think it's strange that Mr. Stoecklein didn't hear anything that night?"

"Who?"

"The farmhand on the River Valley Farm."

She shrugs. "Maybe. I don't know. Why don't you ask him yourself?"

The horrible truth hits me. Karen Westwood is glad Nancy Clutter is dead. Not that I think Karen had anything to do with it. She's awful, but not *evil*. Still, the murders have done two things for her: they've conveniently gotten rid of her competition in the popularity department, and they've supplied her with the biggest windfall of wild rumors she could have ever dreamed of.

"You're a peach; you know that, Karen?"

"A peach." She laughs. "I've been called a lot of things—but never a peach."

CHAPTER TWENTY-THREE

THE HOUSE IS EMPTY. IT'S only 8:15 P.M. Mom and Dad are spending the evening with Mr. and Mrs. Hope, and Asher has reluctantly agreed to be with his teammates, to honor Kenyon and to celebrate making the team. So it's me, alone, for the next couple of hours at least.

An idea goes from a thought to a plan: zero to sixty in a matter of seconds, as fast as Karen Westwood would gun her accelerator.

But first I call the Hope residence. When Dad is handed the phone, I tell him that I'm home early, safe and sound. Mom asks if I had a good time. She sounds concerned. I lie and tell her that I did. They'll be home late.

I debate changing out of my ruined dress and into some comfortable pants and a sweater, then decide against it. It would waste too much time.

Pulling my hair into a bun in the bathroom, I smile at my reflection in the mirror. Lying on Nancy's behalf seems like the right thing to do. It's what she would have done.

The hall closet is where we keep our double-barreled shotgun and the box of ammo.

Grabbing the shotgun and six rounds, I head for the garage, plucking the keys off the peg. The Porsche awaits: a shiny, silver, two-seated standard. There's one place I can go to get my answers.

Swinging the gun around, careful not to scratch the car, I lean it against the passenger seat. Then I toss the ammo onto the passenger seat and stick the key in the ignition. The engine revs. A shiver runs down my spine as I put the car into reverse and shift into drive. Out on the dark prairie road, the wind blows my hair right out of its bun. It flops into a mess. *Little Bastard* is what James Dean called his car. I understand that now. Turning onto the Arkansas River Bridge, I slam on the brakes, coming to a complete stop. My head almost meets the steering wheel. The shotgun falls and hits my thigh.

Taking a moment to breathe in the cold night air, I press on the gas and it sends the Porsche down the abandoned River Valley Farm lane. My throat feels tight. I suddenly realize I'm crying, and I'm not sure why.

Mr. Stoecklein heard Bobby's truck when he left Saturday night and Landry's the other day, but why didn't he hear the killers? What about the screams? Let alone the gunshots? The gunshots were a hundred yards away. Am I missing something?

Parking off to the side, I grab the weapon and the shells and get out of the car. Aiming the double-barreled shotgun toward the sky, I remember what Seth taught me: *"Look, it's pretty self-explanatory. Point. Shoot. That's all you really need to know."*

I squeeze the trigger not once but twice. BOOM. BOOM. A porch light flicks on at Mr. Stoecklein's house. Loading two more rounds, I aim the gun at the sky. BOOM. BOOM. Leaning over the car, I grab the remaining rounds and load them.

"Who's there?" Mr. Stoecklein shouts, bursting out the front door.

When he see me, he freezes and points his sawed-off shotgun at me.

I don't lower my weapon like you see on TV shows; I aim *my* gun at *him*. I'm squinting in the glare of the porchlight. Wearing my punch-stained Chanel and heels and holding a double-barreled shotgun, I look like Calamity Jane—with the added bonus of tears rolling down my cheeks. I don't brush them off.

"Carly Fleming!" I shout.

"Lower your gun, little girl," he says, his voice loud and even.

"No." I straighten, collecting myself. "Lower yours."

My entire body trembles, not with fear, but with adrenaline.

He walks closer. His face is a mask of darkness; he's silhouetted by the light behind him.

"You're threatening me, my family," he says. His voice is softer now.

"Consider it a warning," I say.

"You . . . you do know that by trespassing on this property and shoving a gun in someone's face, you're breaking the law."

I sniff. "I don't care about laws."

He cocks his gun while I aim mine at his unreadable face.

"Why didn't you do anything that night?" I ask him.

He stops and lowers his weapon. Blinking, I can see now that his expression is one of tired disbelief. "What the hell are you talking about?"

"You heard—you had to. Why didn't you stop them? Why didn't you save Nancy?"

"I didn't hear anything," he says. His voice sounds sad, rueful. He takes a deep breath.

"But you heard Bobby leave. If you heard Bobby leave, then why didn't you hear the killers as they drove up—or away?" I ask him.

His gun at his side, he approaches cautiously. My shaky finger dances over the trigger.

"Carly, listen," he pleads. "Put that gun down. You're scaring me."

Loosening my grip on the gun, I lean back on the car and try to breathe. "Why didn't you hear? Why didn't you hear?"

He takes the gun from my hands just as I hear the wail of a siren. Lights flash through the trees. A patrol car turns onto the property. "It's going to be okay," he soothes. He reaches for me, to stroke my hair or pat my shoulder, but hesitates at the last moment.

"You called the sheriff?" I ask him.

A smile flits across his face. He rubs his eyes. "Carly, you fired a gun on my property. I didn't know it was you."

Covering my face with my hands, I start to cry again.

"Please believe me," he adds. "I would have done anything that night to save them. I would have run over there and blown them to bits if I heard anything."

The siren falls silent. A car door slams. I lower my eyes to see Sheriff Robertson standing next to his patrol car with his handgun drawn.

"It's okay, sheriff, it's a misunderstanding," Mr. Stoecklein begins. "You don't need to . . ." His voice trails off.

"A misunderstanding," I whisper.

Clearly this isn't a misunderstanding to Sheriff Robertson. I'm escorted to the back of his patrol car. He puts his hand on the top of my head and pushes me—somewhat gently, at least—into the backseat, slamming the door shut.

If Sheriff Robertson is doing this to scare me, it's working. He talks to Mr. Stoecklein before laying my double-barreled shotgun in the trunk. Then he starts up the siren again, red and blue lights flashing, as he takes me to jail. The whole ride, I'm numb. I have only one thought. Did he put the shotgun in the trunk to use as evidence against me?

I'M ARRESTED, BOOKED, FINGERPRINTED. When my mugshot is taken, I feel as if I'm onstage again. Maybe it's the bright lights. But this is no act. I hold a tiny black sign with white letters: CARLY ANNE FLEMING. GARDEN CITY POLICE KANSAS 11/21/59 5'5" 110 POUNDS. I recognize the police officer who takes my picture; he was a senior at my school when we first moved to Holcomb. He pretends he doesn't recognize me. Or maybe he really doesn't. I swear I might pee my pants.

An older deputy takes me upstairs to the "ladies' ward." He's grim and silent. He looks disgusted with me. Keys rattle on the belt under his paunch. The ward is actually a tiny cell, built in the sheriff's residence—in the kitchen no less. White bars separate me from the sink and countertops. It's not even a cell. It's a cage. It occurs to me that maybe it really *is* some sort of animal pen—a place where the police dogs can curl up on quiet nights when there are no lady criminals to arrest. There's a window, but it's too high for me to look out.

After what seems like an eternity, a woman appears to offer me a glass of milk and a homemade chocolate chip cookie. She's not

Sheriff Robertson's wife, though she looks familiar. She's plump, maybe a bit older than my parents. Maybe the same age. I'm too tired to tell.

"Don't be scared," she says.

Before I can reach through the bars to accept, the kitchen door bursts open again. It's the sour deputy and Sheriff Robertson.

"Sheriff, is she going to stay the night?" Deputy No-Name asks, as if I'm not right here, five feet away.

"Deputy, I don't think it's necessary," Sheriff Robertson says. "She's learned her lesson." He turns to me. "Haven't you, Carly?"

I bite back my fear and anger. "Yes, sir," I say. "Never point a gun at a grown-up."

Sheriff Robertson laughs. "Well put."

The deputy unlocks the cell door and grabs my arm as if I'm a flight risk. Sheriff Robertson closes the door and escorts me out of the residence and down the stairs. I sit on a wooden chair, handcuffed to the stair rail as my parents talk to both of them. I catch a glimpse of Asher, lurking off to the side. Poor kid. He came home after his big day and what must have been an emotional night to *this*.

Then I spot Mr. Stoecklein. Now I feel sick.

BEFORE I KNOW IT, my parents are standing in front of me with their arms crossed. They look more exhausted than upset. "Dad, I'm sorry," I say.

"Not now," Dad grunts.

"Not *ever*," Mom corrects.

The deputy bends over and unlocks the handcuffs.

I rub my wrists. "Am I free to go?"

The sheriff nods. They agree that since it's my first offense, I should be let off with a warning. Mom drives Asher and me home while the deputy takes Dad out to the Clutter farm to get the Porsche.

CHAPTER TWENTY-FOUR

IN SUNDAY SCHOOL, AUDREY GLEEFULLY points out that I broke three of the Ten Commandments. She adds that attempted murder is just as much of a sin as *committing* murder, so technically she believes that I have broken four. Needless to say, I'm glad to join my parents in the sanctuary after such a true display of Christianity by Audrey Phillips.

At least Reverend Cowan is on a more positive biblical high, exhorting us not to judge and to love thy neighbor. But as I listen, I consider (not for the first time) how the New Testament totally contradicts the eye-for-an-eye message in the Old Testament. Reverend Cowan wants us to pray for whoever committed "this unimaginable atrocity, in the sacred confines of a family home." He's adamant about this part. Now I'm angrier than ever. His language makes my blood boil. It *was* an unimaginable atrocity.

"We need forgiveness, not revenge," he says.

I roll my eyes. How can we even think about forgiveness? It's just another reminder that people are ignorant. Maybe Holcomb is particularly ignorant. Never underestimate the power of the uneducated in large groups. I know I'm judging everyone here, but I can't help it.

Honestly, right now, I'd like to treat the killers the way Audrey Phillips treated me. I want to see whoever did this pay with their own lives. I want revenge, Old Testament style.

Reverend Cowan invites those who feel the need to come to the altar to pray. Mom practically grabs me by the arm and pulls me out of the pew, leading me down the aisle.

All eyes are on me. There are whispers throughout the sanctuary. I catch a hushed snippet: *". . . Shouldn't she be in jail?"*

Maybe judgment isn't all it's cracked up to be. The New Testament might be on to something with forgiveness after all. I slump down on my knees at the altar. Mom stands behind me with her arm on my shoulder, making sure that my head is down. Asking God to forgive me seems impossible. What did I do wrong? Okay, maybe I shouldn't have pointed a gun in Mr. Stoecklein's face.

Mom's hand is gripping my shoulder so tightly, I'm sure it's leaving a mark.

Okay, fine, God. I shouldn't have pointed my gun in Mr. Stoecklein's face. I'm sorry. Forgive me, please?

INSTEAD OF GOING HOME, we go to the country club to have lunch. The omelet bar and an unlimited supply of Shirley Temples are exactly what I need right now.

I stand in line, waiting for Chef Daniel to cook up my spinach, tomato, and cheese combo. "Extra cheese, please," I say, watching him dump a handful of sharp cheddar into the pan.

A girl behind me coughs. I glance over my shoulder. Karen. Of course. She looks as pleased with herself as ever. Her Sunday dress is pink. She reeks of purity, even though I didn't see her at the service this morning. If only people knew the truth. On the other hand, *I* know the truth about her, and she knows I know. And perversely, that's what makes her so happy.

She smiles. "Funny how people treated you in church."

I don't say anything.

"What? No comeback?" she asks.

"No comeback."

She waits for me to say something more. I don't. She edges closer, standing right behind me. I can smell her perfume. Finally, I can't take it anymore.

I whirl around. "You didn't even *go* to church this morning," I snap at her.

She shrugs, eyeing me up and down. "Audrey told me. You know her dad's chief deputy. She also told me you were arrested last night. She told me every last detail." She pauses dramatically and shakes her head. "*Arrested?* Really, Carly."

Amazing. It figures that the sour, pudgy deputy, who never even bothered to identify himself—which, come to think of it, might even be illegal; I should ask Dad about that and get that guy in trouble—is Audrey's father. Why didn't I know that? This town is so small. But then, Nancy always teased me about how I'm the last girl in Holcomb to figure anything out. It hurt me when she did that, and she knew it. She had a mean streak—not all the time, but more than most people know.

On the other hand, she was right. I'm a fool.

Too bad she isn't here now to share a smug little moment with Karen. I feel a pang as I take the plate and start to walk away. That doesn't stop Karen from following. She's baiting me. But I'm not going to acknowledge her. That's exactly what she wants.

"You planned this, didn't you?" she whispers loudly. "With Bobby."

I almost drop my omelet. Now I *can't* ignore her. I turn again. "Excuse me? What did you just say?"

"Don't act so surprised," she says. "We know that you're not so innocent in this situation."

"What are you talking about?" My voice is louder than I'd like it to be. "Are you making up a story as you go along?"

She laughs, glancing around the dining room. A charged silence has fallen over the guests. "Don't go all mental on me," she murmurs. "I was there. I saw everything. Friday night at Nancy's after the play, you and Bobby were talking alone."

Now it's my turn to laugh. "That doesn't mean a thing."

"Come on, Carly, don't be so naïve. It's what people *think* it means."

Lies.

Only then do I realize I'm not hungry anymore. I slam my plate on the nearest table. My omelet goes sliding off and onto the tablecloth. I storm toward the door.

"Watch out; she's dangerous!" Karen shouts after me with glee.

On the way out, I catch a glimpse of my mother, her jaw hanging slack. She avoids my eyes and stirs her cup of tea. I wonder what she believes about me. I wonder what everyone else believes.

WE'RE HOME EXACTLY TEN minutes before a police car pulls up in front of our house. No siren or lights this time, though I'm not sure if that's good or bad. I cower behind a living room curtain. It's Audrey's father. Just my luck. Three loud knocks and my heart beats so fast I swear it's going to jump right out of my chest. Dad answers while Mom stands beside him, clutching her pearls. The deputy and Dad exchange a few hushed words, then Dad waves me over. I'm not handcuffed, but he takes me by the elbow to escort me out and put me in the back of a patrol car.

"Is this really necessary?" Mom asks.

"It's protocol," Deputy Phillips says. "We have to follow every lead."

So it's official. I'm a suspect. I poked my nose into all of this for Nancy, and for Bobby, and this is my reward.

SHERIFF ROBERTSON WAITS FOR me in an interrogation room. He's not alone. Agent Nye and Agent Dewey lurk in the doorway. They nod as I arrive, and step out into the hall. They both pull cigarette packs from their suit pockets at the same time, as if they choreographed this moment. I stare at them as they light up. My parents exchange a private disapproving glance and back away. The sheriff beckons to me, gesturing to a lone metal chair on the other side of his desk.

On the scuffed wooden desktop there's a notebook open to a page covered with illegible scrawl (why do all policemen have terrible handwriting?)—and a tape recorder. Aside from that, the room is barren.

I turn to Dad, who nods for me to follow instructions. My legs tremble as I enter. The chair is cold, unforgiving. It hurts to sit down. The tiny room has no windows. It's dark and damp, and it smells like stale cigarette smoke.

"Carly?" Sheriff Robertson begins. "I want you to know—"

"I didn't kill Nancy," I blurt out, loud enough that the two KBI agents fall silent in the hall; loud enough that I hear my father's footsteps draw closer.

Sheriff Robertson stands. He walks over to the door and slams it shut.

My shoulders sag.

"Now, listen to me, Carly," he says. The soft way he says my name reminds me of the way Mr. Stoecklein spoke to me when I broke down in front of him. He reaches for the tape recorder but stops short of pushing any buttons. "I don't believe you had anything to do with it. But I have to follow every lead. Your father can explain the reasons why. He understands the way an investigation works. By clearing your name, we narrow the possibilities and get closer to the truth."

The sheriff says all this while looking at the door.

"Do you understand what I'm telling you?" he asks.

I nod, swallowing. "Yes, sir."

He presses the record button. "Okay, let's get started."

The questions seem silly at first. Stuff he already knows: my name, my age, where I go to school, how long I've lived in Holcomb, when I first met Nancy. I answer truthfully every question he throws at me. I don't know how much time has passed; there's no clock in here. But just when I'm starting to relax, he leans back in his chair, crosses his arms and legs, and asks, "What happened that Friday night?"

"What happened Friday night?" I repeat.

"Yes, November thirteenth."

I blink, my mind racing back in time. "Well, I had school and then the play that night. We put on *Tom Sawyer*. I was Amy Lawrence. I told this all to Agent Dewey—"

"I know. But I want to hear it from you."

My mouth feels dry. I rub my palms on my Sunday dress, wilted now after the long day. My skin is clammy. "Hear what?" I ask. The question sounds squeaky in my ears.

"Someone mentioned that you were talking about Nancy." He speaks in a cold monotone.

"Who said I was talking about Nancy?"

"I cannot say."

"It was Karen, wasn't it?" I ask.

"I cannot say," he repeats.

"Then it was Audrey. She has it in for me. Did she say something to her dad?"

"Carly," the sheriff warns. "Listen very carefully."

"*I am.*"

With a sigh, he leans forward, glancing at the tape recorder. "Do you remember anything unusual from that night?" he asks quietly.

"No. And I don't understand why this is happening. You *know* I'm not involved. I didn't have anything to do with the murders. Why would I want to kill her?"

"Because you weren't as good friends as you thought," he says.

The swift response is like a slap. I want to answer, but no words will come. I stare at him, cold all of a sudden.

"I know you tutored Nancy in math," he adds. His eyes are on me, unblinking.

"How do you know that?" I ask.

"Never mind that," he says. "Let's talk about a different night. Why don't you tell me about the football game?"

"The football game?" I repeat, at a loss.

I wonder if this is some kind of police trick, to make me confused. Holcomb High School doesn't have a football team. Then it hits me. *Garden City.* The Buffaloes: Holcomb's nearest team, the one the guys in town root for. Sheriff Robertson is talking about "the big game." Not that I even cared, which is why it hadn't occurred to me. But I was there.

Dad drove us—me, Asher, and Mary Claire—to Dodge City to see the Buffaloes versus the Red Demons. We met up with Seth and Alex in the parking lot. When we got inside the stadium, Mary Claire made herself comfortable with Alex, but I stuck with my father at the top of the bleachers, bundled under the blankets he brought. Seth moped. It was cold. That's all I remember. I'm wracking my brain to think of something, *anything*, but I can't.

"Sheriff, I—I just watched the game," I stammer.

"Did you talk to anyone?" he asks.

I throw my hands up. "My father? My brother? My friends?"

He pulls a pair of reading glasses out of a pocket and peers at his notebook. "Carly, someone overheard you say, and I quote, 'Since she's gone, I can maybe make her my best friend.' End quote." He looks up, gazing at me over his wire rims.

Oh, no. It can't be.

The realization crashes over me: a nauseating wave. I see it all now. I relive it.

Dad ran to get us some pop and some hot dogs. I asked Asher where Kenyon was, why he hadn't come. Asher wasn't in the mood to chat. I should have dropped it. I should have kept my mouth shut. But I started talking about their friendship. How I envied it. I was talking to my brother, but not really, because I assumed he wasn't listening. I was mostly talking to myself about things I never should have shared with anyone . . .

Asher not only heard every word; he told the police.

Does he think I killed Nancy? I can't bring myself to believe that, but I also know that Asher would never think to hide anything from the police. The interrogation room spins. For an awful second I'm worried I might be sick. I grab the edge of the desk and squeeze my eyes shut until the feeling passes. Then I try to compose myself.

"Sue," I gasp. My eyelids flutter open. I'm unable to meet the sheriff's gaze.

"Beg your pardon?"

"Sue," I repeat. "I . . . wasn't talking about Nancy. I was talking about Sue." I can feel my throat tighten. I don't want to cry, but I fear I will anyway.

"You're really going to have to explain," he says.

So this is what an interrogation is like when you're guilty. This is what it feels like to be a criminal. I know that now. I never thought I would. But here in this terrible place, with this terrible weight on me, all I want to do was confess. The urge to cry has passed. In its place there is only sorrow and regret. I *do* have some sins to atone for. All I can do now is hope the sheriff will be forgiving. Too bad that, like Karen, I don't remember seeing him in church, either.

"I thought . . . here's my chance," I say. The words seem to come from someone else.

The sheriff's blank face fills my field of vision. "But it wasn't?"

"No, sir," I say, shaking my head. "Not like I wanted it to be."

THE PLAN WASN'T A long time in the making. It wasn't some big secret plot. It was an idea that just popped up, the day before the game. An innocent idea, or so I thought.

I was just arriving at Nancy's house to tutor her when Sue came running out the front door, crying. It was already getting dark. The sun had set a few minutes earlier.

"Sue, are you okay?" I asked.

She shook her head and coughed. I offered her a tissue from my bag. After taking it and dabbing her eyes, she blew her nose. Then she sniffled and looked up at me.

"I had to tell Nancy some bad news. I don't think she's up for tutoring today."

My face went hot. I could feel that I was blushing, and I hated myself for it, but I couldn't help it. "Wait, you know about the tutoring?" I whispered.

Sue smirked at me through her tears. "I'm her best friend, Carly." Then she glanced back at the house. "Or I was."

She shoved the used tissue into my palm and bolted down the street, vanishing into the shadows.

Tucking the tissue into my pocket, I opened the front door. The hall lights were on. I could hear the wailing from the first floor. Nancy's room was at the top of the stairs, the one on the right, across from Kenyon's. The door was slightly ajar. I knocked but I don't think she heard me. Tentatively, I pushed it open.

"Nancy?" I whispered.

Her lights were low. Her books weren't even on her desk; they were strewn across the rug. She was lying on her bed, clutching her teddy bear, crying into her pillow. She glanced up and groaned.

"What's wrong?" I asked.

"I'm fine," she said in between deep sighs. "I just need a minute."

She sat up, clutching her wet pillow to her chest, trying to get a grip on herself. "Sue just gave me some bad news, is all."

I hesitated. Nancy's eyes drifted to the mess on the floor. She groaned again.

"If you don't want to tell me, you don't have to," I offered.

"No—it's okay. Everyone will find out anyway."

I sat on a chair by her desk.

"She's transferring next year," Nancy said.

"What? Where? When? Why?" I asked.

Nancy shot me a cold glare. "That's a lot of *w* questions. I'm not in the mood to be quizzed right now."

"Sorry," I mumbled. "Do you want me to go?"

"No," she muttered. "I probably need a lesson anyway."

I took a tissue from the box on her desk and handed it to her. "Do you want to talk about it?"

"Nothing to talk about," Nancy said. She cleared her throat. "She's being selfish. That's all. She thinks that by transferring to good ol' GCHS she has a better shot at going to college."

"Why?" I asked. "Is Holcomb High for dumb kids?"

Nancy scowled at me and wiped her cheeks dry. "No. Why would you say that?"

"Because you said—"

"It doesn't matter what I said," Nancy interrupted. "She's transferring so she can get into K-State, leaving me all alone here."

I turned my attention to my book bag. "You're not alone," I quietly replied.

She stood and shambled over to her closet, then started rummaging through the dresses hanging down. "We'd share clothes," she mused. "Who am I supposed to share clothes with now?"

"You can share clothes with me, if you want," I said softly, glancing up.

Nancy turned abruptly. She gave me a sour look. "You're kidding, right?"

I'm not sure why, but I burst out laughing. And miracle of miracles, so did she.

That was it. She sat at the edge of her bed and we went through our regular tutoring routine, just like always. But when I left that night, I felt as if I were floating on the bitter November wind. Something had changed between us. Hadn't it? With Sue gone, there was an opening. A void. And maybe, just maybe, I could fill it. But it wasn't just the hope. It was something more.

Because right before I left, she offered to lend me that red dress for the Sadie Hawkins dance.

WHEN MY STORY IS finished, the sheriff leans forward and stops recording. *Snap*: the button cuts the whirring of the tape. In the sudden quiet, the air feels thick and heavy. But neither of us speaks for a while.

Finally he leans toward me. "Carly, living in a small town is not for the faint of heart. Everyone knows everyone's business. It's hard to find your niche. Friendships are established from the moment you are born. And if you move into one of these small towns when you're—"

"An outsider."

He shakes his head at my interruption. "No, miss. I wasn't going to say that."

"But it's true. New York might as well be Mars. I had friends there," I say.

"You have friends here."

"I know. But I thought Nancy could see me as her best friend, not just her friend from the wrong Manhattan."

He laughs.

"Sue's from California and *she's* not seen as an outsider," I say.

"Does that make you upset?" he asks.

I frown at him. "Yes. But it doesn't make me upset enough to kill. *This* makes me upset. I don't like being interrogated like a common criminal."

"Well, we're almost done." He pushes the record button again and asks, "When did you decide to go to the spook show after the cast party on Friday, November thirteenth? And I need you to give your answer loudly and clearly for the microphone to pick it up."

I look at the machine, its hubs turning slowly. "It was Seth's idea. He mentioned it while we were at the concession stand. He wanted to go. Why don't you talk to Seth?"

"I will. Did anything out of the ordinary happen at the spook show?"

Now it's my turn to laugh. "Well, besides peeing my pants at the sight of the deranged psychotic little girl, then no."

Sheriff Robertson flashes a tired smile. He opens his mouth, then closes it and shakes his head. "Okay. Thanks, Carly. We're done. I'll let your parents know you're free to go." He looks me in the eye. "Just don't leave the state."

"Not planning to," I say.

He shuts off the recorder and rewinds the tape. I wonder if he thought this was a waste of time. I would. Why aren't they out there scouring the countryside? Agent Dewey is convinced that it's someone local. But I'm beginning to wonder if there are any real suspects at all.

CHAPTER TWENTY-FIVE

THREE DAYS UNTIL THANKSGIVING, AND Mary Claire's going to Great Bend to pick up a turkey. I decide to tag along on her little expedition, even though I don't have permission from my parents. It's risky, but the possibility of getting away from Holcomb is too irresistible. Once it lodges in my brain, it feels essential. It's what I need. Most important: the police in Great Bend might have clues that Sheriff Robertson and Audrey's dad don't.

I still haven't talked to Asher about what he told Sheriff Robertson, or even when they spoke or why. *More w questions*, Nancy would say. I don't ask them. Asher is still so remote, still suffering over Kenyon. He's so exhausted after basketball practice, anyway, that there's no point in saying anything.

I tell my parents that I have a school assignment to work on with Mary Claire. It isn't a lie, but it's not exactly the truth, either. They don't know that I left town and the county. But Great Bend is still in Kansas, so technically I'm obeying Sheriff Robertson.

Mary Claire is delighted. Of course she is. "I'm harboring a felon," she says as we pick up speed on the highway. She smiles wickedly, checking her mirrors. "Just like you said."

"I'm not a felon," I protest. "Not . . . technically."

"You'll probably be arrested again if you get caught. You'll be in so much trouble."

"The charges were dropped," I snap back at her, flustered. Then I frown and face forward. "And besides, there weren't any charges *to* drop. I am free and clear."

She laughs. "Well, if you do get arrested, *again*, I cannot bail you out."

"Thanks," I say. I pull out the steno notebook Agent Nye gave me. I hadn't given this little gift much thought until I was arrested, especially given his snooty attitude. But after that interrogation, things changed. I want to take control. Maybe he gave it to me as a joke, but I want to show him what I can do with the clues I have.

Great Bend—hunting knife. An abandoned car. Two Negroes were seen driving. '53 or '54 Mercury, Colorado license plates. Bloody western-style shirt with the sleeves cut off found in ditch north of Hugoton.

I try to concentrate, but all I can think about is Mary Claire, rolling her eyes. I'm not processing what is written down. The words that once seemed so important are a riddle now. I can *remember* the feeling I had when I put my pencil to the paper, the fierce urgency, but I can't remember *why* I felt it. Well, other than it would clear Bobby. But Bobby isn't the reason I've been running myself so ragged. Not entirely. I thought I was so certain of what I've been doing.

"Carly, are you sure you want me to drop you off at the police station?" Mary Claire asks in the silence.

"Yes," I say. I snap the book shut and turn to glare at her.

"Carly, you're taking this too personal," she says.

"It *is* personal," I say.

"How? You weren't that close to her."

"I could have been. We could have been real friends."

"I'm your real friend," she says.

The words are quick and breezy. They sound just like any other offhand remark Mary Claire would make. She's staring at the road, hands on the wheel, relaxed. Hardly anyone would notice any difference in her, but I can see that her jaw is tight. Her cheek twitches, freckles rippling in the cold glare of the afternoon sun.

"I know you're a real friend," I tell her.

"So what is this all about? You're acting strange, like when you moved here. Like when you were trying too hard to fit in."

My eyes fall back to my closed notebook. I want to answer her, but I don't *have* an answer. Not one that I want to say out loud, anyway. Besides, she already knows the truth. Nancy was the real friend I wanted. Mary Claire has always just been Mary Claire. A friend, yes. But not the same. Not the one I wanted.

Before I know it, she's pulling over to the side of the road.

"Carly, maybe you shouldn't come with me to get the turkey." When the car rolls to a stop, she turns to face me with a blank smile. It's polite, but there's no warmth. It's as if we're strangers meeting for the first time. "I know how you can be when farm animals are killed in front of you. I'd rather not drop you at the police station, either. It doesn't feel right."

I nod. "I understand," I say. "If you don't mind driving me back home—"

"Not at all," she interrupts, putting the transmission in gear. With a screech of the tires, she swerves back onto the deserted highway and makes a U-turn back toward Holcomb.

MOM IS WAITING FOR me inside the house. She's sitting on the sofa, reading a book. When she looks up, I can tell right away that she knows I've been doing something I shouldn't have been doing. I'm home earlier than I said I would be, and I haven't gotten into any trouble at all . . . and still somehow she knows. "Mom, I'm sorry," I begin.

She doesn't say anything. She pats the cushion beside her with her left hand. I narrow my eyes at the book in her lap—its thick black cover, the delicate pages, the tiny print in columns. For a moment I can't quite believe what I'm seeing.

She's reading the Bible.

I look up at her.

Without a word, she stands and leaves it open for me on the coffee table, then heads to the kitchen. As I flop down onto the sofa, I notice that a passage is underlined and circled in red ink: Deuteronomy chapter 21, verses 18–21.

> *If a man have a stubborn and rebellious son, which will not obey the voice of his father, or the voice of his mother, and* that, *when they have chastened him, will not hearken unto them: Then shall his father and his mother lay hold on him, and bring him out unto the elders of his city, and unto the gate of his place; And they shall say unto the elders of his city, This our son* is *stubborn and rebellious, he will not obey our voice;* he is *a glutton, and a drunkard. And all the men of his city shall stone him with stones, that he die: so shalt thou put evil away from among you; and all Israel shall hear, and fear.*

A not-so-subtle hint from my not-so-religious mother.

I just hope that she's reading the Bible because she wants to get more out of Reverend Cowan's sermons.

CHAPTER TWENTY-SIX

I'M STARING AT MY NOTEBOOK when Mom calls for me from her bedroom.

> *10 days since Nancy was killed, no leads.*
> *Yesterday Mary Claire told me that Agent Dewey made her take a lie detector test. Not sure if that's a lie. Was happy to talk, though. She's still giving me the cold shoulder.*
> *Want to talk to Bobby. He avoids me at school. Why?*

"Carly?" Mom shouts again.

"Coming," I yell back.

I close the notebook and shove it in my desk drawer. Maybe I should rip that page out. I wonder what Agent Dewey or Sheriff Robertson would think if they read those words. I wonder what Karen or Audrey would think. Or Mary Claire, for that matter. Or even Asher.

Mom is addressing place cards for the Great Turkey Extravaganza that the Junior League of Southwest Kansas is hosting; ladies from Garden and Holcomb and as far as Dodge and Liberal are coming. She's been helping to plan the event for months. Up until ten days ago, she was excited about it. Since the tragedy, she's hardly mentioned it.

"I can't believe I did that," she mutters as I walk in, ripping the card in half and throwing it in the wastebasket beside her desk.

"Did you need me?" I ask.

She nods. "Can you take Asher to practice? I've got to finish up these place cards."

"Does that mean I'm not grounded anymore?" I ask. I feel a prickle of excitement. Even though it's only 4:15 P.M., the sky has been cloudy all day and it's already dark out.

"Don't be silly. I'm not giving you an inch of freedom. Straight to the gym and back." She fixes me with a stern glare. "And since my car's still in the shop, you're going to have to take the Porsche. No funny business." I wince a little inside. The last time I drove the Porsche, I ended up in the jailhouse.

"I've got to go. I'm going to be late," Asher hollers from the living room.

"Whose was that? The one you threw away?" I ask, glancing at the trash.

She looks up at me and says in a whisper, "Bonnie's."

ASHER AND I DRIVE to the school in silence. It's the first time the two of us have been alone together in a while. I keep stealing glances at him as I drive, but he stares out the passenger window. I want to penetrate his shell. I want to ask him about his conversation with the police. But I can't bring myself to do it. He'll have to open up to me in his own time, when he's ready.

When we pull up, there are a bunch of boys waiting in the

parking lot, huddled in their winter coats. They aren't horsing around. They're shivering.

"The coach keeps the gym locked now," Asher says. "We have to wait for him to open it up."

He doesn't have to explain why, and I don't have to ask. Then he stiffens. I follow his gaze. Bobby's truck has just pulled into the lot. I squint and can see that he's at the wheel. Bobby is dropping his little brother off, just like I'm doing. Just going about his business. But Asher squirms.

Bobby scares him now. He thinks Bobby did it. Or he's scared of me, and he thinks I did it. Maybe he thinks Bobby and I did it together. Or maybe I'm just being ridiculous.

When my brother reaches for the door handle, I reach for him. "Asher? Can you—"

"Tell Dad to come pick me up when practice is over," he interrupts. "Okay?" He hops out of the car and slams the door shut, bolting for the pool of light at the locked gym entrance.

ON MY WAY BACK home, I'm about to jump out of my skin. I can't keep going on like this. I don't want to go home. Maybe I could drive around for a little while. I'm already grounded, so what could my parents do? Ground me again? I can always make up an excuse. I could go fill the gas tank; that would kill some time. If my mom questioned me about it, and I told her the truth, I wouldn't be *lying*. But still, somehow, she'd know. She always does. Like she knew when I took a ride with Mary Claire. It's as if she has a built-in lie detector—

I jerk in the seat.

Lie detector. Mary Claire.

In a flash, I'm gunning the accelerator. If I hurry, I can get to the courthouse in Garden before 5 P.M.

I CAN HEAR AGENT Dewey's voice as I race up the stairs at the end of the long ground-floor hall. He's loud. He sounds mad. Maybe he's arguing with someone. His words echo across the walls.

"I'm convinced it's somebody local who had a grudge against Herb. I have a feeling . . ."

"And are we just basing everything on a feeling rather than theory or fact?" I hear Agent Nye grumble.

When I reach the second floor, I run toward the sound of their voices. The offices are all brightly lit, bustling. The place still seems to be open for business, at least. They must hear my footsteps, because Agent Church peers out the door. He's wearing that same blue suit and striped tie. I wonder if he owns more than one, the way my dad does.

"Need something?" he asks.

"Um, I think I need to talk to Agent Dewey. It's about his feeling," I say. Agent Church smirks and stands aside. "Alvin, there's a little girl here to see you," he says.

Giving him the evil eye, I walk past him through the doorway.

"Carly, what do you want now?" Agent Dewey asks from behind a desk. He rolls his eyes at Agent Nye, who's slouching against the wall. I almost feel like telling them I don't want to hang around three tired-looking men in suits any more than they want to hang around with me. The room reeks of cigarettes, though nobody is smoking.

There's an empty chair in front of Agent Dewey's desk. I sit without an invitation to do so and ask him, "Do you honestly have *no* leads?"

"Listen to me, Carly," he says, motioning for Agents Nye and Church to leave us alone. He shoos them with the back of his hand, but they both laugh and stay put. "I have plenty of leads. And I have to follow those leads. It's like a big jigsaw puzzle. Get it?" He's softened his voice, and his tone is condescending. "I'm looking at everyone. I have a long list of suspects, and I'm doing my best in narrowing them down until I have the culprit."

"Can I see the list?" I ask.

"Not protocol."

Agent Nye laughs.

I whirl around. "What's so funny?" I demand.

He bites his lip and looks at Agent Dewey. "Come on, Alvin, you've let that fella and his woman see the list and more."

I turn back to face Agent Dewey.

"Not protocol," he repeats, glaring at Agent Nye. I take a deep breath and ask the question I've come here to ask. "So what do I have to do? Take a lie detector test?"

He blinks and stiffens, as if he's just awakened from a nap. With an unreadable glance at Agents Nye and Church, he tilts his head at me and smiles. "Will now be good?"

CHAPTER TWENTY-SEVEN

So I've solved one mystery today.

Mary Claire wasn't lying.

Agent Dewey escorts me to a room with no windows. It looks like the interrogation room in Holcomb, furnished only with a table and two chairs. But it's scarier, somehow. Maybe because this time I know my parents and brother won't be waiting for me when I'm done. Or maybe because I'm not going to be recorded here. I'm going to be hooked up, analyzed, *examined*.

There's a black rectangular box in the middle of the table. It's got cords coming from sockets, cords that will soon be attached to me.

Agent Dewey straightens the graph paper on the machine and tightens the needles. He's already explained that they will move up and down as I answer yes-or-no questions.

Those are my only choices. Yes or no. It should be easy. But I already feel anxious.

I sit facing a wall as a deputy attaches sensors to my body. The sensors will record my respiration, heart rate, and blood pressure. He puts two air-filled rubber tubes around my chest and abdomen to measure the rate and depth of my breathing. A blood-pressure cuff is wrapped around my upper arm. Fingerplates are slipped around my middle and index fingers.

"The agent will ask you ten questions, and you will answer yes or no to each question. Your responses will be recorded as well as how your body changes during the questioning. Now, don't worry, everyone has been asked a version of these questions," the deputy says.

It won't make an alarm sound if I speak out of line—but I won't; I have nothing to hide. Agent Dewey coughs, drinks from a coffee cup, and lights a cigarette. He turns on the machine. The spindles go up and down, measuring my blood pressure, spiking when I get nervous or anxious or scared. I think I'm going to wet my pants. Will that short out a circuit and electrocute me?

"Okay, let's begin," he says, blowing smoke toward my face.

Instead of saying a word, I nod, mainly because I don't know if I'm allowed to speak or not.

Agent Dewey takes a deep breath. "I'm going to ask you some questions. Please answer with yes or no; don't explain, just respond. And no nodding—speak. Are you ready?"

"Yes," I say.

Agent Dewey: "Okay, question number one, is your name Carly Fleming?"

Me: "Yes."

Agent Dewey: "Question number two, are you fifteen years old?"

Me: "Yes."

Agent Dewey: "Question number three, do you suspect anyone of killing the Clutters?"

Me: "No."

Agent Dewey: "Question number four, were you arrested Friday, November twentieth?"

Me: "Yes."

Agent Dewey: "Question number five, were you born in 1945?"

Me: "No."

Agent Dewey: "Question number six, were you born in Kansas?"

Me: "No."

Agent Dewey: "Question number seven, do you know who killed the Clutters?"

Me: "No."

Agent Dewey: "Question number eight, do you live in Holcomb?"

Me: "Yes."

Agent Dewey: "Question number nine, did you help kill the Clutters?"

Me: "No."

Agent Dewey: "Question number ten, did any of your friends kill the Clutters?"

Me: "No."

Agent Dewey: "Question number eleven, is today Tuesday?"

Me: "Yes."

Agent Dewey: "Question number twelve, did you kill the Clutters?"

Me: "No."

CHAPTER TWENTY-EIGHT

IT'S FRIDAY NIGHT. THE GYMNASIUM'S full. I've never seen the bleachers so packed. Everyone in town is here to support the Long-horns, and I know why. They've come because of Kenyon, because he's *not* here. I duck away from my parents once we're inside. Officially I'm still grounded, but they've given me permission to sit by myself or with any friends who come. They want to sit close to the floor. It's Asher's first game, after all.

I want to be here for him, too, but I don't want to be too close to a sweaty game I don't care about.

As I climb the steps, I search the crowd for Mary Claire.

Instead I spot Sue Kidwell.

Her eyes meet mine. I ignore the strange knot in my stomach and wave, and she waves back. She smiles. I make a beeline for her. She scoots to make space beside her on the bleachers.

"Hi, Sue," I say.

"Hi, Carly," she says.

We turn to the court and sit in silence.

The starting lineup is announced, and then the game's under way. Asher is among the starters, but he and his team might as well be playing on the moon. I can't force myself even to watch, let alone care. Guiltily I turn to Sue and ask if she wants anything from the concession stand.

"My treat," I offer. Dad gave me a whole five dollars for snacks. He and Mom knew I wouldn't want to watch the game with them, and maybe they didn't want to watch the game with me, either.

She smiles again. Her eyes are tired and puffy. "A Coke would be nice. Thanks."

I nod and hurry away. The knot in my stomach is back, and again my eyes search the crowd for Mary Claire. Why isn't she here?

The concession-stand line starts at the baseline. The grown-up couple in front of me—probably the parents of some player; I recognize them from around town—are talking about Truman Capote, the author of *Breakfast at Tiffany's*, the strange little man from the courthouse who Aunt Trudy knows. Well, claims she knows. My ears perk up.

The man chuckles with his wife. "He's interviewing everyone, hon. Should I talk to him? I didn't know them, but I can probably come up with a couple of stories. I could be famous!"

I bite my lip to keep from screaming. I'm disgusted. Stories? Meaning lies? Just so he can see his name in print? I glare as they take their food. Stepping up to the counter, I order two Cokes and a bag of popcorn.

"Need a hand?"

I turn, and Landry is there behind me.

My heart flutters for a second. Maybe I *should* have sat with my parents. I wasn't expecting to see him here, though I should have. I'm so disoriented I just want to hide. Landry's cheeks are ruddy, his eyes bright, as if he just slept twelve hours. His jeans and shirt are crisp. His hair is wet. His coat smells fresh, as if it just came from the Laundromat. He dressed up for the occasion. I wonder why. "Yeah, a hand would be nice," I say.

He takes the two bottles and I carry the popcorn, sampling it as we walk back to the bleachers. But when he spots the empty space next to Sue, he pauses.

"Doesn't look like there's a whole lot of room," he says, his voice flat. "I'll just give this to Sue. See you later, okay?"

Before I can respond, he hands off the pop, first to Sue and then to me, and hurries back down the stairs.

Sue barely even looks at him. Does Landry think that Sue and Nan Ewalt did it? They were the ones who found the bodies, after all . . . I wince. The thought is unbidden, an unwelcome guest, but there it is just the same. It sickens me. Maybe Sue thinks that Landry and I did it. Maybe they both think Bobby and I did it. Whoever really killed Nancy and her family must be laughing right now. They've poisoned all of Holcomb.

I sit back down next to Sue. She sips, her eyes on the game. I place the bag of popcorn between us.

"Thanks for the pop," she says finally.

I nod, looking at her, sipping my own bottle. Holcomb scores a basket. The bleachers erupt in cheers.

"Carly, I don't really want to talk about it," she says out of nowhere.

I don't answer.

She turns to face me. "It's like I'm living in a dream or watching some movie and I have a part to play."

"I know exactly what you mean," I say, remembering how I felt around Nancy, how I was always playing a role.

"I don't know if you do," she says.

I nod. I don't look away.

"She was my best friend," Sue adds.

"I know."

"The last time I saw her—I mean, alive—was right before you came over to tutor her . . . We got in a fight." She places the bottle on the floor and puts her hands over her face. "I can't get it out of my head. Did you know that Mr. Clutter, Mrs. Clutter, and Kenyon were gagged—but Nancy wasn't? I bet Nancy talked to them. I bet she screamed for someone to help her, and no one did. Sometimes, I think I hear her screaming."

My throat is tight. I try to speak, but the words stick. I wipe my eyes and put my own bottle down. "It'll be okay," I manage.

She turns back to me and looks me dead in the eyes and asks, "Will it?"

I nod, not trusting myself to respond.

"My mom wants me to talk to that strange man, that writer from New York," Sue adds. "But I can't. Why is he here, anyway?"

I search my brain for something to say, something that will reassure her. I feel sick again, knowing how badly I wanted Sue to move away and leave Nancy without a best friend.

"Maybe for the truth," I finally tell her, even if I don't believe it.

CHAPTER TWENTY-NINE

HUBBARD'S DRUGSTORE HAS A LINE out the door Monday morning. There are exactly ten copies of *Time* magazine when I enter, and exactly two copies when I leave. But I got the third. I make sure to get to school early and sit on a bench near the front office. Pulling the magazine from the paper bag, I flip to page 18.

NATIONAL AFFAIRS: IN COLD BLOOD.

Seth bursts through the front doors with Alex, a blast of cold air trailing them. Seth spots me and of course repeats a rumor that's blowing through town like a snowstorm. The killer is someone local because of some kind of con that was happening at the farm.

"Everyone knows Bobby did it. I just wish he would confess already. I think we should do the town a favor and take care of him. We don't even need a trial," Alex adds.

My grip tightens, my fingers wrinkling the pages in anger. A group surrounds Seth and Alex, spewing what they all feel, that Bobby killed the Clutters.

"All of you shut it," I say. "He's been exonerated by the KBI."

"Big word for such a pretty girl," Seth says, erasing even the slightest trace of fondness I ever felt for him.

"Honestly, stop. You know it's not true, none of it. You're just embarrassing yourself."

"Embarrassing ourselves? You're embarrassing yourself. You think we even care what you think . . .Yankee?"

My jaw drops. I can't believe what I'm hearing.

"They're only nice to you because of me," he goes on with a sneer.

"Nancy only pretended to be your friend because you were my girlfriend. Karen told me that you tutored Nancy in math, and she thought you were a drip."

"You're a jerk," I say. "If you even had—"

The doors swing open again, and I clamp my mouth shut.

It's Bobby.

He keeps his head down as he walks right by us, not saying a word.

HOT DOGS AND CHIPS are on the menu for lunch. I want to ask Mary Claire why she wasn't at the basketball game Friday night, except it's the first time I've seen her all day, and I assume the conversation is going to be all about the fresh suspicion surrounding Bobby. She always jumps right in at lunch. I ask about Bobby first to get the subject out of the way. But Mary Claire brushes me off; she has no opinions on that. She's squirmy with excitement. She wants me to guess whom she met yesterday.

"We talked for an *hour*," she finishes, sounding giddy. "Guess!"

"I hate guessing," I say.

"Please—"

"Just tell me who." She rolls her eyes and turns to her lunch, but she's smiling. "Mr. Capote," she says. "He came to our farm and ate a piece of cake that I made, and we sat at the kitchen table."

"Why did he want to talk to you?" I ask, shocked. Maybe I'm a little envious. I'm the one who's been investigating, after all.

"He asked me if I wanted to tell my story," she says.

"*Your* story?" The words pop out of my mouth before I even have a chance to consider them.

Mary Claire's smile falls away. She shifts in her chair. "I've known Nancy my whole life," she tells me.

"I know—"

"You're not special, Carly."

"I didn't say I was."

"You're acting like a spoiled little brat," she says, picking up her hot dog.

"I don't mean to. I'm sorry."

"Forget it." She eats for a while in silence.

I don't have an appetite. I am also dying of curiosity. "So, how did it go with Truman Capote?"

"Okay, I think. He talked, mostly. I just sat there. Hardly said a word. And when I did say something, I had a feeling he didn't exactly care what I had to say."

"So what is he *like*? I've asked my aunt, but all she says is he's fabulous and knows the right people."

Mary Claire sips her milk and shrugs. "He's weird, very weird."

"What do you mean by weird?"

"He's just different," she says. She cracks a grin and shakes her head. "This one question he asked . . ."

"What?" I whisper.

She glances around the cafeteria and leans close. "He wanted to know if Nancy's cherry was popped."

"No he did not," I gasp. "What did you say?"

"I didn't say anything." I turn this information around in my head. I shouldn't be surprised. *Breakfast at Tiffany's* features a nameless narrator who's a teenage . . . "party girl." Those are my dad's words. Truman Capote's are different. My dad has defended girls like that in court—girls who are hired for a very specific reason by men who have money and think they have class.

Mary Claire looks at me. "If you want my advice, just say his name right. Don't call him Mr. Cappuchi. He gets pretty annoyed. He'll correct you like he did with me: '*it's Ca-po-TEE.*'"

LATER THAT NIGHT, MY family sits at the country club, pretending to look at Monday's menu, pretending to celebrate Asher's win on Friday night. I'm thinking of Sue's words again. *"A part to play."* That's what we're doing here right now. Saturday or Sunday would have been the right time to celebrate. But Dad was working. On what, he wouldn't say. He didn't have to tell us. What else could he be working on in Holcomb—here and now? I wonder if Sheriff Robertson and those KBI agents, Dewey and Nye and Church, talked to him about Bobby and me.

"I'm thinking a steak and a twice-baked potato," Dad says.

If I talked to Mr. Capote, what would I say? I also wonder.

"Dad, did you read that article in *Time* magazine everyone is talking about?" Asher asks, as if reading my mind.

"I did," Dad says, not looking up.

"Honestly, I wish they would leave us alone," Mom says.

"Well, he wants to talk to me," Asher says.

I stare at him. First Asher talked to the sheriff without my knowing, and now this famous writer wants to talk to him, before talking to *me*.

"Why does he want to talk to you?" I demand.

Asher stares right back at me with a look of disbelief. "Kenyon was my best friend," he says coldly.

"Right," I say, remembering the truth. I wish I could melt into my seat and disappear. Asher is actually worth talking to. He *had* a close relationship with a Clutter. One that didn't consist of trying to get someone to understand that $x+y=z$. He and Kenyon *were* friends.

"Well, it's out of the question," Mom says.

"Don't you think people need to hear what they were truly like?" Dad asks.

"Like Frank Beggett?" Mom asks.

Dad's face clouds. "We made a promise," he says.

She looks down. "I know," she whispers. "I'm sorry."

When Dad talks like this, in absolutes, his words are a gavel: *case closed*. He doesn't need to elaborate. We all know what he means. The entire family swore an oath never to mention that particular name ever again.

Several years ago in New York City, nineteen-year-old Frank Beggett allegedly murdered thirteen-year-old Angela Susanne Dunn.

According to the police, the newspapers, the prosecution—*everyone*—Frank asked Angela if she needed a ride home from school. She accepted. The next day she was found in an alley two blocks from her home, strangled with a leather belt. All evidence pointed to Frank's guilt, including eye-witness testimony: people had seen Angela get into his car.

But Dad defended Frank in court, because that is Dad's job. And he is very good at his job. Frank Beggett was found not guilty. He did not get death by electrocution. He was released with a clean record. Apparently the police had mishandled some evidence. Dad made the case about *that*, about how Frank Beggett was a victim, too. It was enough to sway the jury.

"Why do you want to talk to that writer, anyway?" Asher asks in the heavy silence. "He's weird."

I open my mouth but nothing comes out. I don't have an answer.

"Didn't you tutor the girl in math?" Dad chimes in.

I nod. And that's *it*, really. Dad just answered the question for me.

I'm always going to be known as Carly Fleming, the math tutor, and I don't want that, because I don't want to *accept* that.

"Well, you can talk about tutoring," Dad says, closing his menu. "If the situation arises."

Mom shakes her head. "He'll twist her words."

"Becca—"

"Honestly," Mom says, stirring her martini with a skewer of two olives. Collecting herself, she flashes Asher a brittle smile and lifts her glass. "Cheers to your victory."

CHAPTER THIRTY

THE INVITATION DOESN'T EVEN COME from Mr. Capote. It comes from his friend, the polite lady with the musical Southern accent. Maybe she followed me after school. I nearly slam right into her on Main Street as I'm hurrying to meet Mary Claire at the diner, my head down in the frigid wind. She's wearing a long dark blue wool coat and holding a cigarette in her right hand.

"Beg your pardon, Miss Fleming; I'm Miss Lee. I believe we spoke at the courthouse? I wondered if you had a moment this afternoon for Mr. Truman Capote."

Did she and I speak? I can't remember. But in the rush of excitement at finally having the opportunity to tell *my* story, I nod. I also forget all about Mary Claire. I follow Miss Lee several wintry blocks to the Wheat Lands Motel, which is really just another coffee shop. She puffs on her cigarette the whole time, then daintily drops it to the curb as she holds the door for me.

"Truman will be right down. But you can have a seat." She gestures to a round table by the window, piled high with papers. There are three empty chairs. "Do you want anything to drink?"

"No, ma'am," I say, sitting across from her. "Thank you, though."

She laughs and orders me a Coke anyway, then starts fumbling through the stack of papers. "The Clutters had so much religious crap in their house," she says under her breath. "Not to speak ill of the dead . . ."

I'm suddenly uncomfortable. "Well, they were Methodists," I say, but she pays no attention.

The Coke arrives. The waitress doesn't look particularly happy about having to bring it to me. I take a sip, wondering how long Miss Lee has been camped out here. I keep stealing glances at the empty chair. Soon I'm guzzling my pop, just to have something to do. I stare out the window at the street, drinking slowly as the last of the sunlight fades quickly. The lamps flicker on. The minutes tick by in silence.

"I swear he'll be right down," she says, looking at her watch.

"It's okay," I say.

I'm done with my bottle of pop, and I'm just about to suggest we do this another time, when Mr. Capote swoops down from the staircase, wearing what looks to be a woman's western coat and cowboy hat. He holds a tin can toward me as he flops down in the empty chair. At first—honestly—I think it's cat food.

"Little girl, would you love some of this delicious beluga caviar?" he asks in that odd high-pitched voice. It cuts through the room. He turns to Miss Lee. "It came straight to room 202 in a care package from Babe."

"Well, wasn't that thoughtful," Miss Lee says without looking up from the papers.

"Well?" Mr. Capote says to me.

"No, thank you," I say, crinkling my nose.

Mr. Capote snaps at the waitress with his free hand. She arrives with a basket of saltines. He spoons some of the caviar onto one of the crackers. "Trust me, it's good." He holds it out for me to take.

Minding my manners, I cringe and gulp it down. It *tastes* like cat food, or what I imagine cat food to taste like.

"Salty," I croak. "Thank you."

"It's better with vodka." He smiles.

"I guess I'll take your word for it," I say. I wish I hadn't finished my Coke.

He shakes his head. "Prohibition lasted for thirteen years, ten months, nineteen days, and thirty-two point five minutes. Most of our great nation came to its senses, but apparently, the law is still alive and well in this backward state," he says.

I'm not sure what I'm supposed to say.

"Miss Fleming, you're allowed to have the initial reaction of wanting to punch him in the face," Miss Lee adds in a dry voice.

Mr. Capote narrows his eyes at her. "I'm too humble a person, really. On the other hand, I'm actually much greater than I think I am." He turns back to me. "So, who do you think killed them?"

I stare at him, taken aback by the suddenness of his question. "I don't know," I say.

"You must have an inkling."

"Are you a sleuth or just a creeper?"

He laughs and exchanges another glance with Miss Lee. "Well, maybe a little bit of both."

"We're here to do a piece on the town, the citizens, and also the family," she says.

"It's not going to be an exposé," he adds, eyes on me as he hands Miss Lee the tin of caviar and the saltines. "It's more of a human interest piece."

"So you're interviewing everyone in town?" I ask.

He nods.

"So, I guess that's why you want to talk to me," I say.

"Precisely," he says, nodding.

I can tell Mr. Capote's sizing me up, deciding how he's going to handle me, the direct approach or the underhanded kind.

"So, you've talked to a lot of people?" I ask, even though I know the answer. I don't want him to know how miffed I am at being one of the last. I want to size *him* up, too.

"A lot," he concurs. "But I'm horrible with names."

"We've talked to the editor of the newspaper," Miss Lee says.

"Oh, Mr. Brown," I say. "He's my Sunday school teacher."

"Well, I don't care for him very much. I found him impolite and belligerent. He's as plain as his name," Mr. Capote says with a sour face.

"Not many people have warmed up to my friend Truman quite yet," Miss Lee says with a smile, eyeing Mr. Capote. "He's like a hormonal teenage girl when he gets his feelings hurt."

He bursts out in a fit of laughter. "What sophisticated man from New York City isn't?"

She laughs, too. "Honestly."

"I'm from New York City," I say.

"Oh *really?*" he asks, obviously not impressed at all.

"Yes, sir. I've lived here since the ninth grade, but I have family that still lives there. Do you know my aunt Trudy? She says she knows you. Her full name is—"

"What does a man have to do to get a drink around here?" he interrupts. Then he shrugs. "As I said, I'm horrible with names." An impish smile plays on his lips. "I remember faces, though, and I remember yours. We're just going to talk here, like old friends, right?"

"I . . . guess?" I say hesitantly.

"Well, you knew the girl?" Mr. Capote asks.

"Nancy."

"Nancy," he stresses. "Nancy Clutter, yes. *Her* name, I know."

"I tutored her in math." Mr. Capote leans back in his chair. He looks disappointed. "Tutored?"

"Yes, sir."

"Was she a dimwit?"

"Truman," Miss Lee scolds, still buried in the papers. She's taken out a pen and has started jotting words down on a blank sheet in a leather-bound journal.

"Forgive me, but isn't the dead girl the town darling and the dead boy the little prince?" Mr. Capote asks. "Isn't that the truth about Nancy and Kenyon Clutter?" It's a question, but it sounds like it's a statement—and one not needing a reply.

I watch his friend. All of a sudden I realize she's taking notes on our conversation. "You don't write anything down yourself?" I ask.

"Everyone has a photographic memory; some just don't have any film," he says with a wink. "Tell me about Nancy Clutter's mom."

"Are you writing a book?" I ask him.

"Not with the information you're giving me."

"So, is that a yes?"

He fixes me with a beady stare from under the brim of his hat. "Do you think the boyfriend did it?"

"No," I say, folding my arms close to my chest.

"I need to talk to the boyfriend. You know the boyfriend?"

I nod.

Mr. Capote pouts. "He won't speak to me. Foxy said he would

help but what does *he* know? Apparently he has no contact with the boy."

"Foxy?" I ask, confused.

"Agent Dewey," Miss Lee clarifies.

I'm still baffled. *Foxy?* But I keep silent, not wanting to look like a "dimwit."

"So, do you think *you* can talk to him?" Mr. Capote asks.

"Talk to Bobby?" I ask, unfolding my arms and sitting straight. "You want *me* to talk to Bobby?"

"Was I not clear?"

"Truman," Miss Lee warns again.

I slump in my chair, deflated. I see now what this interview was all about. They don't want to hear my story at all. They just want to get as close as possible to whoever killed the Clutters.

CHAPTER THIRTY-ONE

WEDNESDAY NIGHT, DAD HAS TO run another mysterious errand at the courthouse, and I go with him. Mom is picking up Asher at basketball practice.

Dad tells me to wait in the car while he goes inside. Maybe he believes that I actually will. The same way he believes that I met Mary Claire at the diner yesterday instead of meeting Miss Lee and Mr. Capote at the Wheat Lands Motel. I wait a good two minutes before I hop out of the car, into the cold night. I tiptoe inside, closing the heavy doors quietly behind me. The knobs are like icicles in my hands. I can hear Dad's voice from the second floor. The place is quiet and dimly lit; it's after hours, closed for business. I creep down the shadowy hall and up the staircase.

The same office, the one that the agents were using last time, is open. The lights are on. But Dad's voice is coming from a room farther down the hall. Holding my breath, I duck inside the closer door. The evidence is spread out across one long table. Looking behind me, to make sure no one's in the hall, I creep slowly in. Careful not to touch anything, I look over all the evidence. My legs turn to jelly. So many photographs. Pictures of death. Bodies.

Mr. Clutter's slashed throat, his wounded head, his duct-taped mouth, and his rope-bound feet.

Kenyon's head on a pillow, a gunshot to the head, his feet bound with rope.

Mrs. Clutter in her bed, her hands over her chest, bound with rope as if she were praying.

Nancy turned on her side, facing the wall.

They knew that they were going to die.

Rope in plastic bags.

A photo of a bloody boot print.

That's all the KBI has to go on. A bloody boot print and some rope?

My head swims. This is all too much. It's too . . . I can't think of a word. I have no thoughts at all. I've been reduced to pure feeling: sickness, dread, horror. It's *real*. Right here. In my face. I rub my hands on my thighs to calm my nerves and to keep from vomiting all over the little evidence the KBI has.

A man coughs.

With a start, I look up to see Agent Church standing in the doorway.

"You shouldn't be in here," he whispers. He jerks his head down the hall. "Your father is talking to the sheriff right now. He know you're here?"

I shake my head. My heart pounds. He shakes his head and someone grabs his arm, pulling him away. I can't see who it is. I crouch low, holding my breath, listening. There's hushed talk. I can catch only snippets. *"Promising lead . . . Lansing . . . Kansas State Penitentiary . . . Alvin's sending Agent Owens . . ."*

"Who are they interviewing?" someone asks loudly.

"A man named Floyd Wells," Agent Church replies. His voice fades as he moves down the hall, away from the stairwell. "He worked for the Clutters back in '49. Did some time, shared a cell with a fella named Hickock. We understand he might have told Hickock about a safe that Herb supposedly had. It's a lead and a damn good one at that." There's an angry grunt. "Alvin told that Capote character? Why in the hell . . . ?"

I hear what sounds like a muffled argument. Taking that as my moment, I bolt out the door and run for the stairs. I'm too terrified to look over my shoulder, but I don't hear anyone yelling after me. I only slow down to open and close the courthouse doors. My lungs feel like they're on fire by the time I slip back into the car.

I repeat the name "Floyd Wells" over and over so I won't forget. My heart thumps and my chest heaves. Luckily it's another ten minutes before Dad appears. I'm not relaxed, but at least I'm not sweating and panting.

I force a smile as Dad starts the engine.

"Was that about what I think it was?" I ask him.

"You know I can't discuss it, Carly."

"I know," I murmur.

He glances at me. "Let me put it this way. I think I know whom I'll be defending," he says. "And . . . it'll be good for the town."

"Do you think they're guilty?" I ask.

He laughs.

Not at the question, of course. He laughs because he knows that *I* know he would never answer—ever—no matter who asked. And he laughs because he knows I'll never stop asking. I'm still smiling, too, I admit. Not because of Dad. I'm smiling because I have no reason at all anymore to introduce Mr. Capote and Miss Lee to Bobby. They wouldn't want to talk to him now anyway.

CHAPTER THIRTY-TWO

AT LUNCH THE NEXT DAY, Mary Claire sees my excitement before I even sit down. I guess I'm not good at hiding things or playing it cool like she is. Or like Nancy was. Maybe I'm not as good an actress as I think.

"What is it?" Mary Claire whispers. "You look like you have a secret."

I sit and lean toward her over my tray. "Can I ask you a question?"

"Sure," she says, her eyes searching mine.

"You've lived in Holcomb your whole life. Would you say you know pretty much everyone?"

She shrugs. "I guess so, why?"

Biting my bottom lip, I glance around the bustling cafeteria. "Last night after school, I went with my dad to the courthouse. I snuck inside. The door to one of the offices was open—"

"And you snuck inside *there*, too," she finishes for me.

I feel myself blushing. I put my napkin in my lap. "Yes. I saw the evidence."

"Carly—"

"I know."

She takes a sip of milk. "Was it as bad as they say?" she asks, very quietly.

I nod, looking up.

She leans back in her chair, staring at me. "You're going to have nightmares, and then I'm going to have nightmares, too."

"Not if I don't tell you what I saw. But listen, here's what I want to know. Do you remember a boy named Floyd Wells? He worked for the Clutters one summer, maybe ten years back. He's older than we are."

She thinks for a moment, her eyes wandering off into the past. "I think so. I'm pretty sure. He moved away when I was little. Yeah. Floyd. He was a teenager. He was kind of odd, if you ask me."

I feel a strange tingle of excitement. I'm onto the truth; I can feel it. "What was odd about him?"

"I don't know." She doesn't seem nearly as interested in this conversation as I am. She takes a bite of her hamburger and lifts her shoulders. "Nancy and I found him swirly. You know: not quite right in the head. He worked for Mr. Clutter one summer and then he was—" Suddenly she drops her food. Her eyes widen again. "Oh, no. You think . . . ?" The unfinished question hangs between us.

"I don't know," I say. I glance around the room again and keep my voice low.

"From what I can tell, the KBI thinks Floyd Wells planted the seed of the robbery in the head of some criminal he met in prison, a man named Hickock. They're going up to Lansing to interview him tomorrow."

"The man's name is Hiccough?" she says with a frown.

I shake my head, frowning back. "Not *Hiccough*—"

"Who has the hiccoughs?" a smarmy voice asks.

Karen is standing beside me, smiling angelically. Her posture is perfect. Everything about her is perfect. I'm half tempted to slap the bottom of her tray and splatter her lunch all over her pristine white sweater.

"No one," I quickly say.

She turns her smile to Mary Claire. "Why so many secrets?" she asks.

Mary Claire smiles back and rolls her eyes. "Carly's just searching for clues," she says.

"Of course she is. Carly's the new Nancy Drew," Karen replies with a giggle.

I glare at Mary Claire, but she pretends not to notice. Karen traipses away. Once Karen is out of earshot, I whisper, "Is that what you really think? That I'm trying to be some kind of Nancy Drew?"

"Maybe I do," Mary Claire says simply. "But I have a right to. Because I know you're going to ask me to help you sneak back into that courthouse." She arches an eyebrow. "Right?"

Now it's my turn to giggle, even though I try not to.

AFTER SCHOOL, MARY CLAIRE drives me to Garden. We park under a leafless tree at the end of the court- house block. The plan is simple: she'll be my lookout. She'll wait on the first floor while I go up to the second. If she thinks I'm in trouble, she'll give me a signal.

But now that we're here, she's getting cold feet.

"Are you sure you want to do this?" She grips the steering wheel. "Can't we just go get a Coke instead?"

"I'm sure," I say, scouring the street for any sign of the sheriff or the KBI agents or my father.

"My treat," she says. "How about we make that Coke a float?"

I turn to her with a smirk. "No."

With a sigh, she opens the door. "If we get arrested, I get the top bunk," she says.

"Deal."

We walk in silence across the street and up the courthouse steps. She goes in first and I follow closely behind. I stiffen the instant the door closes. Men are coming down the stairs. I can see their shiny shoes and suit pants. In a panic we both hide behind one of the big potted plants. Mary Claire gives me a dirty look. Both of us hold our breath, waiting for the men to exit. Once I'm sure they're outside, I let out a pent-up gasp of relief.

"We shouldn't be here," she whispers.

"But we already are," I whisper back.

"How am I supposed to signal you?"

My mind is blank. I should have thought of this beforehand. "Cackle like a chicken," I tell her.

She purses her lips. "A chicken? Yeah. *That* won't be weird."

"Well, what do you want to do? Moo like a cow?"

"I'll whistle," she says.

"Whistling is good," I say, nodding.

At first, I'm cautious. I creep around the plant. But then fear overtakes me. The longer I'm here, the better the chances are I'll get caught. Before I know it, I'm pulling off my Hush Puppies and handing them to Mary Claire.

She gapes at me in either bafflement or disbelief. Or both.

Then I sprint for the stairwell. I'm silent in my stocking feet as I race to the second floor. Every single office door is cracked open.

The empty hallway is teeming with the quiet voices behind them. I make a beeline for the office I know. If the agents are there, fine. I'll make up a story about how somebody stole my shoes. The office is deserted, thank goodness. But the desk has been cleared, too. No photos. No stacks of documents. Just a slim file folder, unmarked. With trembling fingers, I open it.

OFFICE OF THE KANSAS BUREAU OF INVESTIGATION

Eureka!

Mary Claire's whistle is soft, but I hear it. I stand frozen at Agent Dewey's desk, clutching the three-page report. Then I stuff it down my dress, dash for the stairwell, and nearly go flying. I have to grab the railing to catch myself. I keep slipping on the smooth marble steps. But within seconds I'm out the door in my stocking feet.

Mary Claire falls in line behind me, and I don't dare look back. She's still whistling.

The freezing pavement is rough on my toes. It hurts, but I don't slow down. Not until we get back into her car can I breathe.

The instant I slam the door, Mary Claire tosses my shoes in my lap. She isn't whistling anymore. She's laughing.

"Oh my God, I thought we were dead back there!" she cries.

I try to muster a smile. "Now, you can't tell anyone we borrowed this," I say, pulling the report out of my dress and scratching my neck in the process. Great. A paper cut I'll have to explain at dinner.

"Borrowed?" Mary Claire teases. "I think you mean stole."

"I mean borrowed."

"With you, I don't think there's much difference," she says, taking it from me.

"Ha."

"Is it a confession?" she asks.

"I don't know."

As Mary Claire's eyes flash over the pages, I slide my shoes back on. I'm wincing a little. The bottoms of my feet are bruised and scraped. I should probably toss my stockings before Mom finds them in the laundry and asks more questions.

"We should get out of here," Mary Claire mutters, handing the report back to me.

"Hold your horses," I say.

"Well, read it out loud," she says.

THE REPORT IS DRY, like a textbook. A list of facts. Floyd Wells worked for Mr. Clutter from 1948 to 1949.

Mary Claire points out that this was before the Clutters even lived at the house where they were killed.

After Wells left Holcomb, he worked a series of odd jobs and drifted into a life of petty crime. A conviction for robbing an appliance store landed him three to five years at the Kansas State Penitentiary in Lansing, where he shared a cell with Richard Hickock. *Or Dick, as he is called,* the report reads. Wells contacted the authorities after hearing about the murders on the radio because he had a hunch Dick was the murderer.

"Why's that?" Mary Claire asks.

"Says here that Floyd Wells told Dick Hickock that Mr. Clutter was very rich, and that he had a safe with ten thousand dollars in it in his home."

She shakes her head. "That's a lie—there was no safe in that house. Mr. Clutter *always* pays by check," she says. "I mean, paid. I remember he once told my dad to do the same, never to keep large amounts of cash on hand. We have a safe. My dad says cash is important in case there's a run on the banks, like during the Depression. What if they came to our house instead?" She turns in her seat to face me. "It could have been my family instead of Nancy's. It could have been us. We'd be dead."

"Floyd Wells didn't work on your farm, did he?" I ask, trying to reassure her.

"No," she says. She still looks shaken. Melodrama is one of her specialties, especially when she's bored. She reminds me of Aunt Trudy that way. But she's not bored now. "What else does it say?"

I flip to the final page, skimming the text. "There's more of his statement . . . He talks about how Dick had a friend named Perry Edward Smith . . . He knew they were dangerous, and so that's why he alerted the prison authorities. He said that Dick would have tortured Mr. Clutter to get to that safe. It ends with 'suspects' possible whereabouts: Carson City, Nevada, and Edgerton, Kansas.' Hickock's last known residence." I look up. "That's it. Well, except for what Floyd Wells is getting in return for the information."

"There *was* no safe," Mary Claire murmurs, gazing out the window.

"I'm just reading what it says here. Where's Edgerton?"

"Near Olathe," she says absently.

"Olathe? That's where Landry's from," I say. I'm not sure why that gives me a funny feeling, but it does. Girls like Sue and Karen—Nancy, too—don't think highly of that area. It's poor. Seedy.

"So, now we know who did it, right?" Mary Claire asks, turning toward me.

"I guess."

"What's wrong?"

"It's too easy," I say. "Don't you think? Floyd Wells just happens to know exactly who did it after hearing the news on the radio? He could be making the whole thing up. You said he was swirly. Maybe there was bad blood between him and this Dick character. They were cellmates. Maybe they were enemies, too. Now Floyd Wells has a horrible crime to pin on his enemy and a get-out-of-jail-free card, all rolled up in one. Pretty convenient."

Mary Claire's eyes widen. "Is that what he's getting out of this? I mean, for talking to the KBI?" she asks. "He's getting out of jail?"

"More," I say. "A thousand dollars. *And* parole."

"Holy moly."

CHAPTER THIRTY-THREE

Dad has to work late, and Mom is meeting with the Parent-Teacher Association, so I'm told to have dinner with Asher in town after basketball practice. Mom even called ahead to alert Mrs. Hartman that we'll be at Hartman's Café. They must suspect I haven't been where I've claimed to be after school. Mary Claire dropped me off here following our excursion after school to the courthouse. I'm sitting at the counter in front of a grilled cheese sandwich and an ice-cold fountain Coke when the door flies open.

It's not Asher. It's Mr. Helms, our neighbor. He's old, about Mr. Stoecklein's age, and retired. He runs in, orders himself "a coffee, no milk and no sugar" in one breath. Then he grabs my arm and says, "I caught a man at the Clutter home. Saw him with my own two eyes."

"Was he arrested?" I ask.

He nods slowly.

"I bet he was the one who came in here last night asking a lot of questions about the murders. They always go back to the scene of the crime," Mrs. Hartman says, giving me a knowing scowl of disapproval.

"He had a .38 revolver in one of those snap-on belt holsters under his coat. In his car he had a .30 hunting rifle, a 12-gauge shotgun, and a hunting knife," Mr. Helms says.

She clamps a hand over her mouth, then drops it. "A hunting knife and a shotgun? Aren't those the same weapons used on Herb, Bonnie, and the kids?"

"Yes, ma'am, they are. They're questioning him about the murders."

She shakes her head. "Menacing creatures."

"He says that he was just curious. That's why he was out there."

"Sure he was," she says. "Sure he was . . ." She heads back to the kitchen.

When the door swings shut behind her, Mr. Helms leans over and tells me what he really saw. Not just the prowler. "A woman—an older woman. She was wearing a housecoat and had the same coloring as Bonnie. It was her, all right. I know what Bonnie looks like."

I try to smile as politely as I can. "Mr. Helms, Mrs. Clutter is dead," I say.

"Don't believe me, fine, but it was Bonnie, all right," he says, nodding.

Mrs. Hartman reappears. "You okay?" she asks Mr. Helms, her brow creased as she pours him another cup of coffee. "You look like you've seen a ghost."

"You have no idea," he says over the rim of his mug.

A few minutes later, Asher appears. He throws his gym bag under the stool next to Mr. Helms. Mrs. Hartman places a hamburger with French fries in front of him. It's all ready and waiting, thanks to Mom's call. I feel like we're being spied on. Maybe we are. Maybe my mom made up tonight's meeting so she could catch me in the act of doing something bad.

I privately vow to lay off the sneaking around. There's no need to poke my head into police business anymore. Mary Claire dropped me off here at Hartman's after we finished reading what was in the file. She stayed in the truck as my lookout while I ran up the courthouse stairs and deposited the file in the mail slot. Nobody saw me. I'm done.

"You know you stink?" Mrs. Hartman says, crinkling her nose at my brother.

He smiles. "I was at practice."

"Uh-huh."

Mr. Helms tells Asher all about what he saw. Asher doesn't believe him but indulges him anyway. He's a model of patience and understanding, even though he's starving. He's not being phony, either. He takes after Dad that way. Me? Not so much. I stare down at my half-eaten sandwich, no longer hungry. Tonight I wanted to grill Asher about why he talked about me to the police and kept it secret. But I've lost the urge. Asher was just doing the right thing, because that's what he does. Always. It's why he and Kenyon were *real* friends.

After jabbering in my brother's ear for what seems like hours, Mr. Helms excuses himself to go to the restroom.

"Have you seen Bobby today?" Asher asks me.

I shake my head. "No. Why?"

"He's acting really strange. He's still at school. He said he was going to stay late shooting."

"I'm going to go talk to him," I say, gathering my bag from my chair.

"Why?" he asks.

"To be there for him," I say.

"What about what you promised Mom and Dad?" Asher says.

"I can take him home if you want," Mr. Helms offers.

I'm annoyed that he was eavesdropping, but grateful, not to mention happy to have a witness that I'm not breaking any rules. "Thanks," I say, grabbing my bag. "You too, Mrs. Hartman. Please tell my mother, if she asks, what happened. I went to console a friend."

She flashes a wry smile. "I sure will, hon. You're a good girl."

With a reluctant nod, Asher turns back to his food.

I head out into the cold. Landry's pickup pulls into a parking spot. Eureka!

"Hey, you going in?" he asks as he hops out.

"Just leaving, actually," I say.

He slams the door and locks up his truck. Everybody locks up everything nowadays. I wonder if that will continue when the killers are finally caught, if they're ever caught. "That's a shame; we could've sat together," he says.

"Asher said something's up with Bobby."

Landry frowns at me. "Oh. So?"

"So I'm going to go see him. Can I ask a favor? Can I borrow your truck? Please. Pretty please with a cherry on top."

"Okay." He gives me a curt nod. "You know, Bobby still loves Nancy," he adds, handing me the keys as he walks by me. His voice is cold. He grabs a hold of the door to Hartman's and pulls it open, avoiding my eyes.

"I know that," I tell him.

"Do you?" he asks, letting the door slam behind him.

THE GYM IS UNLOCKED, to my surprise. Tossing my bag on the floor, I take a seat on the bleachers. Bobby is alone, but he doesn't see me. He's still in his basketball uniform, practicing all by himself. I watch as he shoots from behind the line. He makes some and misses some. Finally, when a shot bounces off the backboard and into the backcourt, he chases after it and spots me.

"I didn't see you come in," he calls, out of breath.

"Yeah, well. I'm sneaky," I say.

He manages a smile. "What are you doing here?"

"Asher said something happened."

"Oh. Nothing happened." He bends over and picks up the ball, his smile gone. "It's just my friends aren't really my friends anymore."

"You don't mean that."

He shakes his head and sits beside me. He stinks like Asher, but I don't mind.

"It's the truth," he said. "I've been cleared by the police, and they still look at me as if I killed them all."

"But you didn't," I say.

"Yeah, I *know* I didn't," he says.

"They're stupid."

He shrugs. "Not all of them. Everything's different. I'm not getting the ball as much during practice."

"It's just a game."

"No, it's not. It's what we do."

Stealing the ball from him, I say, "Okay, then I should learn, too. Show me how to shoot."

He laughs, which was what I was hoping for. "I don't think there are enough hours in the day," he teases.

"Har-har-har."

I try dribbling the ball. It doesn't go so well. The ball hits my foot and bounces over to Bobby. He hops off the bench, scoops it up, and dribbles past me, whizzing toward the basket.

"Show-off!" I call after him as he makes a layup.

"Come on, I want to see you shoot," he says. He throws the ball and it hits my chest.

"Ouch."

"Two hands," he says as I try to catch my breath.

"I know, I know," I manage. "Asher tells me the same thing."

Standing at the free-throw line, I lob the ball into the air, underhanded. It doesn't even come close to the basket.

He laughs and shakes his head. "But I guess he didn't tell you how to shoot, huh?" he asks, chasing down the ball. "Like this." He stands beside me at the line, holds the ball in his right hand, and pushes off with his knees. It goes straight into the basket. "Nothing but net. Now your turn."

For some reason, I actually want to do this. I've never felt like I had to prove something to Asher. In fact, I secretly get a kick out of being so awful at sports, because it aggravates him. So I concentrate when Bobby hands me the ball. I do exactly what he did, pushing off with my knees, releasing with my wrists, watching my shot go through the basket without even hitting the backboard or rim. I blink twice. I can't quite believe it.

"*Swish?*" I say.

"Carly!" He cheers my first-ever basket. "You're a natural."

He grabs the rebound and stands in front of me; only the ball is between us. Then he lets it drop to the floor; it rolls toward the door. I look up. His eyes are inches from my own. My breath catches.

"Bobby?" a voice yells.

We both spin. It's Coach Eck.

"I've got to lock up," he says.

I swallow when I realize he's not alone. Someone emerges from the shadows on the other side of the gym. *Seth*. He stands in the doorway, his face blank. Then he turns and walks out.

"Yeah, okay, Coach," Bobby says, hurrying toward the locker room. "I'll see you tomorrow, Carly."

"Yeah," I mumble without looking at him. I race to the door.

Seth is sitting on the hood of Landry's truck, smoking a cigarette.

I approach slowly and stand at the driver's side door. We stare at each other. Seth doesn't seem to be in any hurry to move. He takes a long drag and exhales. I shiver in the cold.

"It'll be hard to drive with you blocking my view," I finally say in a flat voice.

He flashes me a disgusted sneer. "Honestly, Carly, you're embarrassing yourself," he says. "I just thought you should know." With that, he stubs out his cigarette on the hood and leaves the butt there. Then he jumps off and walks away.

CHAPTER THIRTY-FOUR

I HAD A HARD TIME falling asleep last night. Now it's morning, and the sun seems too bright, and I'm irritable. I'm sitting on a bench in front of the office, waiting for Seth to walk through the front doors. He has to know what he saw between Bobby and me at the gym wasn't what he thought it was. Not that I should even care. Our relationship is over. But I know how rumors get started in Holcomb.

At least he's alone when he arrives. Talking to him is harder with Alex around.

"Seth," I say, but he just walks past. I grab my bag and catch up with him at his locker. "Seth, you've got to listen to me."

"Do I?" he says.

"What you saw last night—"

"I don't care about what you do, Carly. I'm going to be late for class."

"We still have a minute."

He doesn't even bother to answer. Instead he slams his locker shut and walks down the hall. I'm about to chase after him when there's a tap on my shoulder. I turn to see Alex. He smiles and hands me a note just as the bell rings.

MRS. FORD—THE SCHOOL'S ART instructor, resident oddball, and my homeroom teacher—nearly shuts the door in my face. I apologize and slink to my seat.

"I have a splitting headache. I need peace and quiet," she says, sitting at her desk at the front of the room. She closes her eyes and rubs her temples.

I start to open the note.

"No notes in my classroom," she snaps, her eyes suddenly open.

But it's too late. I can't help but gape at what's on the scrap of paper: a crude drawing of a tree with two stick figures holding hands, ropes around their necks, hanging from a tree branch.

Mrs. Ford stands up and walks over to me. "Carly, I told you," she says, grabbing the note from me. Then she lets out a little cry. Her face turns as white as a ghost. If it wasn't the drawing that did her in, it was the line underneath it.

Carly and Bobby hanging from a tree, D-Y-I-N-G.

She turns to me, her jaw slack.

"I didn't draw it," I say, shaking my head.

"Who then?"

Everyone in the classroom points to someone else.

A FEW MONTHS AGO, some troublemakers locked all the doors to all the classrooms at school and hid the keys. We were stuck sitting in the hallways, talking so loud that the teachers got tired yelling at us to be quiet. At least we had no homework that night. The janitors went around unlocking each door. It took a while, and when we got inside the classrooms and took our seats, we couldn't stop laughing. The teachers were frazzled.

The boys who were responsible got a lecture, but that's it. I think Principal Williams was just too glad the day was over to deal with punishments. There was a group of them, from out near where Landry lived, who were always pulling those types of pranks. Especially on Mrs. Ford. She's gullible. She's also a jumpy mix of very bohemian and very religious. Not a great combination in a teacher. The result is an unfortunate habit she has of running to the storage closet in the back of the room, shutting herself inside it, and praying for us. We can hear her through the door. It's always the same prayer, too.

"Dear Lord, they do not know what they do. Please take away their sins. Cleanse them, dear Lord, cleanse them."

As she stands there now in shock, looking over all the kids, the classroom door opens. It's Bobby. He's late. I want to crawl under my desk and hide. Mrs. Ford looks at him and then at me. She pushes the paper into my hands and heads straight for the storage closet.

Alex and Seth chuckle. Soon we're all listening to the muffled words we know by heart now.

Bobby looks over at me. "What's going on?"

I hand him the piece of paper. He takes it, gives it a once-over, and tears it up. The pieces fall to the floor. He sits in silence for the rest of the period, avoiding everyone's eyes—including mine. The instant the bell rings, he's out the door. Running.

Mrs. Ford slowly emerges from the closet.

Once everyone is gone, I scoop up the fallen bits of paper and hurry out of the room. I spot Landry in the hall. He's grinning.

"So, Mrs. Ford was praying again?"

"Yes, we're all cleansed now," I mutter. I toss the bits of paper in the trash can and head to my locker. Landry follows. He's in a better mood than he was last night, and I'm relieved. It means the rumor mill hasn't begun to churn. It's still too early in the morning. He leans against the lockers as I dial my combination and grab my history book and composition notebook.

"She and Mr. Helms should spend some time together," he cracks. "I bet they'd hit it off."

I turn to him. "Did he tell you about the ghost he saw?"

"Yeah, he did."

"Do you really think he saw something? I mean, other than the guy that they arrested?"

Landry shrugs. "I don't know. Maybe he did see something."

"Do you believe in ghosts?" I ask.

He's still smiling, but his eyes are distant. "Maybe, I don't know, though sometimes I think I feel my uncle's spirit," he says. He pauses and looks right at me. "About yesterday, I didn't mean what I said outside Hartman's Café. I was just . . . frustrated. Okay?"

I nod, but I'm not listening. My mind is a thousand miles away. Thanks to Landry and Mr. Helms, I'm suddenly thinking of Aunt Trudy.

CHAPTER THIRTY-FIVE

MARY CLAIRE'S ON BOARD FROM the moment I say the word *séance*. The problem is that, according to the Ouija board Aunt Trudy sent me, we need four people.

"What about Landry and Bobby?" I suggest.

"No way," Mary Claire says.

"Why not?" I ask. It makes the most sense, not to mention that it was my plan all along. Plus, I wouldn't even have had the idea if it weren't for Landry. Besides, maybe with Bobby being there, the spirits will talk. Not that I'm sure I believe in this mumbo-jumbo. But anything is worth a shot if it will clear Bobby's name once and for all.

"It's too risky," she says. "Most of all, it doesn't look good for *him* to be there."

I try to think of a comeback, but she has a point.

"Don't worry, Carly, I've already recruited a pair," she says.

"Really? Who?"

"Karen and Audrey," she says.

I sigh heavily. I can already picture what this will turn into: a convenient excuse for them to snicker at me and get the rumor mill churning nice and steady.

"Listen to me, Carly." Her voice grows serious. "It's better to be friends with them than not. Besides, Karen and Audrey believe in this séance thing. Don't you think we need four people that actually do? I mean, if you're serious?"

Mary Claire is right. For all kinds of reasons. Not that I'm happy about it.

MY PARENTS KNOW THAT I'm not only spending the night with Mary Claire, but with Karen and Audrey, as well. That means four different sets of parents know exactly what we're doing, or believe they know what we're doing. They believe we're going to see *Journey to the Center of the Earth* at the movie theater in Garden City.

I know I vowed not to sneak around anymore. But this is worth it, for all kinds of reasons. There was no way I could tell them we were going to the Clutter farm. It's not just the best place to hold a séance. It's the *only* place.

Mary Claire drives us out in silence. We sit at the end of the long driveway for a good five minutes before we have the courage to go any farther. I try not to think of the gruesome photographs I saw at the courthouse.

Karen and I get out first. We move the police barricade out of the way. We'll move it back when we leave. We don't have to worry about Mr. Stoecklein; he moved off the land shortly after my arrest, to a property along the highway. My father told me it was because he couldn't stand to be so close to the Clutter house anymore. Who can blame him?

Tucked under my arm is the Ouija board. While Aunt Trudy insisted she believes in its powers, she also suggested I could make a game of it with my friends. Her note concluded, *It works either way.*

This does not feel like a game, and two of the three others don't feel like friends.

I think of my aunt's words in the note right after Nancy and her family were murdered: *"Things will be back to normal."* And here I am, breaking into the Clutter house to conjure their spirits. Is this what she meant? Maybe. But then "normal" to Aunt Trudy might seem to some Holcomb locals like a direct link to Satan himself.

Mary Claire carries a bag full of candles and a box full of matches. Audrey has a couple of flashlights. None of them work, though, because she forgot to change the batteries. Karen holds a huge blanket that we plan to lay on the hardwood floor.

The front door's locked. But Mary Claire has planned for this. She remembers where Nancy hid a key just in case she forgot hers.

It's still there.

Somehow, that gives me the chills. The house is empty. We tiptoe up the stairs and down the hall to Nancy's bedroom. Karen and Audrey lay the blanket on the floor, and Mary Claire starts to light the candles around the room. Taking the Ouija board out of the box, I place it in the middle of the blanket. My hands tremble. It looks like a game, but spookier: square-shaped, marked with the twenty-six letters of the alphabet, the numbers zero through nine, and the words *yes*, *no*, and *good-bye*.

I read the rules last night so I'd know them by heart.

"It says we should never ask questions about our death or another's death," I tell them.

"Nonsense," Mary Claire says. "We want to talk to Nancy and find out the truth, don't we?"

"Wait, can we ask her about how she died?" Karen asks.

"Yes," Audrey chimes in before I can answer. "I read about it in a magazine. I know exactly what I'm doing. We can't ask how *we're* going to die—that's the rules."

At least they seem to be taking it seriously, even if they get on my nerves.

"We'll have to each put our fingers on this to help guide the spirit to speak to us," I say, holding the movable planchette.

We make a circle.

"Should we say a prayer first?" Audrey asks.

"Like, to God?" Mary Claire asks.

"Doesn't that defeat the purpose of dark magic?" Karen asks. I see her smiling wickedly in the flickering candlelight. She's having the time of her life. Maybe that's what such a strict religious upbringing will do to you.

"Probably. But shouldn't we cover all our bases?" Audrey says.

Karen rolls her eyes. Audrey mumbles a prayer anyway. Afterward, we hold hands and say in unison, "Let there be no evil forces or demons . . ." Just like the directions say.

"Someone has to be the designated medium," Karen points out. She must have read the directions, too.

"I volunteer Carly; it is her board," Mary Claire says.

I scoot closer. When we each put our index and middle fingers on the planchette, my heart beats so fast I think it's going to jump out of my chest.

Leaning forward in a huddle, we watch the board intently, moving the planchette around in circles to get the board warmed up.

"Be careful," Audrey whispers.

I take a deep breath and start, "I, Carly, ask for my spiritual guide's protection. Spirit, please come forward and give us guidance."

The planchette comes to a complete stop and then forcefully moves to the bottom left-hand corner of the board, spelling out the word *H-E-L-L-O*.

"Hello."

Mary Claire laughs.

"This is absurd," Karen says with delight.

"Shhhh!" I whisper.

"Ask it who it is," Mary Claire says.

"Who are you?" I ask.

It takes a second, but then it starts to spell *Y-O-U-R-F-R-I-E-N-D*.

My heart is thumping again. I can hear it in my ears.

"Make sure it's Nancy," Audrey says. "It could be a demon for all we know."

"Are you Nancy?" I ask. The words lodge in my throat.

The planchette moves forcefully to the top of the board and lands on the word *yes*.

"It's working! It's really working!" Audrey cries.

"Shhh!" we hiss at her in unison.

She squeezes her eyes shut and covers them with her hands, shaking her head.

"Do you remember the night of November fourteenth?" I ask the board, fighting back my own fear.

The movable indicator moves to *yes*.

"Ask her if she knows who killed her," Mary Claire whispers.

The planchette starts moving at a rapid pace. *B-O-B-B-Y-D-I-D-N-O-T-K-I-L-L-M-E*. Mary Claire and Karen are barely touching it, and Audrey has taken her fingers off it. The rules say that all participants need to be touching it. I blink at the triangle shape in the uncertain candlelight. Did it move on its own or did I move it? I don't know anymore, and maybe it doesn't matter, because I know the truth. Right now I want to prove it. And then I want to leave.

"See, I told you," I whisper, looking at Karen.

"But you can't ask that; it says not to ask about their death," Karen protests, suddenly serious. "Carly, you're making this up as you go, aren't you?"

"I am not," I fire back.

Our fingers linger on the planchette. Without warning—and I swear I don't move it—it slides abruptly to the bottom of the board.

good-bye

Audrey peers between her fingers and decides to scream.

That seems as good a reason as any to bolt.

CHAPTER THIRTY-SIX

MONDAY MORNING KAREN WANTS TO tell the entire school what happened at the séance. I know she's going to lie and make it seem creepier than it was. But she listens to Mary Claire and me when we warn her that the wrong people might overhear and start talking.

I don't let her out of my sight until the three of us make a pact not to utter a word. I try to make my voice like Dad's. *Case closed.*

I'm not worried about Audrey. She goes to GCHS, and she was so petrified by the whole thing, there's no doubt she'll keep her trap shut. Besides, what would her father, the deputy, say?

So I'm not sure why I tell Landry. Not that it matters. He thinks its hooey.

WHEN I ARRIVE HOME after school, I find Bobby sitting on our porch swing. I can tell right away that something's wrong. I try to make a joke.

"You know you can ring the doorbell. We will let you in."

"I don't know what I'm doing here," he says. He sounds as if he's talking to himself. His skin is pale and dark circles ring his eyes. I realize that I didn't see him in school today.

I wrap my arms around myself, shivering in my coat. The sky is gray. In homeroom, Mrs. Ford talked about the possibility of snow today. In the way only Mrs. Ford could, of course, marveling over "every individual snowflake's miraculous and unique beauty" while fretting over "the problems they cause when falling from heaven by the millions." I think she was right about the forecast, though.

Sitting beside him, I ask, "Shouldn't you be at basketball practice?"

"Yeah, I should, but I'm not."

"Why?"

He stuffs his hands in his jacket pockets. "It's like I told you the other night. Everywhere I go, I get strange looks. My friends have turned on me. I thought you would understand."

I glance toward the windows of our house. The sun is already low in the sky. The living room lights are on, and I know Mom is home. I wonder if she's watching us. Lowering my voice, I tell him, "Don't worry, they've got suspects, real suspects. And they're going to be caught soon."

He shifts away from me and looks me in the eye. "How do you know?"

I blink. I'm at a loss for words. What have I done? The truth came out because I wanted to be honest with him. *I know because I've stolen confidential material from the Garden City courthouse, because I wanted to clear your name. But I returned the report at least* . . . Nope. Not saying that. Not even thinking that. Banishing that from my brain.

"Bobby, I've—"

"Carly, what have you done?"

I laugh miserably. If only I could tell him I just asked myself the same question.

"Did you do something again?" he presses.

I feel all my defenses melting away. All I want is for him to understand. I turn and stare at the ground, trying to formulate my thoughts. The swing jerks beneath us, almost violently. He must be angry. "Nothing bad, I swear. Nothing . . . well, some people might say it's illegal—or not even—but not if they knew it was for a good reason . . . because . . ." When I realize I'm rambling, I look up.

Bobby is gone.

I stand up. I frantically search for him, catching a glimpse of the back of his coat, vanishing down the sidewalk beyond the hedges. He's running away. To distance himself from me, from trouble. My shoulders sag.

When I turn to go inside, I see my mother at the living room window, looking at me.

CHAPTER THIRTY-SEVEN

TUESDAY MORNING. I CAN'T BEAR the thought of going to school. I've barely slept. I'm sitting at the kitchen table with my family, eating cereal in grim silence, when the doorbell rings. Dad answers it. I can hear Bobby's voice.

"I thought Carly might need a ride to school," he says.

Depression falls away like some ugly winter coat I've just shed. I jump up, but Dad has already let him in. Bobby is here. He has returned. He's running his fingers through his damp hair, standing in the kitchen doorway. He looks much better rested than I feel, much better rested than he looked yesterday.

I muster a smile.

"Hey, Asher," Bobby says.

Asher doesn't look up from his textbook and cereal bowl. But his tone is friendly when he responds, "Hey, Bobby."

"Are you hungry, young man?" Dad asks, returning to his chair and his newspaper.

Mom pours herself another cup of coffee and stands beside me at the kitchen sink. "What about Landry?" she whispers in my ear as she sips her coffee.

"What about him?" I say, grabbing my lunch.

She and Dad exchange a look. Dad returns to his newspaper, snapping it so that it remains upright. Asher remains oblivious as always, his face buried in whatever he's reading. Or pretending to read. Now I wonder about what he notices and what he doesn't. But I don't have time to dwell on Asher.

"Carly, have a good day at school," Dad says.

"I will. Bobby . . . I just need a moment, okay? Thanks for the lift."

"I'll wait in the truck," Bobby says.

After dashing upstairs for a last peek in the bathroom mirror, I vow again not to do anything bad or dishonest. I look terrible. *Ugh.* But this is my just reward. I hurry back down. "Bye, Mom," I say.

She stands between the kitchen and the living room, leaning against the door frame. "Carly, be careful."

"I always am," I say.

"*Please* be careful," she says, more sternly this time.

I race outside. Bobby starts the engine. I close the truck door.

"It's really nice of you to pick me up, but I know it's a little out of your way," I tell him.

"I bet you're wondering why I came to your house last night," he says.

I nod several times. "Why did you?" I ask.

"Because *you* know what it's like."

"What it's like?"

"You understand," he says.

"Understand?"

"You know . . . what it's like to be an outsider. When Nancy took you under her wing—"

"She didn't take me under her wing," I point out.

"Didn't she?" he asks.

"No."

"You were over the house a lot," he says.

"I was tutoring her."

He jerks to a stop and turns to look at me. "Tutor?"

I nod again.

"But . . ." He scowls and shakes his head. "She didn't need a tutor."

"Yes, she did," I say.

"I think I would know if my girlfriend needed a tutor or not," he snaps.

The words sting. But I'm too tired for a fight. I turn and look out the window. "We're going to be late," I tell him. "Let's just get going, okay?"

He puts the car back into drive. "Carly—"

"What?"

With a sigh, he says, "Nancy told me she was trying to help you fit in. Teaching you things. About Holcomb."

"That's true," I say shortly. "Don't worry, Seth made it perfectly clear that I was only friends with you all because I was dating him. That's true, too, right?"

"Well, not exactly. Seth can be a real zero sometimes. I know that now. But when a new girl—"

"I thought he was your friend," I interrupt.

"Things change," he says. "See, I know what it's like for you now."

"But you *have* friends," I say.

He laughs sadly. "*Had* friends."

"Well, me, Mary Claire, and Landry are still your friends."

"I don't really know Landry," Bobby says with a shrug.

"He's great," I say, maybe a little too enthusiastically. My voice sounds shrill in my ears. "He's helped me prove your innocence. You should get to know him."

"Maybe," he says. "Like Nancy thought you should get to know Holcomb?"

I nearly explode, but instead I take a deep breath. "It's different. Listen to me, Bobby. Landry doesn't think you killed Nancy and her family. I *know* you didn't. You asked what I did. I saw a report about the investigation. One of the suspects lives in Edgerton. Near where Landry's from."

Bobby slows to another stop. "You think he might know the person. Can you ask him?"

I nod.

Bobby grins.

FRIDAY, ASHER'S GOT HIS second basket-ball game—against Satanta High School. The school lets us out of our final class early for a pep rally. The cheerleaders work themselves into a frenzy as the basketball team is introduced one by one to the crowd. Mary Claire and I sit next to Karen on the bleachers, applauding along with everyone else.

Since the séance, Karen's actually been friendly. Friendlier than usual, anyway. She's even kept her sarcasm to a minimum.

I'm bored with all the school spirit I can't bring myself to feel; my attention drifts. I see Landry standing by the wall behind the pep band. He sees me and waves.

"I'll be right back," I say to Mary Claire and Karen, but neither hears me.

It's better that way. I hop up and scramble toward the aisle.

I'm suddenly on a mission, one that's just occurring to me. I don't have to get Bobby involved in clearing his own name. I can leave him out of it. I can talk to Landry myself and tell him the truth.

Somewhere in the dim recesses of my brain, I hear my mother's voice at breakfast on Tuesday, warning me to be careful.

Be careful of what? I wish I'd shouted back. Mom couldn't care less about what it means to be an outsider in Holcomb. She *wants* to be an outsider. If you ask her where her home is, she won't hesitate to tell you: it's New York City. Holcomb is temporary. She clings to the silly dream that we'll be back on the East Coast in no time—back to the world of Jack the Presidential Hopeful and Handsome and Aunt Trudy. Back to all those rich, sophisticated, colorful lives. Back to where Truman Capote belongs.

It's sad. But what's really sad is that I only see it now.

We're never going back.

Dad has said it a hundred times: most people consider the defendants he represents to be monsters. It doesn't matter if a jury finds them not guilty. It's *worse*. When that happens, the victims and their families see Dad as a monster, too. People believe that he puts—well, *put*—dangerous criminals back on the streets of New York. It's impossible for us to ever go back. But Mom just pours another martini and laughs him off. "Always so dramatic," she says.

Landry is staring at me.

"Outside," I mouth to him, pointing at the exit.

He follows me out of the gym and into the hall. We sit on a bench across from the restrooms. For a second I don't say anything. How do I say this? How do I *ask* this?

"Landry, I know you lived in Olathe," I begin. "Well, I know for a fact that the main suspect in the Clutter murders lived and might still live in Edgerton. That's close to Olathe, right? Well, what I'm asking is—"

"How do you know this?" Landry interrupts me.

I shake my head. "It doesn't matter. Listen. Do you know a man named Richard Hickock? He'd be called Dick, probably."

Landry doesn't answer. He squirms on the bench, turning away from me.

"What is it?"

"Dick?" Landry says in a paper-thin voice.

"Yes. It's—"

"Dick Hickock?"

I nod.

Landry looks a little green. He bends over and clutches his stomach. He's going to be sick. Thankfully, he runs to the restroom. The door closes behind him. There's coughing and gagging. I run after him, pushing right through the door. I don't care if there are other boys in here or if I see them. I have a little brother; I've seen plenty. This is an emergency.

"Landry?"

"You shouldn't be in here," he shouts from inside a stall. His voice is strained. He's retching.

"I want to make sure you're okay," I tell him.

The toilet flushes and the stall door opens. He's got his color back. Now he just looks embarrassed. He washes his hands and rinses his mouth with some cold water, then dries off with a paper towel. For a very long while, he stands at the sink, the faucet still running. Finally he straightens.

"I'm sorry," he says to me in the mirror.

"Don't be."

I hold the bathroom door open for him. He turns the faucet off and heads back into the hall.

"His family's nice people," Landry tells me. He wipes his mouth with his sleeve. "I helped out on their farm sometimes. In the summer. Mrs. Hickock would give us lemonade. I . . . talked to Dick. Not much. It makes sense, though. He wasn't like them. His parents, I mean."

"Do you think they know that their son did this?" I ask.

He looks at me. "I don't know. But why would they want to?"

I don't have an answer. Honestly, I hadn't even thought of the question.

CHAPTER THIRTY-EIGHT

IT'S A SIX-HOUR TRIP—BOTH WAYS.

Landry talked his parents into letting me tag along with them to Olathe for the weekend. I talked my parents into the same. It wasn't as hard as I thought it would be. Mr. and Mrs. Davis have to go to their farm to check on their crops and animals before the freeze sets in; they're worried about the place. Meanwhile, Landry and I want to check out KU. We might want to attend college there after we graduate.

So it all makes sense.

Secretly, I do make Landry promise we'll visit the campus. It may not be as close to home as the "right Manhattan," where KSU is, but it's still Kansas. I *know* Kansas is my home, unlike Mom. Shouldn't I go to college here?

Truth. Not a lie. Not that part.

Dad is impressed by my "initiative." That's what he calls it. He's proud that I seem to have moved on from the tragedy of Nancy's death and that I have started to think about the future. He has no clue that I'm not telling the whole truth, or that I know what he knows. Besides, since he represented Landry's uncle a long time ago, there's a built-in trust between him and the Davis family. They know we're friends.

Even Mom is silent. Maybe she thinks I've chosen Landry over Bobby, as if that were even a choice. Maybe Landry is the choice she prefers. Or maybe she just can't be bothered, as long as I'm "not sleeping overnight in the same room as this . . . boy."

She actually says this part out loud when his parents pick me up.

We all laugh together, the Davis family and the Fleming family, standing in the freezing cold. (Asher had the good sense to stay inside.) We clumsily reassure ourselves such a scenario could never happen—not in Olathe or Holcomb *or* New York City. Of course not. I wonder if Mom's already had a martini. It's ten o'clock in the morning.

I wave good-bye.

Landry and I exchange a secret smile as we head to his parents' car. None of the adults know that our trip is a ruse to pay a visit to the Hickock home. Is a ruse the same as a lie? I should ask Mr. Capote what the difference is, if I ever see him again. He would know.

THERE'S NO DRIVEWAY AT the Hickock residence, just dirt and gravel. Landry turns off the engine and I reach for the door handle, but he grabs my arm.

"What?" I whisper.

He shakes his head.

"You're not getting cold feet, are you?" When he doesn't answer, I add, "We've come all this way."

It's Saturday evening and not even dinnertime but already pitch-black. Squinting, all I can see in the inky void are hints of a dilapidated farmhouse off to the right. Curtains obscure the dim lamps within. This is deep Kansas, far from everything. Everyone thinks we're at KU.

"Carly, wait. You can't just go on in there and accuse their son of a crime," he says. "They won't talk to you if you do. Let *me* do the talking."

I nod. He's right. "Okay."

Getting out, we brace ourselves against the cold. Landry hurries up the walkway. I follow, head down, noticing empty flowerpots. He knocks forcefully on the door.

"Who's there?" a woman yells.

"Landry Davis, ma'am, you knew my dad. We own the farm down the road from here . . ."

It takes a while, but the door opens. The woman who answers is stooped and gray. She smiles, and invites us inside. The light and warmth are blessed relief. Landry and I sit on the couch, and before I know it, she's offering a plate of sugar cookies cut out like bells and Christmas trees. Then she gives us each a cup of coffee. He drinks his. I do not.

"Oh, my, you've grown, child!" Mrs. Hickock exclaims. "I seen many a picture of you when you were a youngster. You were just yea high. So what brings you here?"

"Orders from my dad. I have to pick something up at the farm."

"Aren't you a good son!"

Landry manages an awkward smile.

She sits in an overstuffed easy chair. The room smells of something. It's not unpleasant, but it signifies . . . what? Not neglect. Sadness? Loneliness? Maybe it just smells of old age. Behind her on a table is a photograph of a man dressed in a mechanic's uniform. Light-colored hair, tall, lanky, kind of withdrawn in the eyes. He's smiling. I can't tell by his picture whether he's destined to become a mass murderer or not.

"That's my Dick," she murmurs, catching my stare.

Landry reaches over and grabs my arm. I get the message. He wants me to keep my mouth shut. "How is Dick?" he asks. "My mom was wondering."

She smiles, revealing blackened gums and three yellow teeth. "Your uncle was so kind. My husband respected him. He's out for the day, my husband." Her smile disappears. "It has to do with Dick, if you must know. He's taking care of some mess our son got into . . ."

"A mess?" Landry says, making sure to sound surprised.

"The police were out here yesterday," she goes on. "I don't really understand why they were here. They searched around for a good while. Took our shotgun. Took it right out there on our front porch and fired it. Took the empty casing. My son's a hunter. I don't understand all the trouble Dick gets himself into, but it's a mother's place to worry. He's a good boy, a *good* son, though his life hasn't ended up the way he hoped it would. But isn't that life, really?"

I'm perched on the edge of my seat. "Was he ever in trouble with the law before?" I ask.

Landry squeezes my hand—hard.

But she just smiles, her eyes far away.

"He tries, he really does. But he's been in trouble, all right." She takes a tissue and wipes her eyes, looking at me. "I'm sorry. What's your name, dear?"

"Carly. I'm Landry's sweetheart," I say, squeezing Landry's hand back. I shouldn't have said that. His skin is sweaty. He looks at me again. He's not happy. He looks even unhappier than when I opened my mouth the first time.

"Oh, how sweet. Landry, your family moved to Holcomb, to run your uncle's farm, right?" she asks.

"Yes, ma'am," he says.

"Who's running the farm here?"

"Some hired hands. My dad tries to make it up here to check on things once a month."

"Oh, I didn't know."

Landry nods.

"Holcomb, right?" she asks.

"Yes, ma'am," Landry says.

"I remember reading about a murder of a family in the paper," she says, clutching her pearls.

"The Clutter family," I say.

Landry lets go of my hand, his smile pained.

Mrs. Hickock shakes her head. "Oh, it was such a sad thing to read about in the paper. How horrible. Did you know them?" she asks.

We nod.

"I'm sorry to hear that," she says. "At least you have each other to lean on."

IN THE MIDDLE OF the night, I wake up screaming, sweating, my heart pounding. Mrs. Davis runs in and turns on the lamp on my nightstand.

She brushes my damp hair out of my face. "You had a nightmare. You're okay now," she says, pulling the covers up to my chin. "Try to get some sleep." She goes to turn off the light.

"Don't!" I croak.

"Carly, it wasn't real. It was just a dream."

"A scary one."

For a moment, Landry's mom hesitates. I don't blame her.

What would my mother do if the roles were reversed, if Landry was in our house and he woke up screaming? Actually, I know exactly what my mother would do. She'd make herself a martini.

"Do you want to talk about it?" Mrs. Davis asks.

I shake my head.

"It's okay, dear," she soothes. "I'm here if you need me. Good night."

In my dream, I was sitting in the Hickock house, listening to Dick's mother talk about her son, about how he was an angel, how he could never do anything wrong. She kept pointing to the picture. *He's safe.* She said this over and over. *He's safe. He's safe . . .* Then Dick leaped from the photo. He was armed with a shotgun. He took one look at me, cocked the trigger, and pointed the barrel at my head. Then he blew my brains out. I saw the explosion of blood. I saw myself on the floor. I saw it all.

CHAPTER THIRTY-NINE

MONDAY AFTER SCHOOL, BOBBY IS waiting for me by the front door. I can tell something is wrong from his expression. He offers to walk me home.

"No ride this time?" I joke.

He shakes his head, his face somber. "No. But I wanted to tell you something. I was going to call you, but I saw Asher on Saturday, and he told me you were away, looking at KU."

I nod, not wanting to explain. So I steer the conversation back to him. "What is it?" I ask. "Why did you want to call?"

"I'm transferring schools, and I thought you should know," he says.

I drag him to Hartman's Café so I can try to talk some sense into him.

WE SIT AT THE booth in the corner, drinking Cokes and sharing a piece of cherry pie.

"But Garden is seven miles away," I say, stressing the importance of the distance.

"It's still the same county. It's nothing. Car—"

"Then why do you think it will be any different at Garden than it is at Holcomb?" I ask, cutting him off.

He shrugs. "I don't."

"You just . . ."

"Have to."

I know why he thinks he has to. I so desperately want to tell him that he should just ignore all the naysayers and stay put at *his* school, in *his* hometown, with me. I know he didn't do it. No one in this town did it. Soon the real criminals will be caught and all our names will be cleared. People will stop looking at Bobby—at everyone—like we're guilty by association.

He takes another bite of pie. "Have you talked to Mr. Capote yet?" he asks.

I nod. "Have you?"

He nods. "Agent Dewey thought that it was a good idea. He said that if I didn't talk to Mr. Capote, he'd probably just make it all up."

I laugh.

Bobby finally cracks a smile. "You know what?" he says. "He told me how he beat Humphrey Bogart in arm wrestling. Sure. Like I believe that."

"I don't believe that."

"You know he has Nancy's diary?" he adds.

I shake my head.

"I think he just took it," Bobby tells me. He leans close, pushing the plate out of the way. "Listen, this is going to sound strange, but have you seen Landry in the past few days?"

"We went to Edgerton this weekend," I whisper.

"You did *what*?" Bobby's voice is suddenly urgent. "Did Landry tell you about Dick Hickock?"

"How do you—"

"Mr. Capote told me about Dick Hickock."

Of course, I think. Unbelievable. Mr. Capote is out there blabbering to everyone about what the Holcomb police know. Doesn't he know he could get himself arrested for doing that? Maybe he doesn't care. I don't care, either. In a way, Bobby's revelation is a relief. Now I can come clean and tell the truth for once, too.

"Landry's parents took us to see KU," I tell Bobby. "They didn't know we went to the Hickock place. I had to see for myself what it was like."

"You could have gotten yourself killed," he says.

"But I didn't."

"Yeah, luckily." He looks around the half-empty café. "Was *he* there?"

I shake my head. "I met his mom. Landry knew the family, not well, but enough to get us through the front door."

"Did you learn anything?" he asks.

"Only that his mom thinks her son can do no wrong."

"That's what mothers are supposed to think."

"Even if it's not the case?"

"What does your mother think of *you*?" he asks. He cuts the last bite in two and takes his share. "All mothers think their children are angels."

CHAPTER FORTY

A FEW DAYS LATER, MARY Claire, Landry, and I are sitting at Candy's Café. It's not the usual spot where Mary Claire and I meet, but we wanted to go someplace where we wouldn't run into people. We order French dips, fries, onion rings, and Cokes. I feel better than I have in a long time. We're so close to clearing Bobby. We're so close to clearing *everybody* in Holcomb. We're getting back to normal. Well, except for Nancy.

But Nancy is the reason we're doing this. That's why it's so important.

Mr. Capote is still staying at the Wheat Lands Motel in Garden, and I have a plan. Or I want to *come up* with a plan. I want to sneak into his room. I want to know what else he's managed to get his stubby little hands on, aside from Nancy's diary and confidential police reports.

"That's breaking and entering," Mary Claire reminds me.

"We've done it before," I say, arching my eyebrow.

"You have?" Landry asks.

Mary Claire flashes me a smirk. "Never mind, Landry." She crosses her arms. "I agreed to come here today, and to go along with you. But after we do this, we're done. No more playing

Nancy Drew." She holds out her pinkie for me to take. "Swear," she says.

I'm a little annoyed that she mentioned Nancy Drew, because that's Karen's favorite way of making fun of me, but I reach forward.

"I swear," I say, clasping pinkies.

Landry snorts. "I don't have to pinkie swear, do I?"

"Girls only," Mary Claire and I say at the same time, and we both laugh.

"So what's the plan?" he asks.

I shrug. "I haven't gotten past how we're going to get in. We need to find a different way upstairs through the coffee shop on the first floor. I met Mr. Capote and Miss Lee in that coffee shop. There's a chance the people who work there will recognize me. *Or* we'll bump into Miss Lee. It's too risky." I look to Mary Claire. "Any ideas?"

A smile spreads across her face. "I know that motel. There's a maids' entrance."

WHEN WE MEET UP at Mary Claire's house Sunday afternoon, I don't ask her how she got the two maids' uniforms. She's lived here her whole life and knows people. And like she told Landry and me at Candy's, she also knows the Wheat Lands Motel. So I'm assuming she borrowed them from someone. Borrowed and not stole. When it comes to Mary Claire's dark side, I've learned that it's best not to ask.

My uniform fits perfectly. For some reason this makes me even more nervous, keeping watch for Mr. Capote or Miss Lee. Mary Claire and I will pretend that we're cleaning Mr. Capote's room.

Either that or just sneak in and rummage through it if there's nobody else around. Landry will whistle if he hears anything. Just like what Mary Claire did in the courthouse.

As we park, I slouch down in the front seat. Just in case we see anyone and they start asking too many questions. Everyone thinks Mary Claire and I are studying for our final exams.

Before I know it, we're out of the car. It's freezing, and I'm not wearing a coat, but I don't even shiver. The maids' entrance is open, and we pass a couple of maids—older women I've never seen before—on their way out. Mary Claire smiles and waves and they wave back. Then we're up the stairs and in the deserted hallway, standing in front of room 202.

"You're sure this is the right room?" Mary Claire whispers.

"That's what he said," I whisper back.

I raise my hand to knock, but she tries the knob instead. It doesn't budge.

"You learn more if you *don't* knock," she says, pulling a hairpin out of her apron. She leans over and starts jimmying the lock.

After a second, there's a click, and the door swings open.

Maybe I should be surprised that Mary Claire is good at picking locks, but I'm not.

In my apron is the camera that Aunt Trudy sent me and told me to keep hidden. I've only used it once before, so I know it works. (I took a picture of Asher's room when he and my parents were out of the house, just to prove what a slob he was, but I never showed it to anyone.) I have to say, the contraption is pretty neat and futuristic. If I see something out of place, I press the button and the photograph develops right here. I don't have to take a film roll to the drugstore and wait for weeks.

Mary Claire and I creep inside. She closes the door behind us.

The room is dark. It smells of cigarette smoke and liquor. There's a stack of papers and a typewriter on a desk, next to a near-empty bottle of scotch whiskey. The top paper is scribbled with a woman's handwriting. Of course: Truman doesn't take notes. We start to go through the stack.

"Listen to this," I say. "'Mr. West is a portly young man of twenty-eight who looks forty and sometimes fifty.' Man, I don't want to know how he describes me."

Mary Claire laughs, pulling out a different sheet. "Here's your answer. 'Carly Fleming—Kind of sad but pretty. An outsider but desperately wants to be liked.'"

I scowl, following her finger. My heart squeezes. She's telling the truth.

Still laughing, she moves on. "'Tall, dark, and just plain handsome, Agent Alvin Dewey exudes a grim determination that helps reassure a community terrified by the massacre.'" Mary Claire snickers. "I feel reassured, don't you? Oh, and here's a good one: 'Hurd's Gas Station: Staffed by cretins.' Ha! He has a point there."

I shake my head.

She pauses on some words and her eyes narrow. "Gross!" She wrinkles her nose. "Listen to this: 'Yes, but nothing beats vinegar for getting the "dead body" smell out of the carpets.'"

"He's sick," I say, eyeing the piece of paper sticking out of the typewriter. "Listen to this. 'Some people in town think that Mr. Clutter was having an affair. The other woman's husband found out. In a jealous rage, the cuckold went on a killing spree.'"

Mary Claire sniffs. "Wow. That's kind of risqué. I didn't think good old Herb had it in him."

"It's not funny," I say. "It's a lie."

But she just smiles as she starts pulling out drawers and sifting through them. "You think so? Because you never know how people act behind closed doors."

There's a business ledger of some kind half hidden behind the desk lamp. Leaning close, I see that there are at least a hundred names on it. Each has been assigned a dollar amount. "I think he's paying people for their interviews," I say.

She stands up straight with her hands on her hips. "I didn't get paid."

"Neither did I."

I snap a picture of the ledger. The blank gray film slides from the camera and I wave it in the air, waiting for the image to appear.

All of a sudden Mary Claire shrieks. I nearly have a heart attack.

"I found the diary!"

Once I've recovered, I grab it out of her hand.

"Wait," she says.

"What?"

"You can't read that."

"*They* did," I say.

"That doesn't make it right . . ." Her voice trails off. Maybe she realizes it's slightly hypocritical to talk about right and wrong when she's the one who made it possible to break into a hotel room in uniforms we don't own. But I can tell from her expression that's not it. She wants to protect her friend, even though her friend is dead. I hesitate, swallowing.

What does it matter now?

Shaking my head, I sit on the bed and flip to the last entry.

Jolene K. came over and I showed her how to make a cherry pie. Practiced with Roxie. Bobby here and we watched TV. Left at eleven.

I glance up and show Mary Claire. "That's it?"

She sits beside me. "What did you expect it to say? 'Jolene K. came over and I showed her how to make a cherry pie. Practiced with Roxie. Bobby here and we watched TV. Left at eleven. Getting ready for bed—wait, two men here, a Perry and a Dick, friendly, scratch that, not friendly, a gun, a trigger pulled . . .'"

"Dot. Dot. Dot," I say.

"Dot. Dot. Dot," she repeats.

Someone pounds on the door. We hop off the bed and onto our feet. I manage to take two pictures—one of the front cover and one of the last entry—before Mary Claire slams the diary shut and shoves it back where she found it. We're about to hide in the closet when we hear a faint whistle.

"It's me, Landry! We got to go; he's downstairs with that woman. They're sitting down but I don't know for how long . . ."

We open up, but Landry pushes us right back in. Maids are coming up the stairs. Out the window we go, climbing down the ice-cold fire escape: Landry first, then Mary Claire, then me. As I close the window of Mr. Capote's room, I remember my pinkie swear.

No more Nancy Drew.

CHAPTER FORTY-ONE

AT SCHOOL THE NEXT DAY, Mary Claire and Landry both avoid me. I'm not sure why. I wonder if it's because they're still nervous about getting caught for what we did yesterday. It's too bad, because I have a little gift for Landry—an early Christmas present in return for keeping watch for us and saving us at the motel. It's more of a joke: an old cardigan I found in a thrift store in Dodge, the last time Dad took us there.

If I'm being honest, I'd bought it intending to give it to Landry all along.

It *is* pretty perfect. It has a cursive *L* sewn on the left breast pocket. Mom is sure it was made for a woman, but I don't care. That's what makes it funny.

The lights are on in his house when I pull up, so I know he's home. I knock several times and stand shivering on the porch.

"Be right down!" he calls.

When the door opens, he doesn't look particularly happy to see me.

"Carly, what are you doing here?"

My stomach sinks. "I . . . I, um, I got this for you," I say, handing the wrapped box to him.

He takes it, but he doesn't open it in front of me. I'm disappointed.

"I didn't know we were doing this. I don't have anything for you," he says, glancing over his shoulder. I can hear his mother puttering around in the kitchen.

"Don't worry about it," I say.

"No—I should have got you a present. I will." His eyes drift past my shoulder. I turn around to see his father driving up. He parks and hops out of the truck, walking to the flatbed.

"I need your help!" his father calls.

Landry puts the gift I gave him on a porch chair and hurries down the steps. His dad hands him some boxes. Not sure what to do, I hold the screen door open for both of them.

"Thank you very much, Carly," Mr. Davis says. He's not grunting or straining. The boxes are empty.

"Landry, what's going on?" I ask as he races past me back to the truck.

"Spring cleaning," he says.

"But it's winter," I say.

"Thanks for the gift" is Landry's reply.

AFTERWARD, SHAKEN BY THE strangeness of that visit, I decide to drive to Mary Claire's. I need to see if everything's fine between the two of us.

Mrs. Haas answers the door and lets me inside. "Oh, Carly, they're upstairs, go on up," she says.

They?

I want to ask her who's visiting, but the lump in my throat prevents me from saying a word. I hear giggling behind the door. It's closed, but I don't even knock.

"Carly!" Mary Claire says, her eyes wide. She's leaning on a pillow, flipping through magazines. Her hands are frozen in mid-flip. "You scared me!"

I see then who's with her. It's Karen. She's sitting beside Mary Claire. She's looking at the magazine over Mary Claire's shoulder. She offers me a smirk.

"It's a sleepover," she says.

"Hush," Mary Claire scolds Karen, turning her attention back to the glossy pages. "As if your mother would let you sleep over on a Monday night?"

They both giggle again.

I bolt. I run down the stairs and straight past Mrs. Haas, out the front door.

Sitting in my car I wait for Mary Claire to come after me, but she doesn't.

I won't let myself cry. I head to Garden. I need cookies. I also need gas for the car.

THE HURD'S PHILLIPS 66 is on the drag where most people stop on their way out of or into Garden when the low-fuel light pops on. An attendant comes running over as I pull up to the pump. Watching him in his grimy coveralls and a ratty coat, his face and hands smeared with grease, I think of the word Mr. Capote used to describe the men who work here: *cretins.*

What a stuck-up jerk he is. Mr. Capote doesn't know anything about these men. I can't wait for him to leave town and go back to New York City.

Rolling down the window, I pull out a dollar from my purse, making sure to smile extra wide. "A dollar's worth, please."

The attendant nods politely. "Yes, miss." He takes the money, unscrews the cap, and starts filling the tank.

A thought occurs to me as I'm tapping my fingers on the steering wheel. I suddenly realize why Mr. Capote came here in the first place. It wasn't for gas. It was for information. I brace myself for the cold and hop out of the car.

"Can I help you, miss?" the attendant asks.

"Were you working on November fourteenth?" I ask him.

He shakes his head. "James Spor was."

"Is he here?"

"Just inside there." He points to the shop.

"Thanks." Ducking down into the wind, I run across the parking lot and into the garage. Another man, also in grimy coveralls, is working under the hood of an old blue Chevrolet.

"Are you Mr. Spor?" I ask.

"Uh-huh," he replies.

"That man out there says you worked on November fourteenth. Is that true?"

He peers out from behind the hood, then takes a rag and wipes his hands. He's taller and older than the attendant outside, and he's wearing a jacket that's too small and a hat lowered over his eyes. "What day of the week was that?" he asks.

"A Saturday," I say.

"I don't think so," he says. "I usually take Saturdays off. But hold on . . . that was the night before the Clutters, right?"

I nod.

"I was working the late shift." He stares at me, his eyes cold. "Now, why do you want to know?"

"Do you remember two men at all? Strangers? They were probably cagey, nervous."

"Again, child, why do you want to know?" he asks.

"Did they say anything strange to you?" I ask.

"Well, the tall one was talking about a score he was going to do."

"A score?" I ask, feeling sick. It had to be them.

"If I showed you pictures, do you think you'd remember them?"

"Little girl, you've got to tell me, what the hell is going on?"

"I will . . . I promise. Later. But now I have to go. Thank you!"

I turn and race back to the warmth of my car. The KBI has to interview this man. I have to tell Sheriff Robertson about this man. The store-bought cookies will have to wait.

THE COURTHOUSE IS QUIET, real quiet, like not a soul in the place except for the janitor. Old Man Miller, Asher and I call him—though never in front of my father, who says that it's disrespectful. *"He's Mr. Miller to you."* When I reach the second-floor landing, he glances up from sweeping.

"Where's everyone?" I ask, reaching the fourth-floor landing.

"Gone," he says.

"Gone where?"

"Vegas. They found them," he says.

"Found them?" I say slowly.

"Found *them*," he says, continuing to sweep the floor. He jerks his head toward the wastebasket by the stairs. "It's over."

I turn and spot a crumpled piece of white paper, the word WARRANT printed at the top.

Digging it out, I read out loud, for not just me, but for Old Man Miller to hear, too.

*The state of Kansas to the sheriff of FINNEY county: Whereas,
Complaint in writing under oath, has been made to me, and it
appearing that there are reasonable grounds for believing that on
or about the 15th day of NOVEMBER, 1959, in FINNEY
County and State of Kansas, one RICHARD EUGENE
HICKOCK and PERRY EDWARD SMITH did then and
there unlawfully, feloniously and willfully and with delib-
eration and premeditation, and while being engaged in the
perpetration of a felony, kill and take the life of Herbert W.
Clutter, Bonnie Mae Clutter, Nancy Mae Clutter, and Kenyon
Neal Clutter.*

*You are therefore commanded, forthwith, to arrest said
Richard Eugene Hickock and Perry Edward Smith and bring
them before me, at Garden City, in said County, to be dealt with
according to law; and then and there return this writ.*

"Like I said," Old Man Miller grunts when I'm finished. He
returns to his broom.

Elated, I run up to him, hug his neck, and kiss his cheek.
"Thank you, Mr. Miller! They found them! It really is over!"

CHAPTER FORTY-TWO

You can tell everyone has started to relax a little. Not to the extreme of locking up guns or unlocking doors. But Christmas feels like Christmas is supposed to. Well, at least more than I imagined it would. It's a relief to have the time off from school. To be with my family. Even Asher is smiling more. He's still quieter than usual. We all are, it seems. There isn't as much socializing around town as in previous Decembers. But we're at the dawn of a new year: 1960. Maybe, like me, the rest of Holcomb is looking to put the tragedy behind us and start fresh in January.

So I'm a little surprised when the phone rings the day before New Year's Eve, and it's Landry. He wants to take me to see *Suddenly, Last Summer*, starring Elizabeth Taylor, Katharine Hepburn, and Montgomery Clift. Tomorrow night. New Year's Eve.

I agree without thinking.

My parents might not let me. Of course, Dad overhears; he's always listening in. But to my surprise, he tells me that I have permission. He looks to Mom for confirmation. She nods. I'm too happy to be annoyed that they're eavesdropping.

It's only after I hang up that I ask myself, *Did Landry just invite me on our first date?*

⌒

LANDRY AND I SIT in the theater, eating popcorn and drinking Cokes. His treat. We got here early enough to get the best seats in the house, smack-dab in the middle. At first we're alone, but then the place begins to fill up. Mostly elderly people. The lights are dim. Landry's anxious, fidgety. It makes me anxious, too. I try to hide it by stuffing my face with popcorn.

"Carly, I've got to tell you something," he whispers as the advertisements begin to roll.

"What is it?" I ask. My mouth is still half full.

"You know the empty boxes I carried into the house the other day?"

I nod. "For spring cleaning?"

"Well, that was a lie. We're moving," he says, staring at the screen.

I nearly drop the popcorn. "What?"

A few grumpy grown-ups turn and tell us to be quiet, but the movie hasn't even started yet. They need silence to watch a dancing popcorn bag? Landry leans in close, his lips nuzzling my ear. My heart is pounding. I wonder if he can hear it.

"The farm up near Olathe isn't doing so well," he murmurs. "We have to tend to it."

"What about school?" I ask.

"I'm going to Olathe High," he says.

My throat tightens. Before I know it, I'm blinking back tears. I keep staring at the movie screen, but I don't see anything but a fuzzy blur.

He grabs my hand and squeezes. "It's not good-bye. We still have the farm here. I'll be back."

I'm trying to think of something to say when he kisses my wet cheek. I close my eyes for a moment. So this *is* a date. Our first, and maybe our last. I'm still crying, but I don't know if it's because I'm happy or destroyed or just confused.

Thankfully, when my eyelids flutter open, the lights go down. Landry doesn't let go of my hand. The movie starts, and we're transported into a world of mental institutions—where the insane are lobotomized, their memories wiped clean. I'm probably the only person watching who envies what they want to do to Elizabeth Taylor's character, Catherine. If I could forget everything that ever happened this fall and just start over right here and now, with Landry's rough fingers intertwined with mine, I'd do it in a heartbeat.

"MOVIES ARE NOT LIKE real life," Landry remarks as he drives me back home.

We promised my parents I'd be back by midnight at the latest. Dad agreed because he knows Landry wears a watch. How did I not notice? *Farmer*, Dad explained, which only begged more questions. Such as, how would Dad know what farmers wear?

"What do you mean?" I ask.

"A doctor will never fall in love with a mental patient," Landry says. "Never."

"I don't know," I say quietly. "Real life gets pretty strange, too."

He shoots me a quick glance. "Don't go all mental on me."

We laugh.

"The mental institution part didn't bother me," I tell him. "What bothered me is that the movie was supposed to take place over twenty years ago, but Elizabeth Taylor's dresses were all the latest fashion. I mean, come on. Get it straight, Gore Vidal."

"Get it straight . . . *who?*"

"The man who wrote the screenplay. Didn't you see his name on the credits?"

Landry shrugs. "I was paying attention to you," he says.

I'm glad his eyes are on the road. I know I'm blushing. "Don't go all mental on me," I whisper with a smile, and he smiles, too.

It's 11:47 when we pull up to my house. The living room lights are on behind the drawn curtains. Asher and my parents are ringing in the new year together and waiting for me.

"We never visited KU," Landry says.

"What?"

"You made me promise that if we visited the Hickocks, we'd visit KU. We didn't."

I turn to him. "You're right. Are you mad?"

"No." He takes my hand. It's odd that for the first time, even though it's so dark inside the cab of the truck, I can see that he dressed up for tonight. He combed his hair. He wore pants, not overalls. "I think you're brave."

I laugh. I don't feel brave. I feel terrified that if I don't get inside in the next thirteen minutes, I'll be grounded for the next decade. I feel terrified that I'll lose Landry when he moves back to his old farm.

"What's funny?" he asks.

"Nothing," I say. "Can we just . . ."

"Stay here?" he finishes.

I nod.

"Just until midnight," he says. "I want you to be my first kiss of the new year." I don't answer. I just sit there, holding his hand.

We're both silent, looking at his watch. It's pretty fancy—at least I think it is—but it makes me sad. I wonder if it's an heirloom, a reminder of better times long gone. Maybe it is. But Landry deserves better times now.

When the second hand ticks to twelve, in unison with the minute and hour hands, he leans over and kisses me, full on the lips. In that moment, close and warm and breathless, I think, *He's right. Movies aren't like real life. This kiss is better. Even better than the one we saw between Elizabeth Taylor and Montgomery Clift.*

CHAPTER FORTY-THREE

YESTERDAY, WE WENT TO THE country club and fulfilled our superstitions for the new year.

Chef Daniel is from the Deep South, somewhere in Mississippi; he talks about Ole Miss a lot. So he cooked up a traditional Southern New Year's Day meal. We "Yankees" stood in line as he scooped black-eyed peas "for luck," collard greens "for money," a hog jowl—which he assured us is similar to bacon; I had my doubts—to ensure "health, prosperity, and progress" . . . and a square of perfectly golden-brown cornbread.

We sat in the dining room, staring at the first course.

Something glinted from the peas. He insisted we eat, even if we had just a bite.

"Superstitions are often true," Chef Daniel said. "The person who gets the money in their portion will be extra lucky in the new year." Apparently this was why he cooked the black-eyed peas with a new copper penny.

SO WHEN I WALK into the kitchen to find Mom holding up a shiny penny—maybe the same one?—as she talks on the phone, I'm naturally curious. Dad stands by the sink, eyes downcast as he examines the *Garden City Telegram* Saturday edition.

Mom hangs up. "That was Liam! Jack's running for president!"

"Did you see the paper today, dear?" Dad interrupts.

I squint at the headline.

PAIR QUIZZED ON CLUTTER CASE
ARRESTS IN NEVADA SEEN AS MAJOR BREAK

I turn to Mom. She's glowing. Nothing will stop her from feeling happy. Not today. And she's not even on her first martini.

"How about we celebrate?" she says.

"Celebrate?" Dad and I ask at the same time.

But Mom is looking only at me.

"Jack Kennedy is running for president!" she exclaims. "We can make cupcakes!"

By *make* she means we go to the bakery in Garden and *buy* strawberry cupcakes with cream cheese frosting. But I don't care. For the rest of the afternoon, the entire family—Dad and Asher, too—devour the box while Mom and I sit at the kitchen table coming up with campaign slogans just in case the senator calls and asks us to help with his campaign for the White House. For that afternoon, Mom manages to get back east.

CHAPTER FORTY-FOUR

I'M STILL ON A SUGAR high by Monday morning, when school's back in session. Once again, the morning edition of the *Garden City Telegram* is being passed around, just like it was back in November.

MURDER CHARGES FILED IN CLUTTER

SLAYINGS HICKOCK CONFESSES PART IN SLAYINGS

I hate the word *slayings*.

Seth stands in front of his locker, a crowd circled around him. He's reading aloud.

"'All four were locked in the upstairs bathroom while Smith searched the house. Hickock apparently stood guard upstairs. It was during this search that Smith took the portable radio from Kenyon's room and placed it outside the car used by the killers. Following the search, Clutter was taken from the upstairs bathroom to the basement, where he was tied up. Kenyon was taken to the basement next and tied to a pipe.

"'Lawmen found strands of cord on an overhead sewer pipe near the body of Clutter, and had assumed Clutter was tied to the pipe rather than his son.

"'Then Mrs. Clutter and Nancy were taken to their respective bedrooms upstairs and tied on their beds. Hickock said Clutter was killed first by cutting his throat. Then Kenyon was shot in the head with a shotgun, and they returned to Clutter and also shot him in the head. The woman and the girl were killed last— both shot in the head while in their beds upstairs. The pair then left the house and drove away in the car in which they arrived. The tragedy was unknown to anyone else until two girl friends of Nancy Clutter came from nearby Holcomb to get a ride to Sunday school—about eight hours later. The girls found the body of Nancy, and the sheriff's office was notified. Exactly seven weeks later, the case was solved. Last Saturday, Jan. second, would have been Nancy's seventeenth birthday . . .'"

"Who did the shooting? Hickock or Smith?" Alex asks.
"Does it matter?" I shout. "They were both there."
Everyone turns to me, their faces aghast.

THE DAY'S A BLUR after that.

Not everyone in town thinks we got the right men. Some think that there might be others involved. Dick Hickock and Perry Smith might have had accomplices.

"It *has* to be someone local," Karen says in the locker room while we change for PE. "Why didn't Nancy and her family try to escape when they were locked in the bathroom? Why didn't they fight?"

"Fear," I say.

"Fear? I'd hope that if I was in that situation, I wouldn't just be willing to be led to slaughter."

Slamming my locker shut, I head for the door.

"Carly, what's wrong with you?" she asks.

But I walk right out of there. I'm not in the mood for what-ifs.

As the winter sun sets, the people of Holcomb gather on the Finney County Courthouse lawn in Garden City. The entire town is here. Mom, next to her Junior League ladies. Asher, with his teammates. Dad's in the courthouse, speaking with Judge Tate.

Since Monday, Dad's been quiet. Too quiet. I don't want to think about where this is going, even though I already have a hunch.

I'm standing next to our county's small version of the Statue of Liberty when Mary Claire runs over, grabs me by the arm, and pulls me toward the press line. Karen is there, giggling and flirting with the photographers. I pull away and shake my head.

The temperature's cold enough to snow. My ears are red and my feet are numb. I blow on my hands for warmth.

"They're coming!" someone yells.

Two dark sedans turn the corner onto 8th Street and pull right to the curb. The crowd falls silent. Mary Claire grabs my right hand. The doors open and flashbulbs brighten the dark sky.

In shackles, the two men shuffle past us—past the friends, family, acquaintances of the Clutters. But there are so many others here whom I don't recognize. So many curious individuals. Agent Dewey escorts the shorter one, but that's all I can see. Reporters swarm after them, shoving Mary Claire and me aside. The courthouse doors slam in the reporters' faces.

After a few minutes, the crowd scatters, leaving behind pop bottles and candy wrappers.

It's not as dramatic as I thought it would be. I expected something . . . different. This didn't take away any of the pain. There is no closure.

CHAPTER FORTY-FIVE

MOM'S COOKING IS CAUSE FOR concern.

Asher and I sit at the table, watching Mom burn hamburgers and French fries. Dad reaches into the fridge and pulls out four glass bottles of Coke. He breathes deeply and loudly. Mom jumps back from the stove, barely missing the grease flying from the hot pan.

"I give up! How about hot fudge sundaes for dinner and hamburgers and French fries for dessert?" Mom asks, heading for the liquor cabinet.

"Sounds good to me," Asher says, licking his lips.

After mixing herself a martini, Mom scoops vanilla ice cream into glass dishes while Dad sits at the table sipping his Coke. He looks as if someone has died.

"Dad, what's wrong?" I ask, even though I know the answer.

"I have some news," he says.

Of course you do, I think. I've been here before. We all have.

THREE YEARS AGO, DAD sat us down in the living room of our row house across from Washington Square Park and delivered the exact same words.

Mom was already lying on the couch. She had a cold compress on her forehead. Asher and I were scared.

It turned out we had reason to be. Dad told us we were moving. To Kansas.

Where the heck was Kansas?

Asher ran to the bookshelf and looked it up in an atlas. Kansas, the rectangular state in the middle of the country. Landlocked. Hours to get anywhere. No trees. All wind. The only people I knew from Kansas were Laura Ingalls Wilder and Dorothy Gale. Frontier women. I was a city girl.

We didn't have to ask Dad the reason. We were moving because of Frank Beggett. The name we agreed never to utter. The name of the man who murdered a teenage girl; the name of the killer my father exonerated. So much of the evidence seemed to prove he committed the crime. Very little didn't. But Dad was like a broken record during the trial, repeating the same two words over and over: *"Police misconduct."* In the end, that was all the jury remembered. The press had a field day. A travesty of justice.

Later, Mom started drinking. Threw a fit. The word *divorce* was whispered. A trial separation was brought up as well.

"You go; we'll move in with Mother," my mom spat.

"Why does it have to be *Kansas*?" Asher asked.

"Because I know Kansas," Dad explained.

This was the first we'd heard of it.

Turned out he'd spent summers near the Colorado border there with his great-aunt Lucille and uncle Olin. He had a cousin who was leaving the "four-seasons-in-one-day climate" for Arizona. Dad wouldn't give the cousin's name, which made me suspicious. Maybe the cousin was an outlaw. Maybe *that* was why Dad had never mentioned Kansas. Especially since this mysterious cousin told Dad about all the small towns "in need of a fine defense attorney." The point being: it was a perfect opportunity. Dad could relax. Take things slow.

And that was that.

It was my freshman year. Asher was in eighth grade. School had already started. None of that mattered. Not even Mom's empty threats to leave him.

Case closed.

NOW, HERE IN KANSAS, here in our new home, Mom walks over and sits beside Dad. He takes Mom's hand.

"What's going on?" I ask.

"I've been asked by Judge Tate to represent one of the accused," he says.

My body turns to ice. "You're going to get them off," I say.

"Carly, now—"

"How *could* you?" I shout.

"Carly—"

"Why *you*?"

"Somebody has to do it," he says.

"But not *you*," I plead. I'm crying now. Dad hands me a napkin to blow my nose. Taking a deep breath, I look at him and ask, "Which one?"

It probably doesn't matter which one, not really. But to me, it does. They confessed. In the paper Dick Hickock claimed that Perry Smith pulled the trigger and cut Mr. Clutter's throat. If you had to defend one, wouldn't you want to defend the one who didn't pull the trigger and cut a man's throat? Dick Hickock. I want my dad to say Dick Hickock. I think of Landry. I met Dick Hickock's mother.

"Which one?" I ask again. "Which one?"

"Perry Smith," Dad whispers, staring at the floor.

Mom is crying, too. I don't blame her.

MAYBE ALL THOSE PEOPLE back in New York City were right to hate Dad. How could he do this to me— to us—again? I grab my coat and my bike from the garage and head straight for Mary Claire's.

It's at least a twelve-minute bike ride out to her farm. My knees ache.

All I can think about is my father standing beside Perry Smith. He's a traitor. He betrayed our family by saying yes. From now on his name will be spoken in the same breath as Benedict Arnold and Judas Iscariot. Judas took thirty pieces of silver in exchange for handing over Jesus with a kiss. Benedict Arnold nearly lost the Revolutionary War by siding with England against the United States. Arthur Fleming broke his promise to his family to free a cold-blooded killer.

What will people do to my dad when they find out?

Dad says he has no choice, that Judge Tate is forcing him to defend Perry Edward Smith. The charge is capital murder—death by hanging.

Forcing him? I don't buy it. Everybody has a choice.

Dick and Perry had a choice that night back in November.

Liar.

I stand in front of Mary Claire's front door at least ten minutes before I have enough courage to knock. I turn back to the road and shiver, blowing into my numb hands. It's dark and cold.

The door squeaks open and a burst of hot air hits my back.

"Carly, what are you doing here?" Mary Claire asks. "It's late. Carly, what's wrong?"

"It's bad. Like, real bad," I say.

She closed the door behind us, wrapping her arms around herself. "What's bad?"

"If I tell you, you'll look at me differently from now on. I just know it."

"Carly, you're scaring me," she says.

I don't look her in the eye. I can't. I'm ashamed.

"What did you do?" she asks, rubbing her hands on her arms.

"I didn't do anything—it was my dad."

"Your dad?"

The door swings open. It's Mrs. Haas. "Girls, come inside, you'll catch your death. Carly, what are you—?"

"I'll explain later, Mom," Mary Claire interrupts, dragging me inside, up the stairs, and down the hall to her room. The warmth feels so good. I flop down on her bed. She joins me. We lie side by side. She grabs my hand and interlocks her fingers with mine.

"Now, will you tell me?" she says.

Looking at the ceiling, I tell her. I tell her what Dad said at dinner. I tell her how I feel. I tell her that I can't take it. I tell her how scared I am to go to school. I tell her I'm afraid of what people will say, think . . . do. I tell her everything.

My stomach growls. I didn't eat my hot fudge sundae for dinner or my burned hamburger for dessert.

Mary Claire runs downstairs and comes back with a peanut butter and jelly sandwich and a glass of milk.

"Here," she says, handing me the plate.

"Thanks," I say, tearing off the crust. I like to eat that part last.

"So, your dad's going to represent Perry," she says.

I nod.

"Carly, I'm sorry," she says.

"Things are going to be different, aren't they?" I ask.

"No," she says, shaking her head. But she's looking at my glass of milk.

"You're not a very good liar."

She flashes me a sad smile. "I don't claim to be."

I sit the empty plate on her nightstand and hold the glass of milk with both hands. "Of all the lawyers in all the towns, Judge Tate had to choose my dad."

"I guess your dad's the best," she says.

"I wish he wasn't."

She's quiet for a moment. "You're not going to be alone. I'll stand by your side."

"Will you?"

"Promise," she says, holding out her pinkie. "You're my best friend."

I wrap my pinkie around hers. "Thanks," I whisper, my chest heavy.

There's a knock at the door.

"Carly, honey?" Mrs. Haas says. "Your dad's downstairs."

Of course she called him. I trudge down the stairs. Dad stands in the entryway, waiting for me. I turn and wave good-bye to Mary Claire. She waves her pinkie back, affirming her promise to me that life isn't going to change tomorrow. Even though I want to believe her, I can't. Human nature always gets in the way.

CHAPTER FORTY-SIX

"So, it's true, your dad's representing one of the murderers?" Karen asks the moment I walk into the school cafeteria the next day.

Of course she knows. Audrey, the deputy's daughter, told her. Or maybe she found out some other way. By now, everyone knows. The ugly truth is on everyone's lips. Dad is the public defender for Perry Smith, *alleged* murderer.

According to our house's resident traitor, the word *alleged* makes all the difference.

I don't answer Karen. I don't have to.

Quickly, I eat lunch. Placing my tray on the stack, I head for the restroom. Usually, it's very noisy right after lunch, but today it's undeniably quiet in the hall. And that's when I see them. There they are, standing outside the girls' restroom. The bullies. Some I don't even recognize. Some I do. I'm not even scared. I try to walk to my next class but they surround me.

It unfolds as if I'm watching a movie I've already seen. Where a nudge turns into a push and that push turns into a shove and then the teachers descend. Without asking any questions, the adults decide who's "responsible" for the fight. I'm one of the guilty ones. I sit in the principal's office with the other delinquents, all because of my dad and his inability to tell Judge Tate no.

CHAPTER FORTY-SEVEN

"Trust me, they won't come," I tell Mom.

She's cutting open a box containing a belated Christmas present Aunt Trudy sent us. It's a film projector. It's amazing. But I feel nothing.

"Nonsense," Mom says.

I've felt the ramifications of my father's actions. My mom has, too. I see the women whispering behind her back at the grocery store and at the department store in Garden. I've even noticed that Mom hasn't received the amount of invites she normally receives this time of year.

Dad says capital murder cases take months to plan. Even though they confessed, they still have to plead their innocence—*or* for their life.

Rope costs less than a dollar at the hardware store or you can go to any farmer and they'd probably be willing to hand some over free of charge. Why don't we save time and money?

"You invited them, right, Carly?" Mom asks.

"Yes, but that doesn't mean that they're going to come," I say.

"They will—they're your friends."

Friends? No.

Mary Claire and I haven't talked since we pinkie swore to stay friends. Karen is back to her usual snide self. Seth rolls his eyes when he sees me. And Landry's moved back to Olathe.

"They love this movie, don't they?" Mom asks, pulling out the reel from another cardboard box.

"Yes," I say.

"Then they'll come."

Last December, thirteen months ago, they came and watched it on our brand-new color TV. Color TVs are expensive, $495 each. Mary Claire doesn't even have one. The *TV Guide* had a huge advertisement: *The Wizard of Oz in Technicolor, a Christmas Season Special on CBS.* It's been on TV before, but we'd never known any difference. When Dorothy enters Munchkinland, it goes from black-and-white to Technicolor, but you can't see the change on a black-and-white TV.

Mom remembers seeing it in the theaters back in 1939. She says it was fantastic on the big screen, and everyone gasped when the color changed on the screen. She says it was the greatest movie she ever saw in a theater—next to *Gone with the Wind*. So, needless to say, Mom was overjoyed to receive this present from her sister—*just* the ticket to get back in people's good graces. Aunt Trudy sent us a projector and *The Wizard of Oz* on 16mm reel in a tin can to watch anytime we want. Funny that I can count on Aunt Trudy more than Mary Claire.

Mom made me send out invitations.

She thought it was a good idea to get all of us girls together before we were too busy with homework and 4-H projects. I called each one personally when I didn't receive any RSVPs. They didn't flat-out say no, which Mom took as a sign that maybe everything would be fine. But it wasn't going to be. Mom has to know this.

The front page has been covered with nothing but the murder case for the past few weeks.

HICKOCK, SMITH WAIVE EARLY HEARINGS

LITTLE EMOTION SHOWN BY PRISONERS IN COURTROOM

ATTORNEYS NAMED

SMITH ADMITS BEING AT CLUTTER FARM HOME

FATHER BLAMES HICKOCK'S TROUBLES ON PRISON LIFE

The one that really gets me is: I WISH NOW THEY HADN'T LET ME OUT.

Me too. Me too.

Mom has Asher set up the equipment while I mix up some cherry Kool-Aid and lay out the store-bought cookies on a tray, and the cream cheese–cucumber sandwiches Mom remembered having as a child with tea.

"They'll come," Mom repeats for the hundredth time.

I start the movie anyway. Mom sits at the kitchen table, muttering angrily. I don't know what she's saying, but it doesn't matter. She figured it out, too; they *aren't* coming. They never were. I'm about to shut off the projector when there's a knock at the door.

Karen stands there, staring at me, on the front porch.

"Don't let her stand out in the cold," Mom says.

"My mom said I better come. It would be rude not to," Karen announces, taking off her coat.

Not even a hello.

Of all the girls I invited, Karen had to be the one who shows up.

Mom calls Asher to come restart the movie, which he does begrudgingly.

We sit side by side on the couch. Mom serves us punch. She even pulls out the popcorn maker.

"If Glenda said only bad witches are ugly; then why did she ask Dorothy if she was a good witch or a bad witch?" Karen asks, grabbing a handful of popcorn and jamming it into her mouth.

"I never thought about that," I say.

"Listen, I was lying before. My mom didn't make me come."

"Then why are you here?" I ask.

"I drew the short straw. Mary Claire looked relieved that she wasn't me," she says.

"Why are you telling me this?" I ask.

"I think you should understand how this is going to go."

"Going to go?" I echo, raising my voice.

"Do you girls need anything else?" Mom calls from the kitchen.

"No, Mrs. Fleming. We're good," Karen says.

We're silent until Dorothy throws a bucket of water on the Wicked Witch of the West and she melts away. At that moment, Karen turns to me, puts her hand over mine, looks me dead in the eyes, and whispers, "Do you really think you're wanted here? Can't you see that you're not? How much clearer do I need to make it? Your father has to see that, right?"

I nod. The funny thing is, I agree with her. I don't understand why Dorothy was so keen on getting back to Kansas. Dorothy might think there's no place like home, but to me, Kansas is lies, *all lies*.

Karen leaves before the movie is over. Mom asks if I think Karen had a good time. She doesn't ask about me. I lie, too, and say she did. Mom's still like Dorothy. She believes that if you click your heels together (and sip a martini) everything will be right as rain. I'm leaning toward the Wicked Witch.

Kansas will get you, my pretty . . . and your little dog, too.

CHAPTER FORTY-EIGHT

HALF THE NAMES I'M CALLED at school don't even make sense. But it doesn't matter—they all sting just the same.

Bobby was smart to transfer to Garden. Landry caught a lucky break by moving away, too. I asked my parents if I could transfer to Garden, but they told me straight out, "You think it will be any better at Garden than it is in Holcomb?"

People come to our house, stand outside, and taunt us. Adults, children, men and women, boys and girls. Age doesn't make any difference.

I've taken to hiding under a blanket on the couch.

Actual classes are easy. You sit and listen, take notes, and answer questions when called on. Lunch is a problem, though. Chairs that I used to occupy are now taken. Dessert is my only friend. Brownies don't judge me or look at me with disgust.

The day before jury selection starts, Karen greets me at lunch with a smile as I search for an empty seat. "You can sit with us," she says, pulling out a chair for me to take.

Standing there with my sack lunch in one hand and a carton of milk in the other, I'm dumbfounded. "Why?" I ask slowly, watching as the other girls at the table whisper to each other.

At least Mary Claire isn't there. I haven't seen her at lunch all week.

"Sit," she says.

Pulling the chair close to the table I take my lunch out of the paper bag.

"So, Carly, is it true that you've dined with the killers?" Karen asks.

"Huh?" I say with a mouth full of peanut butter.

"I knew it was true. Carly, how could you?"

Swallowing hard, I say, "That's not true. I haven't eaten with Perry—"

"That's disgusting," she interrupts, gagging.

"What is?" I ask.

"That you call the murderers by their first names."

I pick up my lunch and walk over to the garbage pail. Mary Claire bumps into me.

Her eyes meet mine. Her lips quiver. She shakes her head.

Starting to cry, I push her out of the way. I run down the hall and out the front doors. Forget school. I'm taking the rest of the day off.

When I get home, Mom's sitting on the couch, drinking gin right out of the bottle.

I almost laugh. We *all* have hit rock bottom.

"Why aren't you at school?" she asks, trying to hide the bottle behind her back.

But she gives up, wipes the mascara off her cheeks with her fingertips, and gulps down the gin as if I'm not standing there. She cries big elephant tears about being kicked off one more committee, asked not to attend one more function, and disinvited to one more dinner party. We're outcasts, all of us. My family is the Southwest Kansas death plague starters. We are the rats.

CHAPTER FORTY-NINE

ASHER SITS IN THE DARK. The curtains are drawn and the TV is off. There's no one in the house besides him and me. He just got back from talking to Mr. Capote.

It turns out my brother was one of the last in town to talk to him.

Not that I'm surprised. He was one of the first to talk to the police for the same reason: he always wants to do what's right, and talking to Mr. Capote didn't fit the bill. But in the end I think he felt pressured to, mainly by himself.

In the shadows, I can see that his face is wet.

"Kenyon was my best friend," he says out of nowhere. His voice is hoarse, and it sounds as if he's apologizing. Maybe he is, to himself. "Mr. Capote *should* know about him. But I'm afraid of what he'll say in his article. I tried talking about who Kenyon truly was. That he was really smart. That he played basketball and was really good, too. Without his help, I wouldn't have made the team. That he had a lot of friends. Mr. Capote didn't care about any of that. He told me he heard Kenyon was a loner and that he didn't talk much. But that's all lies. That's not the Kenyon that I know . . . *knew*."

I stare at him, not sure what to say, until he starts talking again.

"I was such a fool. I told him about the last time I saw Kenyon angry," Asher mutters. "It all started with a lie. Kenyon had this Ford Model A. It was from the twenties. It was an antique. It was painted blue but you could see the rust from underneath the chipped paint. Kenyon hated when anyone touched it, let alone drove it. Everyone was banned. But two weeks before Halloween . . . something happened."

I open my mouth to tell him, *I know this story*. Because I do. Mary Claire told me.

But I also know it's important just to let Kenyon talk right now. He's been so quiet these days.

He repeats pretty much what Mary Claire told me at the time: that it was all Nancy's fault. Nancy stole the keys and made Mary Claire and Sue take it for a joyride with her. They made it to Coolidge, west on Highway 50, an hour from Holcomb, before it died. As in *dead*. Wouldn't move. Wouldn't start. They tried. It was as if the car were mocking them or knew what they had done.

They had to get out and push it off the road before a semitruck rear-ended them. It honked its horn as it sped by. They sat on the side of the road with the engine smoking for a good part of a day. They couldn't just leave it there, but they had no "carrier pigeons to contact anyone, either." (Those were Mary Claire's words, not Kenyon's.) When it started getting dark, they started getting scared. It was Landry who drove by and found them. Pure luck. A coincidence. He was on his way back from picking up some grain in Holly, Colorado.

"Kenyon was madder than I've ever seen him," Asher concludes. "I tried to calm him down. But he stayed mad at his sister, even after Landry and I helped tow his Ford Model A, his baby, back to Holcomb." His voice breaks.

That was three months ago. But now Asher stays on the couch, staring at himself in the mirror on the wall across the room. I sit beside him.

My fists are clenched at my sides.

Dad has no idea what he's doing to us.

Asher made the basketball team; he is—well, *was*—the leading scorer. His minutes have dwindled in recent weeks, though. Now he doesn't start. He plays less than half of each game. Coach says it's his conditioning, but Asher doesn't buy it. My parents aren't the types to go make a fuss and demand to know why their son isn't playing. So Asher's left dealing with it himself. Sitting on the bench. Keeping it warm. Waiting for his name to be called again as part of the starting lineup. Calling out, *"Fleming!"* doesn't go over so well.

The son of the appointed defense attorney for Perry Smith isn't someone you want making the crucial game-winning shot. When Asher does play, a hush falls over the bleachers. I wonder how long this will last. Through the end of basketball season? Forever?

"I asked Dad yesterday if I could transfer to Garden," Asher mumbles out of the blue. "But he said no."

I laugh grimly. "I asked, too," I say. "He doesn't understand what we're going through. And Mom? Forget it."

"I don't think Dad even took our feelings into consideration when he told Judge Tate yes," he says. "He ruined my life."

I can tell he's crying, but I don't say anything to him about it.

"If I did transfer, even though Dad's being an ass—"

"Asher."

"Sorry." He sniffs. "But I'd have to sit out athletics for an entire year. Bobby has to sit out. It's a waste of time. Life is such a waste of time."

"You can say that again," I say, tucking my legs under my bottom.

"Life is such a waste of time," he says.

I laugh. He does, too. He turns to me, smiling through his tears.

"I hope the killers get death. Is it sick that I want to see them hang?"

"I kind of want to see it, too, you know, for closure," I say.

"Closure? Is that what you're calling it?" He flops back into the cushions. "That's better than me. I want revenge."

"And how are you supposed to get that?" I ask.

"I don't know."

"Well, if Dad could hear you now, you'd be cruising for a bruising," I say.

"Carly, do you think revenge brings closure?" he asks. "Because I've thought of revenge almost every day. No one remembers Kenyon. And Mr. Capote didn't even care to get to know him. He asked questions, but he didn't write anything down."

I nod ruefully. "That's what he does. The lady with him is the one who takes notes."

"She didn't. That's the problem. Their minds are made up on Kenyon. They don't care what kind of person he was. The chapter on Kenyon Clutter has been written."

CHAPTER FIFTY

AT FIRST, WE THINK IT'S a car backfiring on our street. Then maybe some rogue hunters on the prairie behind our house. But it's neither of these things.

"Don't go outside!" Mom screams.

Asher's already out the door.

We've been shot at.

Asher finds a casing on the driveway. He holds it up.

"Get in the house, *now*!" Mom yells from the front door.

She and I hide behind a chair, as if the cushions are going to save us from stray bullets. Our first phone call is to Dad. He's at the courthouse. Our second is to Sheriff Robertson, who instructs us to stay inside.

Minutes later, Dad arrives. So does Audrey's father. The sheriff doesn't even come.

"We'll find out who did this," the deputy says. He sounds bored. He smirks as he takes our statements.

At this point, I do not trust police officers. I think of the words that got us to Kansas in the first place: *Police misconduct.* I find myself smirking back.

PERRY SMITH'S ATTORNEY'S HOME SHOT AT

Children, Carly and Asher Fleming, students at Holcomb High School, were at the home at the time.

I tried faking sick, but Mom saw right through that.

I sit at the back of the classroom during English, my nose buried in one of the books Aunt Trudy sent me for Christmas, *Catcher in the Rye* by J. D. Salinger. She said I would love it. She's right; I do. Holden Caulfield, why do people hate you?

"Karen, do you think they were destined to die?" Mr. Hendricks asks during our class discussion of *Romeo and Juliet*.

"They should have listened to their parents. They were being rebellious," she says.

With my head down, still attempting to read about Holden's being kicked out of school, I say, "That's ridiculous. It was their fate. Death was their only option."

"It's your only option, too, *right*?"

I look up. Karen is snickering at me. The rest of the class is, too.

I close my book and throw it at her face.

"Principal's office, Miss Fleming—now," Mr. Hendricks says, pointing at the door.

I don't even acknowledge Mr. Hendricks or any of my classmates. I grab my bag, pick up my book, and slam the door shut. I march myself down the hall and out the front doors. I'm not going to the principal's office. I'm out of here.

IT'S LIKE I HAVE a piece of toilet paper stuck to my shoe and no one's willing to tell me that it's there.

Trying to stay clear of people who recognize my face, I drive seventeen miles to Lakin to go to a grocery store.

I almost laugh when I open the door. There's only one other person shopping here. It's Mrs. Smith, the wife of Dad's new best friend at the courthouse: Dick Hickock's appointed attorney. I barely knew Mr. and Mrs. Smith before January. Now Mr. Smith is at our house four out of five weeknights.

When Mrs. Smith sees me, she runs right over. She places her arms around my neck and hugs me tightly. I don't pull away. I need this hug. Besides, I like the way she smells (not of martinis); I like her soft skin and no-nonsense hairdo. I like that she's what Karen wants to be but never could be: a real Holcomb woman.

"Heavens to Betsy, I'm so glad that you're all right," she whispers. "Your family, too, I hope?"

"Yes, ma'am," I say, trying to breathe.

"Someone shooting at your house—thankfully, no one has tried anything at our house—at least no one was hurt."

"Yes, ma'am."

She pulls away and stands straight. "Don't worry, child, things are going to get easier," she says, flattening the fabric on my shoulders.

That's a big, fat lie she just told. My shoulders sag.

"It's been a rough couple of months," I say.

"Well, I heard from a little birdie that this Truman Capote and his friend, Miss Lee, are leaving soon. That's a relief."

I smile up at her. "I agree."

"Well, it was nice seeing you. Have your mother call me, dear. I would love to go have lunch with her." She pats me on the arm and disappears around a corner.

Grabbing a bag of chocolate chip cookies; I head for the

checkout counter. I wait behind some lady with a screaming toddler and distract myself with what my mom calls the "grab and add," the things that you pick up on the racks in the front of the store that you don't need. *Time* magazine sits between *Ladies' Home Journal* and *Cosmopolitan*. I pick up *Time* for me and *Cosmopolitan*, with Lucille Ball on the cover, for Mom.

There's a new article about the case in *Time*. I get distracted until a man behind me taps me on the shoulder. I move up, placing all my items from my cart on the counter. Some high school student rings me up. He doesn't know me, and I don't know him. He smiles, hands me my bags, and tells me to have a good day. And I think he means it.

I should come to this store more often.

AT HOME, I GIVE Mom the paper sacks and she fixes herself not one but two martinis. I watch as she gulps down the first, then starts to sip the second.

"Mrs. Smith wants you to call her," I say, trying not to sound disgusted. "She wants to have lunch with you soon."

"Oh, she does?" Mom says breezily. She smiles at me as if just noticing I've arrived and starts flipping through the pages of *Cosmopolitan*.

"Do you want the number?" I ask.

"No." She swirls a green olive around in her drink. "I think it is best that Mrs. Smith and I aren't seen in public with each other, at least not until all this passes."

"Suit yourself," I mutter. I take my cookies and *Time* magazine and head for the kitchen. With a big glass of cold milk, I sit at the table. I turn to page 18 and read KANSAS: THE KILLERS. It's short, three paragraphs, but it's the last sentence that gets me: *Why did they kill the Clutters? Well, Hickock had an explanation. "We didn't want any witnesses."*

I dunk cookie after cookie into the milk until the bag is empty. Mom has her way of coping, and I have mine.

THE PHONE RINGS AFTER dinner. Dad instantly thinks something bad has happened at the jail and quickly gets up to answer it. "Fleming residence," he says. He frowns. "Wait, okay please . . . Slow down." He turns to Mom. "Becca, it's for you."

Mom's forehead creases. Her eyes are glassy and bloodshot. But she jumps up from the table and takes the receiver. "Hello?" she says. Then she lets out a little whimper. "Oh, no! What's wrong?"

"Dad, who is it?" I whisper.

"Aunt Trudy," he says.

There's dessert in front of me, but I've lost my appetite. Asher stirs melting ice cream with his spoon. We all look at Mom. Eyes wide and focused now, she turns to us, clutching her pearls. "I love you, too. I'll be there soon," she says into the phone.

She shakes her head and slowly puts the receiver on the hook.

"What?" Asher asks.

"Aunt Trudy broke her leg."

"Is she going to be okay?" I ask.

"Of course she's going to be okay," she says, trying to be reassuring. Whether that's for herself or for me, I'm not sure. Her eyes meet Dad's. She walks toward him. "I'm going to go there and be with her. She needs me. Trudy doesn't handle pain well—"

"Wait," Asher says, sitting up straight. His tone is flat. "What do you mean? You're going to New York?"

"Yes."

"When?" he demands.

"As soon as I can," she says.

Dad reaches out and squeezes her hand. "That's so sweet of you, dear."

Asher pushes his chair away from the table. It screeches on the floor. After a cold glare at Mom, he storms upstairs.

Dad sighs. He probably doesn't even understand why his son is so angry. But I understand perfectly. Mom has seized her first opportunity to run away. She could have easily said no. She could have insisted on staying with her husband and children. And the timing is suspiciously convenient, isn't it? I wonder if she's even telling the truth. Maybe she wanted to escape this nightmare so badly that she cooked up a plan with Aunt Trudy.

If she did, I don't blame her. I only wish they'd brought me in on it, too.

"Oh, don't worry, Carly," Mom says, catching my stare. "Everything's going to be fine."

Lies. More lies.

"What a world," I finally reply, thinking of the Wicked Witch of the West.

DAD IS STILL IN the kitchen after ten o'clock. Instead of dessert plates, the table is strewn with legal papers. Late at night, he's been turning this place into his office. I pour myself a glass of milk to take upstairs.

"I'll make a grocery run tomorrow morning after I go see Perry," he says distractedly.

"Can I come?" I ask.

"No, you cannot come," he says. He sounds tired.

"But I don't want to be here alone," I say. "Please, Dad?"

It's a teacher in-service day tomorrow. We won't have school the next day, either. Asher will be leaving for Deerfield for the basketball tournament. And that means I'll be stuck here, at home, all alone.

Dad rubs his glasses on his shirtsleeve and shakes his head.

I want to shout at him. *How can you do this to us? How can you defend a guilty man?* But I already know his answer. I've heard it before. *"A lawyer's job is to believe that his client is innocent."* End of story.

All my friends have stopped calling. Even Landry, though he promised me he'd stay in touch. I wonder if he feels the same way they do.

It's been a while since the shots were fired at our house. Some people may have put away their guns. But not us. Our shotgun is still by the door.

DAD AND I SIT on a hard, cold bench inside the jail. The police officers watch us but don't say anything to us. Dad taps his fingers on his briefcase in rhythm to the music playing over the radio while I keep the beat with the bottom of my shoe.

"Fleming," an officer calls.

We stand.

"I don't think it would be right to take your daughter in there with a murderer," the officer says, looking at me.

"Alleged," Dad corrects.

The officer laughs.

"And I don't think it would be all right to leave Carly out here," Dad says, ushering me into a tiny room.

The officers in the bullpen, who are in earshot, groan.

The room is familiar. I've been here before. We sit in silence waiting for Perry to be brought in. Within minutes the door swings open and an officer escorts a short man in shackles, cuffs on his hands and feet, across the room, shoving him down on the chair. He takes a key and unlocks the cuffs on his hands.

"Be good and no funny business," the officer scolds.

Perry doesn't say a word. He doesn't even make a sound. He just sits there, staring past Dad, past me, rubbing his leg.

"He's all yours," the officer says to Dad, closing the door behind him.

There's a pitcher of water sitting on the table, with three glasses.

"Perry, would you like some water?" Dad asks.

He mumbles something, and Dad takes the pitcher and pours water in all three glasses. I take one and sip, as does Dad, but Perry doesn't.

"Do you need some aspirin?" Dad asks, opening his briefcase.

Perry nods. He doesn't look like the type of person who could kill four people with a shotgun and cut one man's throat like Dick claims Perry did all on his own. But I guess looks can be deceiving. Dad pulls a bottle of aspirin from his briefcase. He takes two pills and lays them in front of Perry, who tosses them in his mouth and swallows without any water.

Dad goes over every detail of what will happen this weekend. Perry and Dick are going to have mental evaluations done at the

State Hospital in Larned to see if they are mentally competent to stand trial. Dad's planning a defense. The "he doesn't know what he did because he is too stupid to realize what he was doing" defense. He thinks Perry's brain-damaged due to an accident back in 1950, which left him maimed.

I don't buy it.

Perry stares at me. He has the biggest brown eyes I've ever seen. But he doesn't smile. He has no expression at all on his face. And no life in his eyes.

"I think that's it for today," Dad says, gathering up the folders scattered on the table. "I'll see you bright and early tomorrow morning."

Perry's eyes leave mine and move to Dad's, who's walking over to the door. I follow, watching Perry grab his water glass and drink the whole thing in one big gulp.

CHAPTER FIFTY-ONE

I'm not sure if it's a good thing I ran into Mrs. Smith at the grocery store. If I hadn't, I might have been able to scream and cry and fuss and beg to make Mom take me with her to be with Aunt Trudy. But now I'm truly stuck alone in Holcomb. With a virtual stranger, no less.

Dad has been called away with Mr. Smith to visit Dick Hickock, wherever he's incarcerated. They'll be gone two whole days. I'll be staying with Mrs. Smith. I have no say in the matter.

On the other hand, I know why Dad chose *her* to watch out for me. He trusts the Smiths. Mr. Smith does the exact same dirty work he does. We're all on board the same sinking ship.

Dad gives me a hug, a kiss on the cheek, and some just-in-case money when he drops me off at the Smith home. It's Thursday night. Tomorrow, she says, I can borrow their car to go to the movies, but after dinner and only if I don't have any homework due Monday.

I force myself not to cry as Dad and Mr. Smith drive off into the darkness.

"If you want, we can make a pie," Mrs. Smith suggests cheerily, tying on her apron.

"Okay," I say.

"I think I have all the makings for a cherry. You like cherry pie?"

"I do," I say.

She hands me an apron and we get started. She talks me through each step. "Your mom doesn't do a lot of baking, does she?" she asks.

"No, ma'am."

Once it's in the oven, Mrs. Smith teaches me how to play bridge, which is really just math disguised as a card game. Apparently it's best played with four people. It's strange, though. How much I enjoy it, I mean. Mom plays, too—or she used to with her (former) Holcomb friends, but she never bothered to show me how. Then again, I was never interested.

"What are you smiling about, dear?" Mrs. Smith asks me.

"Nothing, ma'am. Don't people usually have cocktails when they play bridge?"

She flashes me a crooked grin. "Nice try, dear."

I start laughing. "No, I don't mean *me* . . ."

"I wouldn't be able to offer you anything anyway," she says. "We're teetotalers."

My smile widening, I turn my attention back to the cards. I savor the delicious aroma of the pie. Maybe staying here won't be so bad after all.

FRIDAY AFTERNOON I HEAD to the State Theater. Mrs. Smith lets me take their car, even though it's only a mile or so from their house. She insists. It's too cold for walking.

I'm probably the last one in the county to see *Ben-Hur.* Not that anyone has spoiled it for me. How could they, when nobody even talks to me anymore? I slump down with a bag of popcorn, staring at the screen as the house lights dim. I never realized how lonely a packed movie theater can be, because I've never been to a movie by myself.

AFTER THE MOVIE, I'M tired. The weird thing is, I barely remember the story. I *know* the story, of course; everyone does. But even though it was nearly four hours long, all I can recall is how sweaty and miserable Charlton Heston looked. I can relate to his misery, if not the heat.

Out in the cold, I stop dead in my tracks when I see Seth, Alex, Karen, and Audrey on the next block, walking toward me. They're headed to Candy's Café. Instantly I turn and head the opposite way. I'll take the long way around back to the car. I can't handle seeing them. I can't handle the persecution.

"Carly?" someone yells after I round the corner.

I keep walking. *No, no, no.*

"Carly!"

Footsteps. Someone is running toward me.

"Carly, it's me—"

My heart beats fast. I stop and turn.

"Bobby," I say with a sigh.

"Didn't you hear me?" He walks closer.

"Um, yeah, it's just—" I look over his shoulder. Seth, Alex, Karen, and Audrey are nowhere to be seen. They must already be inside.

"Where are you going?" he asks.

"To my car. Well, Mr. Smith's car. I'm borrowing it."

"I'm going to see *Ben-Hur*," he says. "I know I'm probably the last guy in town who hasn't seen it."

I chuckle.

"If you're not busy, do you want to come with me?" he asks.

"Well—" If I say no, I'll have to walk right past those big open windows.

"I'd sure like the company."

"Sure, why not."

I follow him to the ticket office, hoping that the ticket guy doesn't recognize me. If he does, he pretends not to.

"Two tickets for *Ben-Hur*," Bobby says, handing the man at the counter some money. The man slides the tickets over and we go in. "Do you want some popcorn?" he asks as I stand behind him.

"Sure," I say, even though I'm full from the last batch.

"Back again," the man at the counter mutters as we turn away. Bobby glances at me. "Carly, do you come to the movies a lot?"

"You could say that." I laugh nervously, hurrying into the theater.

We sit in the exact spot I did before. A few kernels of my last batch of popcorn litter the floor. The music starts, the title appears on the screen. I want to concentrate; I really do. But four hours later, I still couldn't tell you what the movie was about.

It's past midnight when I return. Mrs. Smith's sitting in the living room, reading a glossy magazine. She doesn't look up when she says, "Did you know that Sammy Davis Jr. is dating a white woman? A Swedish actress. May Britt is her name. People say that they're going to get married later this year." She grins absently. "Good for them."

"I'm sorry I'm so late," I say, sitting on the couch. "I ended up seeing *Ben-Hur* twice."

She nods, her eyes still on the pages. "Was he worth it?"

I blink. "Ma'am?"

"The boy you sat through the same movie twice for?" she asks. She finally looks up, peering at me over her glasses. "Was he worth it?"

I burst out laughing. "I . . . I don't know." I shake my head. Bobby seemed eager to leave me and go home the instant the movie ended. It was late, but still, he wasn't very polite. Not as polite as Landry would have been. "No."

She closes the magazine and sets it on the end table. "Well, just as long as you weren't with Sammy Davis Jr. I'd hate to think he's the cheating kind."

THE NEXT MORNING, WE sit around reading gossip magazines from cover to cover. I know more about Elizabeth Taylor's love life than one should. But it's fun.

At lunchtime, Mrs. Smith instructs me to call my mother. She insists that she's just following the instructions Dad gave her. I don't want to, but I oblige. Mom answers after the first ring. Apparently Aunt Trudy's getting better, but Mom doesn't know when she's coming home. Of course not. I know that she wants to stay in New York until after the trial. I don't blame her.

"Do you want me to bring anything back from New York, honey?" she asks.

"A bridge partner," I say.

"What's that, Carly?"

"Never mind. Give my love to Aunt Trudy."

Mrs. Smith stands at the counter, kneading dough. She opens her mouth, then closes it. I know she wants to ask me something, but before she can, the doorbell rings.

It's a neighbor, Mrs. Neely. After introducing herself, she starts peppering Mrs. Smith with questions about the case. If Mrs. Smith is perturbed or upset, she doesn't show it at all. She's as genial and polite as ever.

"It was a miracle, a stroke of luck, that these two were ever caught. In my humble opinion, some thanks goes to that Floyd Wells. If he didn't tell the KBI what he knew, they'd still be looking for the killers—sorry . . ." Mrs. Neely says, looking at Mrs. Smith. "*Alleged* killers. I know how your husband gets."

"Yeah, let's give credit to Floyd Wells," I mumble sarcastically.

"Now, now, little girl," Mrs. Neely says. "He didn't know they would go and kill the poor family."

My fists clench at my side. "Floyd Wells bragged about Mr. Clutter's nonexistent safe to a conman. What do you think about that? He knew what he was doing. Without Wells's doing that, the murders would not have happened. They'd be alive!"

Mrs. Smith clears her throat. "Carly, shouldn't you go upstairs and call your mother?" she asks me.

I nod, swallowing. I'm ashamed. I know what she's doing. She wants me out of the kitchen so she can apologize for my inappropriate behavior.

After washing my face, I go to the guest room and sit, staring at the telephone. I actually *do* have someone I can call. I pick up the receiver and dial the operator. "Davis, Olathe, Kansas," I say.

The operator connects me. It rings and rings and rings until I hear a man say, "Hello, Davis residence."

"Is Landry there?" I ask.

"Hold on . . . Landry? Telephone!" the man shouts. He must be covering the mouthpiece with his hand; his voice is muffled. "I don't know. Some girl. Here."

"Hello, who is this?" Landry asks.

"Carly."

Silence.

"Landry?"

"Carly," he says in a dry voice. "Do I *know* a Carly?"

"I know. It's been a while—"

"I moved. I didn't die."

"I'm sorry. I should've called you sooner."

"Yeah, you should have. I'm sorry, too."

"Why are you sorry?" I ask.

He laughs, his voice softening. "I could have called *you*."

"Yeah, you could have."

I flop down on the bed. It feels so good to talk, so easy. We talk about school, about my not-so-friendly friends, about our parents, about the case.

"Are you going to go to the trial?" he asks me.

"I—I don't know. I want to, but I don't want to go alone."

"If I was there, I'd go with you."

"You would? Thanks."

Mrs. Smith knocks on the door.

"Landry, I've got to go," I whisper.

"Okay, talk to you soon—*really*, I'll call," he says.

"Me too," I say, hanging up the phone.

After a moment, Mrs. Smith slowly opens up and leans on the door frame. "Feel better?" she asks.

"I'm sorry. I shouldn't have gotten upset at Mrs. Neely. I'll apologize to her."

She waves it off. "We've all been there, trust me."

I smile.

"Dinner?" she asks.

We have leftover stew and homemade bread for dinner. Then we sit in front of the television set and eat while we watch *Perry Mason*. For the very first time, I realize how silly and unrealistic this program really is. Mrs. Smith agrees. We finish the cherry pie and are in our beds by ten-thirty.

CHAPTER FIFTY-TWO

MONDAY AFTER SCHOOL, I STAY to finish up the last of the yearbook layouts. They're a pain. You have to take each student's photograph and place it just so on these blue-and-white templates. Then type each name, in each grade, in alphabetical order. I've been waiting to the last possible minute to finish two of the students. But I have a deadline.

Mrs. Newsome sits in her office one door down. Needing a break, I pop out to say hello. She asks me how I'm doing.

"Not great."

"Don't worry, I've seen it time and time again. They'll pick on someone else once they get tired of picking on you," she says.

That really isn't a comforting thought. "You know why they hate me, don't you?"

She nods.

Before I can add anything, she stiffens, peering over my shoulder. I turn and see Mary Claire in the hallway. She doesn't say a word. I thank Mrs. Newsome, then leave her office and go back next door. I return to my task as Mary Claire sits at the other end of the table—watching me.

I feed the sheet in backward in the black Olympia typewriter and set my fingers on the keys and type. *"Kenyon Clutter {deceased}."* Lifting the lever, I slowly remove the piece of paper and put it in order with the other pages.

Mary Claire gets up from her chair at the end of the table, walks over, pulls out the chair beside me, and sits down.

"You know I don't believe everything they're saying," she whispers.

"Then why are you whispering?" I ask. "No one is here, except you and me."

"And Mrs. Newsome," she says.

I roll my eyes.

"Don't be that way," she snaps. "I took pity on you when you moved here—from the wrong Manhattan, I may add—and this is how you act?"

"Seriously? You're talking about how I'm acting . . . You've lost your mind, Mary Claire, seriously, lost your mind."

She slumps forward. "I don't want to fight," she says.

"Then what do you want?"

"I . . . I'm sorry to hear about Asher," she says, biting her bottom lip.

I shrug. He's been benched. Not a team player, apparently. The conditioning excuse no longer holds up. Why else would the coach suddenly bench the second-leading scorer on the team?

"It's not right," she says. "He's a good player. I like watching him."

"You like watching *him?*"

"Not like that—"

I laugh.

"Is your mom still in New York?" she asks softly.

"Yeah, I don't think she's coming back," I say.

"Seriously?"

"Not until the trial is over." I turn to her. "You know I don't want them to be found not guilty, right?"

"I know that," she says, looking down.

"Then why are you acting like I'm on their side?"

"I'm not."

"Yeah, you are."

"I don't mean to. I wanted to . . . I wanted to show you something." She's choking on her words.

"What did you want to show me? A picture Alex drew of Bobby and me, swinging from a tree? *D-Y-I-N-G?*"

She looks up, her eyes fierce.

"You're being horrible."

"I'm being horrible? You're treating me as if I'm personally standing behind the people who killed Nancy Clutter and her whole family. Look, I know she wasn't my friend. But she was your friend. She deserves better than you."

"Girls?" Mrs. Newsome calls from her office. "Everything okay?"

Mary Claire shakes her head and bolts. I'm too numb, too tired to feel anything.

My fingers on the keys, I type, *"Nancy Clutter {deceased}."*

SINCE I KNEW I would be staying late at school, I told Dad I'd pick him up outside the courthouse. Bad idea. The moment I get out of the car, I nearly slam into Mr. Capote. He's wearing that big cowboy hat again and a scarf that hangs down to his knees. With him is someone I've never seen before, a tall, gaunt man, younger than he is. He wears an overcoat and is carrying a briefcase.

"Carly, Carly, Carly," Mr. Capote says.

"You remember my name?"

He grins. "Don't get used to it." He waves at his friend.

"We're on the way to see the wizard."

I don't bother to ask what he means. I couldn't care less.

"Can I take your picture?" the tall man asks, setting his briefcase on the ground.

"Why?" I ask.

"*Life*," Mr. Capote says.

His friend looks up and smiles at my confused expression. "He means the magazine."

"Of course the magazine," Mr. Capote grumbles. "Honestly, this girl."

"I don't know."

"Oh, yes, you must," the man says.

He opens his briefcase. There are at least five different cameras aligned in a row. He pulls one out and wipes the lens with a rag.

"What kind of camera is that?" I ask, suddenly fascinated.

"A Rolleiflex TLR," he says.

Truman whispers something to him, and he whispers something back.

"She's the daughter of Perry Smith's court-appointed attorney," Mr. Capote says, so kindly that it makes me want to vomit.

"Really," the man says with a sparkle in his eye. "This could be good."

He's taken pictures of all your friends," Mr. Capote says impishly.

I glare at him. "My friends?"

"Yes, your friends." He smiles. "The girls that found them and your best friend, what's her name—"

"Ex-best friend."

Mr. Capote laughs. "Children can be so fickle. She'll be crushed."

She will? I wonder.

"And of course the boyfriend," the man adds, zooming in on my face.

"You took Bobby's picture?" I ask.

"Yes. And I would very much like to take yours," he says, extending his hand for me to take. "My name is Richard, but you can call me Dick."

I hesitate. "Not Dick like the killer," he says, as if reading my mind. "Different last names. Mine's Avedon. Don't confuse me with a suspected murderer of a quadruple homicide." He messes with my hair. "Your hair reminds me so much of Audrey's."

"Audrey?" I ask.

"Audrey Hepburn," he says.

I smile like an idiot.

"He's taken everyone's photograph, from celebrities to socialites," Mr. Capote muses.

"Have you taken a photo of my aunt?" I ask.

"Who's your aunt?" Mr. Avedon asks.

"Trudy Huntington," I say.

"Her." He laughs. "My apologies."

I'm confused.

"He just wants you to stand right here," Mr. Capote says, taking my shoulders and forcing me to stand still.

"Like this?"

"Don't smile," Mr. Avedon orders. "It's not natural."

I drop the smile.

"That's better," he says, snapping away. "I want you to be natural, as if it was an everyday occurrence. Perfect, that's absolutely perfect. Good girl. Soon this will be over."

"Promise?" I say.

He looks over the camera and smiles. "Yes. Soon *all* of this will be over."

THERE'S A BENCH ACROSS the street from the courthouse. My dad is running late, but I don't mind the time alone. The bells from one of the nearby churches ring loud at the top of the hour. It's five o'clock. Odd how nowadays I can't hear a church bell without thinking of Nancy's funeral. I wonder if that association will ever go away.

I shiver under my coat.

I wish Nancy were sitting beside me. I would talk to her. I would tell the truth.

Nancy, I can't believe you're not here anymore. I know we weren't best friends—or close friends—but I like to think you saw me as a friend.

Tears fall from my eyes, then roll down my cheeks. I sniff and wipe them away.

No one talks to me anymore. Mary Claire won't even say hi in the hallway at school. You would be happy to know that I dumped Seth because he was being a jerk. You were right. When you did give me advice, I should have listened.

I stretch my legs and recline on the bench. The sun is starting to set. There's now a chill in the air.

It's weird that you aren't in school. It's weird that I'm not going over to your house to tutor you in math. You don't need math anymore—sorry, I shouldn't have said that. Honestly, I'm not doing so good in school. I think I might need a tutor. How ironic is that. It's not the same anymore. You should be here.

I stare up at the sky. It's starting to get dark. The bench is bathed in cold, pale lamplight.

It's easy to talk to you now. Easier than talking to you in real life. I wish you saw me as a friend and not just the outsider. I don't know what to do. I can't go back to school. I can't go to the trial. My dad doesn't want to represent Perry Smith. He has to. It's his job. But it's not fair. I wish he had said no. Everyone looks at me as if I think Perry Smith is innocent, and I don't think he is. Neither is Dick Hickock.

They murdered you, your parents, and your brother. They killed something in all of us. Holcomb has changed. People look at each other as if everyone did something wrong, or maybe it's just me—it probably is just me.

I miss you. Holcomb was a better place when you were here.

AN ELDERLY MAN SITS next to me.

"My son is doomed," the man says, looking down at his feet.

I listen to him speak but I don't respond.

"There's no use in having a trial at all—they should just hang him now." He turns to me, grabs my hand, and says, "But Perry is the one who should hang—not Dick."

Looking at the man's wrinkled face and his pained eyes, I see that he's at the end of something. He's been beaten. His striped blue double-breasted coat is too big, sagging over a clashing plaid shirt. I can tell it is not his usual attire. He doesn't want to be here; he's been dragged here.

"I'm Dick's father," he says, heaving a sigh. "Who are you?" he asks.

Shaking his hand, I say, "Carly Fleming. My dad is—"

"Your dad's representing Perry," he says, removing his hand from my grip.

I nod.

"You know this is just a bunch of hoopla," he goes on. "Those boys didn't go to that house to kill. Dick isn't the kind of boy who would do a thing like that. I've known him for twenty-eight years. You know what? Dick didn't even know when Perry killed the man. My son wasn't even in the basement at the time. Dick told me exactly what happened. They were in the basement. My son was holding the shotgun, *his* shotgun, but Perry grabbed it out of his hands and killed that father and his boy. He went upstairs, killed Mrs. Clutter and then the girl. It ain't what they are saying here or what the newspapers been saying, but that's the way it was. He didn't have anything to do with it—it was all Perry."

I don't know what to say. Fortunately, I don't have to say anything. He stands and wanders away, as abruptly as he appeared.

When I turn back to the courthouse, Dad is approaching.

"Ready?" he asks me.

I nod. I *am* ready, I realize. But not the way he thinks I am.

CHAPTER FIFTY-THREE

NO ONE KNOWS I'M HERE. No one would even guess I am *me*.

I'm wearing a pair of sunglasses and a black wig my mom had in her closet from a past Halloween costume. I sneak my way up the stairs and into the sheriff's residence of the Finney County Jail. It's where the undersheriff and his wife live.

A police officer sits outside the door, but he's too engrossed in *Life* magazine to notice me.

The cell that houses Perry is in the Meiers' apartment.

Mrs. Meier's a nice woman, sort of forgetful, but always smiling and never had anything but a kind word to say about a person.

It's a small cell, a shoe box really, next to the kitchen. Bars extend to a back wall. It has a window, a small one, but it lets in a good amount of sunshine on this day, and it overlooks the square. It looks like the cell where I was held. Back when I trespassed and threatened Mr. Stoecklein with a loaded gun.

"Perry?" I whisper, sitting in the chair beside the cage. It's still warm.

I wonder who was here. Not my father; he's at home. Perry Smith, Nancy's murderer, is right here. Right in front of me. Is he asleep? He lies still on his bunk in jeans, a blue button-down shirt, and white socks.

"Perry," I whisper again.

He turns his head and stares at me through the bars. "No more visitors," he says.

"Please," I say.

"Who the hell are you?" he asks.

I think for a moment and say, "Elizabeth Taylor."

He sits up straight. "I ain't in the mood for jokes. Where's Mrs. Meier?"

"Shh," I urge. "Okay, my name is Carly, Carly Fleming. I'm your attorney's daughter."

His nose wrinkles. "I can't talk to you," he says with a scowl.

"Please. I just have a few questions, that's all."

He lies back down. "I ain't answering any of your questions."

"I just have to know . . . I just have to know . . ."

"Know what?" he asks. He crosses his arms over his chest. The tiger tattoo on his biceps looks as if it's going to come to life and roar.

"Why?"

"Why what?" He groans suddenly, wincing.

"What is it? Are you in pain?"

He laughs shortly. "Is that the question?"

"No, but—"

"I was honorably discharged from the army," he interrupts. He says it so proudly, as if I should be impressed with his service to our country. "I went to work for a friend in Washington. I painted cars. I bought a motorbike. It was raining and I lost control. I spent six months in a hospital. But I won't show you my disfigured legs. I'm a gentleman."

I stare at him, not knowing if I should believe a word, wondering if he's playing me.

He gives a sly smile.

"Why did you do it?" I ask.

"Do what?" he asks.

I want to reach through the bars and slap him across the face, but I don't.

"I can't talk about that night," he grumbles. "If you're really my attorney's daughter, you'd know that. You with that little queer who wants to write a book?"

I shake my head.

"Because it's none of his goddamn business," he says. He sits straight again, using the bars to prop himself up. A religious pamphlet falls from the mattress to the floor.

"Are you religious?" I ask, looking at the cover. *Jesus Saves*.

He shrugs, lights a cigarette. As he takes a drag, he winces again.

"Do you need some aspirin or something?"

He shakes his head and exhales. "Some pain is good."

"Just like a shotgun to the head, right? Isn't that what you did? And a knife to the throat, right?"

"Funny, you're trying to trick me into talking." He abruptly stubs out the cigarette under his stocking feet. "*Elizabeth Taylor*, I bet I'm making your life miserable, aren't I?"

"Did you talk to Nancy like you're talking to me before you shot her?" I ask.

He turns away. "Dick didn't touch her, if that's where you're going," he says, looking at the wall. "I made sure of that."

"So you killed her because Dick wanted to touch her?"

"Are you calling me a liar? Because I ain't no liar."

"Why didn't you just leave?" I ask.

"No witnesses. Dick—Dick said we had—"

"Do you always do everything that Dick tells you to?"

He grabs a hold of the bars, gripping them so tightly that his knuckles turn white.

"Are you in love with Dick?" I ask him.

"I ain't no queer." He slams his hand on the bar and raises his voice to a shout. "I ain't no queer!"

"Is that worse than being a cold-blooded murderer?" I say, my voice a shaky rasp. "You killed them for forty dollars. Ten dollars a life—"

"Smith?" the guard barks, hurrying toward us. "What the hell is going on here?" His eyes narrow at me. "What are you doing here? You shouldn't be here. Go!"

"You heard the man," Perry says, grinning. "Visiting hours are over."

Afraid to speak, I pull my purse over my shoulder and put my sunglasses over my eyes. I hurry away as quickly as I can. I'll never know the truth. I see that now. Nobody ever will. The truth died with the Clutters.

"Who are you? What's your name, girl?" the guard calls after me.

Perry Smith cackles. I hear him clear down the stairs. "Oh, don't you know? It's Elizabeth Taylor, all the way from Hollywood, California, to visit."

CHAPTER FIFTY-FOUR

THE TRIAL IS ALMOST OVER. I wish school were almost over, too. I wish spring break started tomorrow. I stand in the stairwell, looking out the window at the snow on the ground. The sun is shining, at least.

Dad has a big day. Today he rests his case; then it goes to the jury. I heard him practicing his closing remarks in the bathroom all night. It sounded like a church sermon. And the Bible verses don't exactly help change that. The prosecution is using the Bible, too. Exodus 20:13, *Thou shalt not kill*. And Exodus 21:12, *He that smiteth a man, so that he die, shall be surely put to death.* And Genesis 9:6, *Who so sheddeth man's blood, by man shall his blood be shed: for in the image of God made he man.* Meanwhile Dad's pleading for mercy.

I try to think of something that will cheer me up.

Mom says she's coming home this week. She says Aunt Trudy's doing better. She asked how things were going. I purposefully left out everything about school and everything with Asher. I sort of make it seem like things have gotten better, even though that's not really the case. I want her home. I miss her, martinis and all.

There's a tap on my shoulder.

"Can we talk?" Mary Claire asks.

I start to walk away.

"Please, Carly, can we talk?" she asks again. "I'm sorry."

I stop on the bottom step and turn. "Are you really?" I ask.

"Yes," she says. She pulls a crumpled piece of paper from her pocket and holds it out to me. "I should have shown this to you earlier. I tried after school the other day, but . . ."

"What is it?" I ask.

"A note that Nancy wrote. Please read it," she says. I take it from her trembling fingers.

> Dear Mary Claire,
>
>   You're right. I should be nicer to Carly. She has kept my secret about tutoring me and not told my parents about my grades. Keeping a secret is a huge asset in being a friend to me. I've thought about your suggestion. I'll ask if she wants to borrow my 4-H red dress. Will this make you happy and get off my back? I'll try to make the effort. That's all I can promise. Okay? Good.
>
>   Your friend,
>   Nancy

I look up. The universe seems to spin and then stop, freezing the two of us in this moment. I was wrong. This place isn't all lies. And it turns out that the truth didn't die with Nancy. Not all of it. Maybe not even the most important parts of it.

"You were sticking up for me?" I ask Mary Claire. The words stick in my throat.

"Of course," she says, sweeping me into a hug. "That's what friends do."

CHAPTER FIFTY-FIVE

I CAN SMELL THE CAFETERIA'S sloppy joes all the way up the stairs. Our English teacher, Mr. Hendricks, stands at the front of the class, reading from George Orwell's *Animal Farm*.

"So, class, what do you think? Are rats their comrades?" He looks around the room, waiting for someone to raise his or her hand before he has to call on a poor soul.

My stomach growls. Seth turns and stares. Mary Claire hands me a piece of gum.

"Carly?"

Apparently I'm the poor soul. It figures.

"In the book they voted that the rats were their comrades; do you think so?" Mr. Hendricks asks.

"Honestly, Mr. Hendricks, right now I'd eat a rat," I reply.

Everyone laughs.

Before he can reprimand me, the door flies open. It's Mrs. Newsome. She's breathless.

"Mrs. Newsome, can I help you?" Mr. Hendricks asks, taken aback.

"The verdict—it's in. I thought you should know," she says, looking at me. "Do you want to . . . ?" She doesn't finish the question.

I can feel everyone's eyes now, too.

Mary Claire taps my arm. "You know you want to go," she says.

She's right. I stand. My knees feel wobbly.

"Call me later, okay?" she whispers. She holds out a pinkie.

I give it a quick squeeze with my own pinkie before I hurry out of the room.

As I RUSH IN, the guard tells me that it took the jury one hour and thirty-nine minutes to deliberate. I sit in the last row in the crowded courtroom. As I crane my neck, searching for my father, someone grabs my shoulder.

I look up.

"Landry!"

He hugs me.

"What are you doing here?" I ask, burying my face in his neck.

"I had to be here—for you," he murmurs.

He tells me he wanted to surprise me. I kiss him on the cheek. I needed a surprise.

"Nice cardigan," I say, tracing the *L* on the pocket with my fingers.

"A very pretty girl gave it to me," he says with a smirk.

"Should I be jealous?"

Before he can crack another joke, the jury enters the room. A hush falls over the crowd. Landry takes my hand. My heart is thumping, but the twelve men seem calm. Relieved, maybe.

Judge Tate asks the foreman if a verdict has been reached; the man stands and says that it has. Dad grabs Perry's arm and helps him to his feet. Landry squeezes my fingers.

Judge Tate reads the verdict to himself and then has the

foreman read it out loud in the courtroom. I close my eyes as he starts to read.

Guilty on all counts.

His last words are, "We, the jury, recommend death."

It's over.

I open my eyes to see Dick Hickock and Perry Smith escorted out of the courtroom and back to their cells. It's how I want it to end. But Nancy doesn't come running through the doors. She never will.

People are leaving, moving on with their conversations; their thoughts are no longer with Dick and Perry. Truman Capote is there, and Miss Lee, and the tall man, Mr. Avedon. They'll leave town in a few days, no doubt, back to New York, and not a moment too soon. Life will go on. Life will *be back*.

Landry stands, takes my hand, and helps me up. We hug again. I tug on his cardigan. I want to hold him forever.

"Come on, it's time to go," he says, taking my hand and leading me down the row.

We wait for the aisle to clear. I see Mr. Hickock walking by. He looks at me, shaking. "I knew it all the time." His voice trembles.

Mrs. Hickock, dressed in funeral black, follows closely behind.

"Landry," she says, taking his hand to shake.

He takes it but she pulls away quickly, breaking into tears. She wipes her eyes with a handkerchief.

"I knew it. I knew it. I knew it," Mr. Hickock repeats. He stumbles. We all move to catch him before he falls.

"Be good, son," Mrs. Hickock says to Landry. Weeping, she leads her husband away.

CHAPTER FIFTY-SIX

MR. DAVIS SITS IN HIS truck, waiting for Landry and me to say our good-byes. I don't want him to go. "Why don't you just stay? I could really use a friendly face at school."

"Dad says we might move back this summer," he says.

"This summer?" I say.

"I'll make sure of it," he says, but I don't believe him. I know he'll try, though. Landry doesn't lie to me.

I sigh. It took forty-six days to find them, three days for them to confess, seventy-six days to build a defense, seven days to find them guilty, and they have forty-six days left on this earth—execution date: May 13, 1960. But Dad's talking appeal and Judge Tate is hearing motions for a new trial in ten days.

"I'll miss you," I tell Landry.

He smiles, brushes the hair out of my face, and kisses my lips. Not long after, Dad comes down the courthouse steps.

THE FIRST THINGS WE SEE when we get home are Mom's suitcases. Before I know it, she's sweeping me into an embrace. I sniff her. She doesn't smell like gin. I smile in relief.

"I'm sorry, dear," Mom says, stepping away and hugging Dad. "Oh—you know what I mean."

"I thought you were coming home tomorrow," Dad says, taking off his coat.

"It was time I faced the music. I caught an earlier flight and rented a car." She smiles at me. "It's good to be home."

Sitting on the couch, I stretch my legs and kick off my shoes and yawn. Dad grabs a glass from the tray on the bar cart and pours himself some scotch, then sits in the rose-colored wingback chair, taking sip after sip. Mom leans against the television set. She's not having a drink. There's plenty to say, but no one says a word.

Later Mom informs us that we're going to the country club for dinner. She's ready to be visible again. And she's got a whole new wardrobe from Bergdorf's.

"I'll pick up Asher at basketball practice," she says, grabbing her gloves and purse, "and meet you there."

I wash my face and brush my hair. Dad changes clothes into something more comfortable. That suit won't be worn again. Bad memories. He has a few. He grabs the keys to the Porsche and we head outside.

The wind pushes through my fingers and blows my hair all over the place. There's a chill in the air and the sun's almost beyond the horizon. This day is almost over. The nightmare is almost forgotten.

We pass the road where you turn to go to the Clutter farmhouse. I almost say, *I wonder if Nancy needs help on her math homework,* but catch myself before I do. We drive by and keep driving until I can no longer see the house in the rearview mirror.

ACKNOWLEDGMENTS

I'D LIKE TO THANK MY agent, John Cusick. I'm so happy you dug my query out of the slush pile and saw the potential of *No Saints in Kansas* back in 2013. You made my dream of having a published book possible.

Thank you so much to editor extraordinaire, Dan Ehrenhaft. You have guided *No Saints in Kansas* into the novel it is today. Honestly, not a day goes by that I don't stop and think how lucky I am to work with you.

And thanks to Bronwen Hruska, Janine Agro, Rachel Kowal, and everyone at Soho for championing *No Saints in Kansas*.

And to Juliet Grames and Paul Oliver for making my first ever book event and signing so memorable. Thank you so much for the tasty food (the Peruvian restaurant was very good) and awesome company.

Thank you to the Kick-Butt KidLit group. To Casey, Jenni, Katherine, Mary, Julie, Lauren, Anita, Kendra, Kara, and Diane— y'all have been the greatest writer friends on this incredible journey.

To my family. Thank you for always being there and letting me follow my writing dream. Thank you Mom, Dad, and my brother, Alex. I love you all.

To Truman Capote—without you, there wouldn't be *No Saints in Kansas*. By writing *In Cold Blood* you helped people remember a loving family that meant everything to the community of Holcomb, Kansas.

And thank *you* for reading my debut novel, *No Saints in Kansas*. Go Hogs!!!